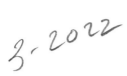

3-2022

DATE DUE

BA		
		PRINTED IN U.S.A.

Hayner PLD/Large Print
Overdues .10/day. Max fine cost of
item. Lost or damaged item: additional
$5 service charge.

EIGHT
PERFECT
HOURS

Center Point
Large Print

Also by Lia Louis and available from
Center Point Large Print:

Dear Emmie Blue

**This Large Print Book carries the
Seal of Approval of N.A.V.H.**

EIGHT PERFECT HOURS

LIA LOUIS

CENTER POINT LARGE PRINT
THORNDIKE, MAINE

For Ben,
the one on the other end of my red thread.

EIGHT
PERFECT
HOURS

An invisible red thread connects those who are destined to meet, regardless of time, place, and circumstance. The thread may stretch or tangle. But it will never break.

—ancient Chinese proverb

CHAPTER ONE

To Noelle. My girl. My best friend.

Here it is. A letter from past me, to future you. God, it's so strange writing this, knowing fifteen years from now, you're <u>actually</u> going to be reading these words. The Future Noelle Butterby! I wonder where you'll be, and who you'll end up becoming. I suppose that's what this is for—to write down our predictions and hopes for each other. (And you'd better have put Leo DiCaprio in my letter, Elle, and not just a date and a measly kiss goodnight either. I'm talking sweaty car scene in *Titanic*, with added Boyz II Men songs and less iceberg-related deaths, obviously.)

Now. On to my hopes for you, Future Noelle, and I have plenty.

Firstly, I hope you're so busy that you almost forget to come tonight—to be there when they take the time capsule out of the ground. I hope you arrive straight off a plane from . . . LA, maybe? Indonesia? Oh! What about Queensland, land of hot scuba diving instructors? Well. Wherever it is, all I know is you'll be so well-traveled that your kids will be named after cool, faraway villages nobody's heard of and you'll be the sort to slip into French mid-conversation "by accident."

Secondly, I hope your life is full of love. Yeah, yeah, I know, classic cliché, classic me, but I do. Bursting with it! Butterflies, goose bumps, can't-eat, make-you-puke love. I'd mention your soul mate—the one on the other end of your red thread—but I don't want to make your eyes roll so much they get stuck in the back of your head, because you want to be able to look at the man. Because he'll be totally hot. A charmer too. And so tall, he'll give you a neck ache. Maybe he'll even have to shop for special shoes because his feet will be that big. Only the best for you, my friend. Just wait and see.

I hope you find that job that doesn't feel like work.

I hope you eventually nail the pizza dough recipe we screw up every single weekend.

I hope you ride that hot-air balloon, that you spend a summer night sleeping outside somewhere under the stars (no tents). I hope you take that all-night sleeper train. But mostly, I hope you're

12

happy, Noelle Butterby. That by now, you see what I see—all that power and kindness and light—and you've let it rip from inside you. Shown the world that you are here.

And lastly (because the size of the paper and envelope they've given us is so small, it's an actual joke), I hope wherever we are, we'll keep on talking to each other, no matter what. And remember, at least when we can't be together, we just have to close our eyes and pretend.

Love you, Noelle.
Always,
Daisy x

I'm not exactly sure where I thought I'd be at this moment in time. If you'd asked me fifteen years ago, said, "So, Noelle, where do you think you'll be on March the ninth, fifteen years from now?" I'm sure I'd have probably said something like, "happy, settled down," or "like something out of those Park Christmas catalog adverts, I expect. You know. Nice house, smiling sweater-wearing husband, one of those posh corner sofas." One thing is certain, though, I wouldn't have expected *this*. Me, alone, stranded in my car at a standstill on a snowy motorway, my phone dead, tears removing my makeup quicker than any fancy product ever could. And my heart, breaking just a little. A bit of a mess, really. Of all the things I might've expected tonight, being *a mess* certainly wasn't one of them. Not even close.

I might've known this evening was set to be a disaster—"go to shit" as my brother, Dilly, would say. The unexpected slow-drifting snow, and in *March* of all months, the painful, stop-start traffic, the phone charger port in my ancient car dying *again,* arriving over a half hour late despite leaving home right on time and having, for once in my entire life, planned the journey bloody meticulously. Someone a little more superstitious might say they were all tiny warning signs or something—hints of things to come. Desperate little waves from the universe to "turn back now, Noelle!" and "Halt! I know you think it's only right that you go tonight, and I know it's been fifteen years, but trust us when we say it'll be shower-of-arrows levels of deflating and you're far better off turning around now and spending two days' wages in that little drive-through Krispy Kreme and eating several dozen all the way home." But despite myself, I was optimistic. Totally sick with a belly full of nervous eels, *yes,* of course, but I was hopeful. Even a little excited. To see my old college again—the place we spent two whole years, before we all turned eighteen and went off out into the world. I'd see old classmates grown up, old classrooms, the cafeteria in which we ate greasy chips and countless rubbery baked potatoes. I'd finally get to read the letter Daisy wrote to me before she died, too, and collect her camera; her final gorgeous moments captured safely on the film inside. Plus, I might see Ed again. We'd talk. Maybe even get a drink together, talk about where we went wrong—where we went *to shit*.

Snow flurries faster against the windshield of my car now, like an upturned snow globe. We haven't moved for ages. I'm not sure how long it's been exactly, but it's been long enough to send a text to Mum to tell her I'm stuck in traffic before my phone died in my hand, and long enough to read Daisy's letter under the lemon-syrup glow of my car's interior light. There's been plenty of time to cry, too, and so much so I've had to blow my nose on the neon-green microfiber cloth we keep in the glove box to demist the windows, hoping no other drivers witnessed it. It was seeing Daisy's handwriting that did it—the tiny *C*s for the dots on the *I*s like new moons—and hearing her lively, smiling, almost musical voice in my head as I read. The little jokes. The mention of the red thread—a quote she'd read in a book and talked dreamily about for weeks. And seeing it all in black and white: everything I haven't done.

Behind me, a driver beeps their horn point-lessly, causing someone else to do the same. As if it'll help, as if it'll even have the slightest

15

influence on the lines and lines of bumper-to-bumper traffic. A hot surge of panic bubbles up inside me. I swallow it down.

Surely we'll be moving again soon. There must be hundreds of us here on the dual highway—*thousands* even, all with homes and places and people to get to. They won't leave us here for long before clearing or sorting whatever's causing this, will they? The taillights of the car in front of me go out, as if answering, "Yes. Yes, they will, actually, Noelle," and again, like fizz in the neck of a bottle, the panic rises in my chest. I turn up the radio.

The camera wasn't there. That's something that hasn't helped with the tears situation, either, the fact that Daisy's camera full of twenty-four undeveloped photos wasn't there in the time capsule. And granted, *lots* of things weren't there tonight, including half of the attendees who'd sent in their RSVPs for the reunion, the photographer from the local paper, and the barbecue and beer tents the college had advertised. The snow and traffic had thwarted everything. But I know Daisy had put her camera in her plastic envelope along with her letter before it was buried all those years ago, and I'd known just from the weight of it when they handed it to me tonight, that it wasn't inside.

"I'm afraid we haven't unburied everything, because of the weather," the new head of history said, sleeves rolled up, her cheeks a flustered cranberry red. "A lot of envelopes are in this time capsule, but the rest are in the other one, which is still in the ground and will be until we reschedule the reunion, unfortunately." The hall behind me echoed and chattered with disappointed ex-students catching up with old friends with plastic cups of cheap wine, condensing lifetimes into ten-minute anecdotes, flapping about the weather, about canceled trains, about what a shame it was that the night had been ruined by snow.

"I know. It's just—the camera was in here," I said. "Inside this envelope."

"I see," the woman said. "As I said, it could be in the other vessel." She handed me a pen and clipboard then. "If you leave your details here, we'll let you know when we reschedule the event. And if we find anything." And that was it—a scribble squashed on the bottom of a wonky register of names, before someone in a high-vis jacket pushed to the front to say they were going to close the doors in ten minutes. And it was then, turning away, heart sagging, my letter and Daisy's envelope in my hand, that I saw Ed. Twenty-six and a half months since we broke up—since he got on that plane to America and flew almost five thousand miles away from me—there he was. Mere meters away in the college lobby, among bewildered ex-students and chattering voices, golden-skinned and bright-eyed and fresh in that intangible way people are after coming home again. New experiences and new places written all over them, a sheen on their skin. And he saw me immediately. Our eyes stuck like glue. And . . . *nothing*. Not a nod. Not even a tiny, awkward smile—just a frozen, icy moment before he turned and the automatic doors swallowed him up. Twelve years of memories together, of Sunday roasts and Christmases and mini breaks and watching me bleach my stomach hairs, and I wasn't even worth a smile you'd toss a stranger in a supermarket, apparently. *God.* Beyond depressing. Doughnuts. I should've chosen the bloody doughnuts.

Snow relentlessly tumbles outside, and as if synchronized, the sea of orange brake lights illuminating the slushy road ahead starts to go out one by one, like blown flames. Drivers giving up, engines killed.

"A tune now," says the DJ on the radio, *"to warm us all up. And what a swizz we can never have this at Christmas, eh, because it* really is *coming down out there."*

And he's right. It is. Snow. Proper bloody thick, settling *snow.* And there is my phone, dead beside me, a black mirror on the passenger seat. No way of being able to pass the time scrolling on Instagram or Twitter, or replying to my friend Charlie's text about Ed (*"the man is a colossal*

18

prick, Noelle. A spineless little dweeb"), no way of dissecting it like two cut-price detectives, the whole non-exchange. And of course, no way of calling Mum—calling *anyone* for that matter. I try the charger cord again. Of course nothing happens.

I let out a pointless *"Shiiiiiiiiiit!"* and cover my damp, hot face with my hands. A Harry Styles song plays on the radio—something about strawberries on a summer evening—and I could laugh at the irony of it, the temperature gauge at minus-five staring brazenly back at me, cars bumper-to-bumper on the road ahead, iced like buns. I can't be stuck here. *I can't.* Mum. What will I do about Mum if I'm stuck here for longer than an hour or two?

It takes twenty tense minutes for the traffic sign ahead to light up its cheery Broadway letters to spell **M4 CLOSED. MAJOR DELAYS**, two minutes for the tears to start again (and for the demisting cloth to enter stage right *again*), and another five minutes before there's a rap of knuckles on my passenger window.

CHAPTER TWO

Uh, hi. Do—Do you need any help?"
I stare at the man through the tiny crack in the passenger window: serious brown eyes, jet-black lashes, squinting as thick snowflakes fall.

"Um. I—I was . . ." My voice is thick, as if there are balled socks in my throat. "I was trying to—"

"It's just I saw you with the phone," he cuts in. He motions, waving his arm in the air in a deranged sort of way, before pushing his hand back into his coat pocket.

"Oh. I see." Brilliant. Just as I feared; other drivers *did* see my in-car meltdown. The tears, the swearing at nobody, the bloody microfiber cloth the color of ravers' hot pants. "I had no signal," I say, clearing my throat, sitting straighter as if to prove I am very stable indeed. "And now I have no battery. I was trying to get through to my mum." I hold up my lifeless phone. "I did manage to send a text before it died. Luckily."

The man glances to his side at the road ahead, then back at me through the glass. "OK, well—if you need to borrow a phone or a charger cord—I guess, just shout." He's American, this stranger. *Very* American. My brother, Dilly, would probably be able to correctly guess which state he's from after hearing just a few words from his mouth. Dilly is obsessed with all things America. The food, the movies, the funky little mailboxes, and how everyone eats cobbler (his words, not mine). He once even dated a man from Boston and spoke for a week in an American accent so obscure, that Ian next door sat us down and asked us very gently if he thought it was possible—and don't be alarmed—that Dilly might've suffered an allergic reaction.

"Ah, thanks. But it's not the charger," I tell the American. "It's the port. The actual, erm—plug socket?"

"*Ah.*"

"Idiot brother broke it. Connecting up a laptop. Two days he was home for, borrowed the car, and that was it. Desperately needed to mix a demo, apparently. He only went out for tomato puree."

"Right."

"It's a super old car," I waffle on, as if this poor bloke cares, but I'm flustered, and short answers or silences beg for it, with me. I can't help but want to fill up the space with words. Plus, he's—well, there's no arguing with science and nature. He's really quite attractive, this man. Like . . . *very.* "The heater gets stuck on cold," I drone on. "And sometimes the car even locks us in and point-blank refuses to let us out again."

"I see" is all he says, but I see a tiny twitch of

a smile through the misty glass as if he somehow knows the heater is only broken because I spilled a can of Tizer on the dial. "Well, if you need to charge it, I'm"—he throws a glance over his shoulder to a parked black car beside mine, the interior light on inside, the door slightly ajar— "just there."

"Oh." I nod. "OK. Thank you. But I'm sure we'll be moving again in a few minutes."

"Optimistic," he says, as if to himself.

"Yes. Well, I *hope*." And I do—I have to. Because Mum isn't used to being home alone without me, and if I think too hard about it, about being stuck here, and about this whole disastrous evening, I might cry again, and this man—this whole motorway, in fact—has seen quite enough. Plus, I'm not expected home until after ten, which means there is still an hour to get there as normal, with no drama, no awkward encounters with strangers and strange cars and Americans with funky mailboxes.

"OK, then." He straightens, gives an awkward nod.

"Thanks," I say, "for offering," and a moment later, my window is firmly shut, and he's back inside his car beside me on the frozen tarmac.

CHAPTER THREE

It's amazing how painfully slowly half an hour passes when you don't have a phone. I don't like to think I'm addicted to my phone, or if I am, I'm certainly nowhere near as enslaved to it as my friend Charlie who spends every Sunday night strategizing how *not* to use her phone. "I've spent a working week on my phone, Noelle, despite telling every poor shit who'll listen that I have no time," she'll say. "I used to get off on meditation. I used to get off on men with beards. But no, not now. Now I get off on a screen and an internet connection. It's sad. A modern-day tragedy." But without my phone, all there is to do is stare through the windshield, nibbling my fingernails raw, watching people duck out of their cars and into bushes to pee, reaching deep inside their car trunks, pulling out dusty old blankets or packets from shopping bags as the snow just keeps on falling. A few moments ago, a driver in the next lane proudly pulled out a five-string *banjo*.

News headlines roll in again on the radio, but they're all the same as they were twenty minutes ago. Something about a footballer and a court case, then the nasally announcements of *"snow blankets parts of the UK. Major delays. Roads closed. The public are advised to not travel unless necessary."*

And maybe I should've listened to Mum— her pleas for me to stay home. "Gary at number twenty-one put on Facebook that it's set to snow six inches, Noelle," she'd said before I left, clutching the collar of her blush-pink dressing gown. "And he's always right. He used to work for Millets." But then, Mum doesn't travel, even when it is necessary. It's been three years since she went anywhere at all, or should I say, any further than the recycling bins in the front garden and the eight-weekly trip to the hairdresser and back, which she attends as if she is under house arrest and only has an allotted forty-five-minute window before the cops turn up to throw her over the bonnet of a car and chain her hands together. In and out, no cup of tea, no small talk at the till. If I listened to her, I wouldn't really go anywhere. And where would the pair of us end up then?

I glance over at the American in his car. I keep thinking he'll catch me looking longingly over, like some sort of perv at a smoky bar, but the more time passes, and the more I try, again and again, fiddling pointlessly with the charger socket, taking out the wire and plugging it back in again, the more I have to accept *I need help.* Because I need to get through to Mum, and it's obvious now, with bush wees and banjos as evidence, we're not going to be moving anytime soon.

I push open my car door and get out. Snow showers my face as I slip on my coat. This borrowed, thin-as-cigarette-paper dress: definitely one of my shittier ideas. It's *freezing*.

The American is looking down at something in his lap when I approach the car. A book, I think, or is that a newspaper? He looks up when I knock against the glass, and the window glides down. The smell of warm coffee and new car leather puffs through the gap into the cold air.

"Hey," he says.

"I really hate to ask, but if I could just use a charger—"

"Sure. Shall I take the phone and let you know when it's charged . . . or do you wanna hop in, or . . ."

He trails off, thumb pointing lazily over his shoulder to the inside of his car.

Ugh, this is awkward, this situation. It'd feel weird passing my phone through a stranger's window, telling him to keep checking whether it has enough charge for a call, hoping he doesn't glance at any of the messages that might come through, because it isn't exactly unusual for Charlie to send a photo of the new tattoo she's penned on Theo's hairy inner thigh on a whim, or a zoomed-in photo of Orlando Bloom's paparazzied knob with the message, **Just some**

more evidence to back up my Some Penises Can Be Beautiful stance. But it also feels weird to jump in a stranger's car, regardless of how stationary it is, regardless of how lovely and normal he seems, and how very much unlike a serial killer he appears to be. I'd rather do neither in normal circumstances. But these aren't exactly normal circumstances, are they? A man, chatting across the lane to a police officer, triumphantly pulls a two-foot-long supermarket baguette out of his back seat as if to prove the point.

"I suppose I'll quickly jump in," I say, "if that's OK?"

The American's car is a grown-up's car—the sort that has heated seats. The sort that has a sensible handful of loose change and a neat package of pocket-sized tissues in the glove box in case of crying or nose-blowing emergencies. I doubt the American has ever drunk Tizer in here. I doubt he's ever spread a McChicken sandwich meal across the passenger seat in Asda's car park and rubbed spilled ketchup into the seat until it blended with the fabric, either.

"Do you want to use my phone to make a call first?" the American asks.

"Oh, um—she won't pick up." I shut the car door behind me. "My mum. She doesn't pick up calls from numbers she doesn't recognize."

"Oh. OK." The radio is on—something folkie;

slow, husky vocals, the gentle picking of a guitar—and the heaters hum quietly. He fishes around in the armrest between us and pulls out a charger, plugging one end into a port below the stereo. He holds the other end out to me. "Here."

"Ah. Thanks." I plug in my phone, rest it in my lap. Warm relief trickles through me like brandy as the charging emblem blinks onto the screen. I blow out a "Phew," and he smiles.

There's silence now, both of us turning to stare ahead through the snowy blur of the windshield. I fiddle with a button on my coat. The American straightens in his seat, picks at a thread on the thigh of his jeans. He glances quickly at me, catches me doing the same, and we both give one of those polite, just-for-strangers smiles. He has a nice face—the sort of intangibly nice face you can't quite put into words. When Charlie was dating, she used to scroll the Plenty of Fish app and say, "I just want a man with one of those *nice* faces, you know? Just one of those friendly, trustworthy, earthy sort of faces that makes you feel like *Yeah*. I'd follow you into the woods, dude, and know there's a high probability I'd remain intact." Yes. The American has one of those faces.

"Coming down out there," I say, because, well, let's face it, I need to say something. "They said on the forecast it'd be light, if at all."

The American ducks to look out the windshield,

two perfect watermelon slices made by the wipers in the snow. "Yeah. Although—I guess it is sort of light."

"Is it?"

He gives a shrug. "Well, light if you compare it to the snow in—Toyama or Syracuse or something."

"Or the North Pole," I add weakly, and he smiles and says, "Sure. Or the North Pole."

Snow flurries down outside, the snowflakes like duck feathers from a gigantic burst pillow in the sky, and a new song begins on the radio. There's a beat of awkward silence. I'll leave. As soon as I have the tiniest drop of charge, I'll get out—

"Are you close to home?" he asks.

"Sort of. Half an hour away," I tell him, and he nods, tells me he's on his way to the airport now, to go home.

"And where is home?" Dilly would give anything now, to place a bet on a state, see if he's right.

"The US. Oregon?"

"Really?" My voice sounds high-pitched, shocked, and his dark eyebrows rise. But I can't tell him why. That it was where Ed went. That it was where *I* was meant to go too, with him, to start anew. Until I couldn't. Until I had no choice but to stay. "I just—I, um, I had a pen pal from Portland once." I change routes. Still true, but

28

not quite the heavy *My Doctor Boyfriend Left Me for a Hospital in Oregon* story he didn't ask for.

"Seriously?"

"I was thirteen," I say. "It was a school thing. We all got allocated an international pen pal and something happened and, I don't know, he was off school for six weeks. Or maybe he just wanted to avoid my letters, which was probably wise . . ."

The American chuckles. He has a nice laugh. Warm, genuine. And it makes me relax a little.

"—so I got this very uninterested genius instead. Only lasted two letters. I think she found me really boring. She talked about prehistory and Socrates, and I just remember listing some facts about Brian from the Backstreet Boys."

He chuckles again. "I'm not far from Portland, actually," he says. "Well, an hour or two. I'm by the coast."

"The coast. Sounds nice."

A traffic announcement bursts through the soft folkie music, and he quickly reaches forward to turn down the volume. He tries to find music again, pressing a touch-screen arrow a few times, then settles on a random station. Another awkward, just-for-strangers smile passes between us.

I click the side button on my phone. The battery sign blinks on and off. Of course. *Of course* it's going to take its sweet time while I'm stuck in a car with a stranger. "My phone's still really dead," I tell him. "Sorry. I just need enough to make a call. It shouldn't be much longer . . ."

He lifts a shoulder to his ear. "It's cool," he says. "Plus, maybe—to pass the time?" He picks up a folded newspaper from the side of the seat and holds it up, showing an unfinished crossword, red Biro scrawled roughly in some of the squares. "Two heads are better than one, right?"

I pause. *"Usually."*

"Usually?"

"In the case of crosswords, one head, and one that isn't mine, is probably better. In the case of geography, too, actually."

He smiles. A comma-shaped dimple appears in his cheek and something glitters inside my stomach, like a spark. "Well, you knew Portland was in Oregon."

"That's true."

"There you go. Most people over here hear me speak and say, *New York? Or Are you from California? Do you know Keanu Reeves?*"

I laugh. "Yeah, no other states exist to us, I'm afraid."

"No?"

"No, afraid not. To us, everyone works for Paramount Pictures and goes to prom and probably knows someone called *Chad*—" I freeze. "God, and of course now I'm worrying you're called Chad and I obviously didn't mean—"

"Sam. I'm Sam."

"Sam." Sam. Makes sense. He looks like a Sam. Sam's a strong, classic, safe name, and I feel certain, somehow, that he is also those things. "I'm Noelle."

"Noelle. Like—"

"Christmas, yeah."

"I was going to say . . . *Gallagher*." His cheek twitches in an awkward, shy smile and I can't tell if he's joking or not.

"That's *Noel*. I'm Noelle. No-elle. Noel, but with an extra *L* and *E* on the end. Very important detail."

He nods. "No*elle*."

I smile. "Correct."

He brings a Biro to the newspaper on his lap. "OK, Noelle *not*-Gallagher. How are you with ancient philosophers? Sixteen down is kind of torturing me."

CHAPTER FOUR

O h, Noelle, I can't believe it. Do you have food? Drink? Are you warm enough? It's all over the local news. Lorry got into trouble apparently. Thank God nobody's hurt. But now with all the snow, too, oh God, it's a nightmare—you're OK, are you?"

"I'm fine, Mum. But are you OK?"

"Ian's here."

"Is he? *Really?*"

"He was passing! How lucky is that? He popped in to see to the gate next door. The new tenants were moaning about it. I said to him—I said, Noelle and I are always saying that new tenant seems stuffy—like she's got a broom jammed up her arse, that you smiled when you took the bins out and she ignored you. Doesn't surprise me that she complained about the *gate,* of all things—"

"Will he stay?"

"Ian, she's asking if you'll stay. He—right. Yes. He says he'll stay until you get back. I'm sure you'll be home by—elevenish, do you think?"

"I don't know if I'll be back by eleven, Mum. We're at a total standstill—"

"Oh, Noelle—"

"I'll be home as soon as I can, I promise. But look, I don't have a lot of battery—"

"Don't you? She's running out of battery, Ian. What? Ian says to switch your phone to airplane mode, save the battery, and to get off the phone now to be safe—"

"It's fine. A guy next to me offered to let me charge it in his car, so I've just been sitting in there. But I don't know how long I can charge it for—"

"A stranger? Oh Christ, please be careful."

"It's fine, Mum. He's fine. He was parked next to me. American. On his way to the airport."

"Oh. *Oh. I see.* Right. OK. Is he . . . your age?"

"Um. Yes, I suppose."

"Tall? Good-looking?"

"I . . . I don't know. Yes? Yes, I guess, he—he seems to have long legs. Look, Mum, I'm getting soaked, I'm standing outside—"

"Well, you know what Dilly said about that American he went out with."

"Mum—"

"Very lively. Full of energy, very fit, you know. And not afraid to show it off either. Walked around nude, apparently, making breakfast, don't you remember? Pancakes. That's what they eat, you know. Not for dessert, either. For *breakfast.*"

"I'm going now."

"With *scrambled eggs.*"

"Bye, Mum. I'll be home as soon as I can."

• • •

It's amazing how quickly an hour and a half passes when you're having one of those conversations—the unexpected effortless kind that makes you feel as though you can't get the words out of your mouth quick enough. Ones where minutes slip into hours but seem to bring the world outside of your little bubble to a complete standstill. A flaming meteor could hit and you wouldn't even look up and say, "Oh, did you feel that? That little tremor?"

My phone sprang to life over an hour ago, yet still I find myself in the warmth of American Sam's car. *Still.* I can't believe it either.

I'd ducked outside to call Mum when my battery charged to 10 percent, awkwardly hovering at the open car door, zipping up my coat on the concrete, unsure whether or not I should just thank him now and say goodbye. Because I had enough charge now to do what I needed to—check on Mum, arrange for Ian to stay with her and help her up to bed. But Sam and I were in the middle of a conversation I was desperate to get back to—ghosts, for some reason, and the best thing we'd ever eaten. And to be honest, simply and totally unexpectedly (and slightly guiltily): I was having such a nice time.

"You could, uh—charge up your phone some more," Sam had suggested, leaning across from the driver's seat, hair bristling in the gentle but icy breeze. He has such nice hair. Thick, dark, probably smells like showers and coconuts. "If you want to."

And I'd nodded from the road, phone in hand, relieved that he'd asked. "Plus, we haven't finished that crossword yet, have we?" I'd joked, and he'd laughed and said, "Yeah, I'm not sure we ever will."

I tingled as I spoke to Mum on the road, snow-flakes falling relentlessly as if from a lifetime supply—that lovely deep exhale of relief once I knew she was OK, and that warm-blooded feeling of having had fun. Away from home. With someone new. Even when I rack my brain, I can't remember the last time that happened. Years. Definitely years. And I'd forgotten the fizz of it, I think—of meeting a fresh, new person, and that purging you can do when you're clean slates to each other and everything shared is new and interesting and a little bit of universe-expanding. Maybe that was part of the guilt too, besides knowing Mum would be worrying—that it had been so long.

"So, this slightly bonkers-sounding alpine-guide thing," I say. Sam is swiveled to face me in the driver's seat, his broad back against the car window. "Your job—"

"My job."

"Do you get to go all over? Travel a lot—go

here and there?" A mountaineer. Sam is an actual *mountaineer.*

He nods. "Wherever I'm needed. Although my base is in Oregon right now—place called Mount Hood? They run summit programs, and I'm a guide with a few other climbers. But not sure for how much longer."

"Mount Hood," I repeat. "I say that like I know it. My mountain knowledge is—well, it's shit, to be honest."

Sam laughs, that little crescent of a dimple in his cheek. "Ah, it's super high, super snowy, super mountain-y. That's all there is to know, right?"

"Wait, so you climb *icy* mountains?"

Sam smiles shyly, taps the side of his finger absentmindedly on the steering wheel. "Are you going to ask me if I worry about plummeting to my death again?"

"You leave me no choice. Sorry."

I keep drifting from my body and watching myself from the other side of the window, and I'm 99 percent sure the Noelle Butterby outside with her nose pressed against the glass is silently muttering, "Kindly, what the fuck is happening to us here?" Because things like this don't happen. Not really, not in real life. Especially to me. People like Charlie, yes, I'd almost expect this to happen to her. Before the baby, she and her husband, Theo, were always out, always falling in instant-love with fast friends on yoga retreats and coming home with stories about people they room-shared with who cured their migraines with enemas and forgiveness, and how they're going to meet up for brunch. But me. These things don't really happen to me. I mean, first of all—stranded due to *snow?* We're barely on first-name terms with sleet in England, let alone proper "Last Christmas" music-video snow, yet here I am, in what is practically a blizzard, sitting in someone's car who only ninety minutes ago was a nameless stranger—a bloke in a car. And I feel—*something.* I don't know what exactly. Alive. Buzzy. Like my blood is rushing with stars, with electricity. And I didn't even want to get into this car. It'd be painfully awkward, I thought, sitting there, looking like a melted waxwork with swollen bee-stung eyes and cried-off makeup, and a ridiculous dress I'd never usually wear in a million years—red, faux satin. Something I'd picked out of Charlie's wardrobe because I thought it said, "worldly adult" and "student most likely to be settled and happy with her shit perfectly together, so what were you thinking, eh, *Ed?*"

But sitting here with Sam—I can't even really explain it. I just know that I don't want to leave. I imagine Charlie's face if she could see me now. "Erm, *excuse me,*" she'd say. "Are you Noelle Butterby? Is that an unidentified male? Are you actually—holy shit—*having fun?*"

Sam stretches in his seat beside me and clears his throat. "Do you think your mom will be all right?"

"I think so," I say. "Our friend, our old neighbor, Ian—he said he'll stay with her. He used to help us a lot with Mum before he moved in with his girlfriend, so . . . best man for the job."

Sam nods, turning a Biro in his hand. "How long has she been sick?"

"She's—not really sick."

"Oh—"

"Well, no, I mean, she *is* sick but—I don't know." My heart clenches now at the mention of Mum. A single icy shot of reality in this tiny, warm bubble, miles from it. "I suppose it's just when you say ill or sick, people think hospitals and meds and being stuck in bed or something, and Mum doesn't really fit in those boxes. She had a stroke six years ago. And she hasn't really been the same since."

Sam is quiet, then says, "I'm sorry to hear that."

"We're lucky really, that she bounced back. She struggles on her feet; she lost a lot of sensation in the beginning, on her left side. But now—mainly it's lost confidence. And I'm not complaining because, well, things could always be so much worse, but she's doing less and less lately, and I'm doing more and more, and—" And then nights like this happen, I want to say, but I don't, and you wonder how much longer you can keep floating on like this, being at the helm of what feels like a gigantic ship you are totally ill-equipped to steer, and one that just keeps getting bigger and heavier. "But we're OK," I say instead. "Most of the time."

I look up at Sam, snowflakes drifting rhythmically beyond the glass behind him like an old nineties screensaver, and I wait for the wince, the eyes widening, the judgment, and most of all, the pity I notice ripple across people's faces sometimes. Pity for Mum, of course, but also for me. Thirty-two years old. Always needing to be close to home. A world the size of a tiny speck in the sky compared to most people's giant planets. Instead, Sam says, "That sounds super tough. Always having to be . . . the shoulders."

Yes. The shoulders. I've never heard it put like that before. "Sometimes it can be. Like tonight, for example—" I look down at the red satin dress, the inky spots of snow slowly drying back to crimson. "Tonight was my first night out in about ten months and I had to plan it with military precision to make sure I'd get home at a certain time and—"

"And look how great that turned out," grins Sam, outstretching his hands, like a magician presenting the end of a trick.

I laugh. "Well, it could be worse."

Sam looks at me sideways. "Yeah. I agree," he says.

The hard buzz of a vibrating phone in the cubby beneath the stereo cuts through the calm of the car, and as if automatically, we both reach for it. My hand collides with Sam's and a jolt fizzes through me, bubbles in my stomach as the warmth of his skin touches mine. Sam snatches his hand away as the phone tumbles into the footwell at my feet, and of course, I realize now, that—*shit*. The phone isn't mine. The name "Jenna" is on the screen on the floor, between my ankle boots, calling, and I definitely don't know a Jenna.

I bend to pick it up. I know my cheeks must be bright shrimp-pink because my bloody ears are on fire and they *always* do that when I'm embarrassed. "Crayfish Face," Dilly calls me when it happens, and I know I must be in full Crayfish Face mode right now. "S-sorry, I thought it was mine, I thought it might be my mum—"

"It's cool, no worries." Sam takes the phone from me as Jenna's name disappears and the screen flashes with a little gray rectangle of a missed call.

"And now you've missed the call. Sorry."

"It's no big deal, seriously. It's just a call," he says, but something in his face, in his dark brown eyes, has changed and I can't put my finger on what. An injection of reality, perhaps, for him

40

this time, in the shape of a phone call. He clears the notification with a swipe of his thumb. "Life was easier when we weren't all so available and easy to interrupt, right?"

"What, when we all wrote to each other?"

Sam nods. "I know nobody does that anymore, but I dunno, it's tempting. Less pressure to answer *right this second,* you know?"

"Some people do," I say. "Steve and Candice did."

Sam's eyebrows knit together and he looks at me. "Who?"

"These two people that work together at an office I clean," I say. "That's what I do. I'm a cleaner. Houses, workplaces. Not exactly *glam,* but it fits in around Mum." And I'm not sure if waffling will help dilute the rising cringe levels in the car, but clearly I'm going to try. Because trying to steal his phone. The touch of our hands. Sam's flinch away like he'd touched shit on a stick. All these things that have ticked the cringe barometer from zero into a firm reading of seven out of ten, and suddenly this all feels a bit ridiculous again. Me. In this car. With him. "These two people who work there, Steve and Candice," I say, "they were having an affair, and I used to find their Post-it Notes to each other screwed up in their bins every Friday evening."

"And what did they say?" asks Sam, a coy shadow of a smile on his face.

"It was mostly tea-based. Like *Steve, tea at three?* And *Candice, your tea is way too hot.* And once there was a very straight-to-the-point *nice tits* one."

Sam laughs. *"Wow."*

I burst out laughing. "I know."

"See, maybe you'd have gotten somewhere with your Portland pen pal if you'd been more like Steve and Candice."

"Or I'd have been expelled."

The buzzing of Sam's phone cuts like ice through the quiet of the car again. His dark eyes drop down at the screen.

"Ah. I really need to take this—"

"Let me leave you, give you some peace. Plus—" I pick up my phone now. "Eighty-six percent charge. I should probably stop stealing your power now and leave you be."

Sam hesitates, Jenna in one hand, car door handle in the other, and I don't know what I want him to say, but I know I don't want to leave. Not really. Not one bit. "No, it's—I mean, you don't have to—seems silly not to let it get to a hundred, if—"

"I—I'll give you some peace," I say again, opening the car door. "I, um—I need to check in at home, anyway."

Sam nods wordlessly.

I slide out of the car as I hear him say into the phone in a new voice—sweet, low— *"Hey, you."*

CHAPTER FIVE

I'm completely freaking out, Charlie. I should go back to my car, shouldn't I? I mean—what part of this is normal?"

"You've hit it off with a stranger, Noelle. You're borrowing a charger; you're stuck in a blizzard. You're not sucking him off and being filmed by his girlfriend, which, by the way, people do all the time in Alston Park car park after midnight, and they're not freaking out. They're having a really lovely time."

"Right."

"So, do you want to stay in the car?"

"*Yes*. But I don't know if he wants me to, and maybe I'm outstaying my welcome, and also this is really *weird,* isn't it? I mean, it—"

"You just said it was his idea to keep charging your phone."

"It was."

"Which is proof—oh, hang on, Theo's saying something. *Ooh. Interesting.* Theo thinks you only called me because you subconsciously wanted to deplete your battery so you have to stay with the hot and funny American for longer."

"Or I wanted to call and have you tell me I shouldn't be sitting in a stranger's car. That maybe I've had a lapse in judgment, triggered by the fact that I had a weird, emotional evening, what with Ed, and Daisy's camera, so perhaps I'm not thinking straight and—"

"No way I'm doing that, Elle. Forgive me, but I like that you're having a nice time with a nice guy. When was the last time you did that, eh? I mean, you wouldn't even go on a date with Jet."

"Jet?"

"*You know*. Who Theo met on the reiki retreat, the one with the torso—"

"Vaguely . . ."

"*And* you wouldn't double-date with us and Simon the chiropodist either, and I have trusted that man with my feet for eight and a half years, Noelle."

"Right. So, do you think I should stay? I mean, this Jenna, she could be—"

"Stay in the car."

"He's so nice, Charlie. I feel—I don't know. Like I've been injected with something. He touched my hand earlier, accidentally, and—"

"Sparks? Energy?"

"Yeah. *Yes*."

"Oh my God, you're so marrying him."

"Charlie, that is ridicul—"

"Theo says he'd give anything to read your aura right now."

"Tell him I've already read it and as auras go, it's firmly shitting itself."

44

"Stay in the car, Noelle."

"OK. OK, I will."

"And maybe after this, you'll be ready for Jet."

"I don't think I'll ever be ready for Jet."

"Shame. Theo says he teaches a class on cunnilingus. They practice on oranges. Oh, and sometimes cantaloupes. Noelle? Elle, are you still there?"

After Daisy died, it took me nine months to be able to bear to even look at a motorway, let alone drive on one. A motorway was loud and fast and unpredictable, where everything could go wrong in the split second it took to make one silly mistake. A motorway took away my best friend. And it should've taken me away too. But tonight, looking at this vast, long road, still and snow-covered and lined with trees, scattered with people, strings of cars lit up inside like distant houses at night, the small orb of fear I still carry fizzles, like the end of a firework. It's just tarmac that Sam and I stand on now. It's just concrete and snow and trees and people trying to make their way home.

"I can't believe your umbrella has *ears*," says Sam.

"Ears on anything adds charm, everyone knows that."

"They do?"

"Of course. Scientifically proven too."

Sam and I are queuing at the back of a bakery lorry, its shutter raised, a butterscotch-yellow light on inside. We stand beneath my umbrella—a Christmas gift from Dilly, and for absolutely no reason at all, designed to look like a koala's face. Sam holds it high above us both, the koala's ears flapping in the icy wind. Sam *is* tall. Six foot three, perhaps, maybe even six four. Mum would definitely be pleased. "I can't abide short men," she always says as if talking about an infestation of roof rats. "Spiteful little things. Malicious."

After speaking to Charlie on the phone, I'd gone for a short walk to find a bush on the hard shoulder to pee behind, which was about as life-affirming as you'd expect, and on my way back, two police officers had told me crisis groups were on their way and that a lorry was giving out free food and water to drivers a little way down the motorway. And as a helicopter circled high above, somewhere in the black sky, I was struck properly by just how serious and real this actually was. *Stranded in traffic. Free food and water. Crisis groups.* For us. For Sam and me, for the hundreds of us stuck here on a motorway. I'd texted Ian to update him, my mouth suddenly dry with anxiety. He'd sent a message straight back, as dutifully as ever, in the way Ian always does—half text, half Trip Advisor review—and it made me smile and thawed the worry, imagining him and Mum safe and warm at home.

All fine and in hand here, he'd texted. **Listening to traffic radio. Very good coverage. Friendly presenter. Welsh. Stay warm.**

By the time I got back to the car, Sam had finished his chat with Jenna.

Food, I'd mimed through the glass of the window, and he'd rolled it down. "Down there, apparently. Back of a truck. I can go and get some? Drop it off?"

Sam had opened his car door then. "I'll grab my jacket," he'd said. "Back of a truck cuisine."

We talked on the way down the motorway, meandering past open car doors and other drivers, about the hungriest we've ever felt in our lives, about the worst thing we'd ever eaten, joking about what we hoped to find being handed out. "Hot Cornish pasties," I'd said, and Sam had said, "Never tried one. Mine'd be oysters."

"*Oysters?* Never tried them, but *ugh.*"

"You should try them before you judge, you know."

"Nope," I'd replied. "Face might blow up. You know, I might have a reaction. You hear of it all the time. One oyster and that's it—your face is a baked potato." And Sam laughed, his breath making clouds in the air. He's smart, that's what Mum would call him—a black duffle coat, buttoned all-but-one to the collar, a charcoal-gray scarf, knotted at the neck. "Very swish," Mum would say. "Such lovely shoulders. And what a *lovely* straight and strong back." I bet Jenna would say the same too, whoever Jenna is, and we haven't quite established that yet, and why should we? He hardly knows me. I'm some woman from the motorway who blows her nose on microfiber cloths and grabs at his phone like it's a bloody life buoy. But it's that *something* again, that feeling I can't name. The alive, buzzy, electricity feeling. Sparks, as Charlie said, and it's that that's making me want to ask, and to know, and I wish it'd stay and piss off all at once.

"Cheese?"

A woman in a sleeveless high-vis jacket smiles down at us now from the inside edge of the lorry, brandishing two sandwiches in cardboard triangles. She hands them to me, followed by two bottles of water, and I balance them in my arms.

"Thank you," we say, and a man squeezes past us to the front of the queue and says, "Got anything gluten-free, love?" and as we walk away, we hear her yet again say, "Cheese?" like a puppet, preprogrammed with only one word. *Cheese.*

Sam and I look at each other at the exact same time, and the knowing smile he gives me makes a wave roll over in my stomach.

• • •

We walk back to the car on the hard shoulder where the snow is thicker on the ground, but less slippery from the lack of footsteps and tire tracks. Spindly, young trees line the border of the motorway, snow balancing on their skinny branches like icing sugar, and we walk together, our shoes crunching on the snow underfoot, the air almost *too* silent in the way it is when it snows. Sounds muted and closer, the snow a natural soundproofer.

Sam looks at me at the same time I glance over at him, the koala umbrella high above our heads, the bundle of sandwiches and bottled water still cradled in my arms. And it suddenly catches up with me in one gust. *This.* The motorway. The snow. Me and Sam. The fact he could be anyone; the fact he is a stranger. The fact somehow—and I really don't know how—I don't feel like he is.

"What's up?" he asks calmly. It's easy to see, even in the short time I've spent with Sam, why he does the job he does. It's what you need, I suppose, if you ever find yourself hanging off a rock face, in need of a life-saving hand. Someone calm and steady. The sort of person that would fare well in an apocalypse.

"Nothing," I say, shaking my head, but it does nothing to stop the heat blooming across my

49

cheeks. *Crayfish Face,* says Dilly's voice in my head. *Seriously, Elle, proper Crayfish Face happening right now. Sort it out.* "I dunno," I say. "It's just—I can't believe this has happened. It's all a bit . . . well, it's mad, isn't it?"

"What, this? The snow? Walking along the freeway?"

"Freeway," I repeat. "And yeah. All of that."

Sam rubs a hand at the dark stubble of his jaw. "Yeah. I guess it is."

And also *this,* I want to say: walking with you, a stranger from thousands of miles away, mere hours ago on his way to the airport; and me, on my way home from an evening that went spectacularly to shit. Daisy's letter. Her lost camera. *Ed.* Yet if it had gone spectacularly *right,* if the snow hadn't happened, if my phone hadn't died, we'd have never met, Sam and me. I wouldn't be right here.

"It's almost pretty, isn't it?" I say. A tactical change of subject. "The trees, the snow . . ."

"Almost," says Sam. "Either that, or you've got, like, motorway Stockholm syndrome, or something."

"Maybe," I say. "But look, if we angle ourselves like this—" I turn my back to Sam, and the gridlocked streams of motionless cars, straggles of drivers, some in their cars, some outside. "And we walk and look this way, at just the trees and the snow—" I look over my shoulder at him, one

50

of the koala ears above his head flapping, as if waving. "We could be anywhere."

Sam gives a grimace. "Oh-*kay*."

"You're not convinced."

Sam laughs, lines at the corner of his eyes crinkling.

"You don't know what you're missing, Sam. Have a little imagination."

Sam pauses for a while. He does that a lot, I notice, before he speaks, as if he lines his words up in his head before he says them out loud, instead of letting everything spill out, like a cluttered cupboard suddenly opened. "I guess at a push, we could be in a park somewhere," he says. "Or in a . . . very bald forest."

"We could be somewhere like *Iceland,*" I say.

"Or Quebec. You ever been to Quebec?"

I shake my head, keep walking. "Never. Not been anywhere like that really. Although I'd love to."

"Well—there it is." I glance over my shoulder to look at him. He's turned sideways now too, his smile amused, like a reluctant teacher who has finally given in to a student's silly joke. "Yup. Here we are. Snowy Quebec. Wow. It is just like the *brochures*."

"See? We just have to ignore the sound of music from cars."

"Yeah, and the police radios and the helicopter and—is that a—" Sam stops walking for a second and so do I. "Is that a *banjo?*"

51

"I have it on very good authority that it is a banjo, yes."

"Right." Sam chuckles, and we begin walking again, still angled away from the road, and just thinking about how we must look to other drivers makes me smile, all hot cheeks and tingles.

"We could just pretend there's a busker in a Quebec park with us," I say. "You just dropped money into his banjo case because Americans always tip and we Brits are terrified of it. Giving too much, giving too little . . ."

"And we're on vacation," Sam says, as if it's factual. "Trip around the world. Planned it for months—years. You printed an itinerary."

"Did I?"

"I think you did."

"I do quite like an itinerary," I say.

"Jetlagged and in Quebec, that's us," Sam carries on. "With a busker and an itinerary."

"And absolutely not on the hard shoulder of the M4. With emergency cheese sandwiches."

"Walking sideways," says Sam.

"With a stranger," I add. And as I look over my shoulder again, Sam meets my eyes with his and shrugs.

"I dunno," he says slowly. "Are we still strangers?"

Then from behind us, a hard thump and a yelp. Sam swoops round quicker than I do, and I see her. A woman on the icy ground, slumped at a bumper, clutching at her head, a single stream of blood trickling down her face, like on those Instagram Halloween makeup tutorials. Sam sprints over, my koala umbrella still in his hand.

CHAPTER SIX

It lands out of nowhere. A plummet—heart to pit of stomach. And I feel it land, like a rock in my gut, in sync with the bang of a heavy car door closing outside. Sam is two cars ahead, crouched in the open door of the woman's car, a police officer standing over him. His smiling, pink mouth moves—chatting, but his eyes are focused as he fixes up the wound. The woman slipped on the ice and bashed her head on the bumper of her own car. The police officer had sprinted over at the same time Sam had. He's first-aid trained, he'd told the officer, fixes up wounds all the time at work. I'd walked over, feeling like a helpless sack of turnips, and Sam had given me a small smile, his hand at the woman's head, and passed me the umbrella. He'd come back to the car to get a large rucksack he'd pulled from the trunk, and I'd told him I'd wait inside. And that's where I am now. My sad, wet koala collapsed in the footwell of Sam's rental car, with the crushed but still intact bottles of water I'd dropped like a sitcom fool as Sam had sprinted over. I watch him now, through the windshield, all wise and tall and handsome and strong and familiar, his lips parted in concentration, snow still falling.

And the voice in my head slides in, as if an actor on cue in a play. "What are you doing?" it says, critical and no-nonsense. "What are you playing at, running away with the fairies like this? This isn't a movie, Noelle, this is real life. *Your life.* And this can't go anywhere. Not in any way, shape, or form. Because Sam will get on a plane back to his life, and you will drive home, back to yours. To Levison Drive, back to Mum, back to your routine and work, and that will be that. Because you are strangers. And you don't know him, and he doesn't know you." I nod in the darkness of the car, like a scolded child, and pull a heavy blanket to my chin. A man from the crisis group, trussed up like a skier, had handed me two of them, plus a freezer bag full of custard creams and two bottles of orange juice a few minutes ago through the passenger door, then he'd joined the policeman and Sam, offering his own aid of ziplock snacks.

Sam's locked phone vibrates in the cubby again—another attempt by the universe to plonk me back into reality, perhaps. A text from—I'm sure—leggy, perfect, and beachy-haired Jenna again, although I can't see what it says. And then my own phone vibrates. A reminder from the gas company, asking me to submit my meter readings. A reminder, on both accounts, that normal life is out there waiting for us both to resume, and this weird situation on the motorway, stuck in snow with custard creams, is just a tiny little stopgap. An interval.

Eventually Sam clicks open the car door and quickly jumps in.

"Jesus, it is *cold.*" He blows into his hands and looks over at me. "You OK?"

I nod. "Fine. And is she?"

"Yup. Good as new. Her friend's gonna drive, so she's in good hands." Sam leans a hand across to the radio, turns it up a little.

"It's cool that you know what to do," I say. "Brave."

Sam chuckles. "*Hardly.* Although, I admit, I kind of like being prepared for the worst. Which sounds dark as fuck as I say that out loud, but I don't know—you never know what's around the corner, right?" Then he looks at me, an eyebrow slightly cocked. "I can hear the cogs in your brain."

"What?"

"Something my mom says—*your thinking's keeping me awake.*"

"Oh."

"Are you worried? About fuel, food, and—being stuck? Was it the blood?"

"No," I say. "Well, yes. Maybe. And I am worried. But mostly trying not to think about it. That's my tactic most of the time."

"We'll be OK. Noelle *Not*-Gallagher," he says with a smile, and I imagine what it must be like to climb a mountain with him, which is laughable considering the furthest I've ever climbed is the steps at Covent Garden station, and halfway up I panicked and told some poor random man with a briefcase that I was having a heart attack and to call for help (and he did not). But I wouldn't do that with Sam with me, I bet. He'd be all heroic, all unshakable, all *there are several mountain lions out there, but if everyone follows me, I'll get us out alive. But firstly, I must remove my shirt.*

"Anyway, the snow's already slowing," he carries on. "The cop said it wouldn't be too much longer."

"Oh. Well. Good."

His brow crinkles beneath his soft, dark hair. "You seem disappointed."

I look at him. "Ugh, I can't."

"Can't what?"

Can't tell you I never want to leave, Sam, I want to say. Can't tell you that I hardly know you and yet I do not want to get out of this car, and I can't even put into clear and concise, sane-sounding words why that is.

"Nothing," I say instead, and groan, hiding my face as I feel it heat up like it's coated in one of those self-heating volcanic face masks. I hear Sam chuckle from behind my hands.

"Seriously, what?"

I peer at him through the gap between my fingers.

"I'm having a really good time," I say, the words muffled through my hands. "With you. Here."

Sam presses his lips together, as if to stop a rogue smile. "*OK,* and that's, what—bad?"

"*No.* No." I laugh, my face as hot as sizzling rump steak. "It's just—this whole thing is so weird. And . . . I mean, we're fucking *stranded.*"

"Yeah?"

"And . . . we have no food besides these sandwiches and biscuits, and I'm peeing in bushes and behind signs for the nearest bloody Burger King, and you're fixing up injuries, and *blood,* and you'd think that all I'd want is to be at home, where everything is normal and safe and *warm,* but—I don't want to go home." I drop my hands to my lap. "There. Said it."

Sam watches me quietly, then looks out the windshield as if considering what I've said. Then he looks over at me and says, "Does it help if I say *same?*"

I smile. "It does. Well, look, maybe we can just stay."

"Build a hut in Quebec," adds Sam. "Out of sticks. Old banjos."

"Deal."

Sam laughs but says nothing else.

I want to ask then, about Jenna. About a wife or a girlfriend. About what's waiting for him at home, if he feels what I feel. This pull. This feeling of . . . *something*. But I don't—I can't. I don't want anything to ruin it—because it's perfect, this night. So unexpectedly, strangely perfect.

My eyes drift to the clock on the dash—two a.m. "God. I can't believe I was meant to be at a party tonight," I say.

Sam yawns, gives a half chuckle. "A party?"

"Yeah." It isn't a lie, not really. The reunion was meant to be a party, of sorts—beer and music and food and catching up with old friends. But if I said reunion, if I said time capsule, out loud, to Sam, I know I might feel obligated to have to give up more. And I can so easily give up more about anything else. I'm that cluttered cupboard, opened, words toppling out, filling silences. But Daisy, losing her, and almost losing myself—it's one of those things I like to keep close to my chest. So close, I sometimes think it's burrowed a hole in the skin, a dark little hollow it's hidden in for fifteen years. "Yep, I had it all planned out," I carry on. "I was meant to bump into my ex-boyfriend, show him I was fine, you know, to prove him wrong or something. And there was also a part of me—a stupid part maybe, hoping it might spark something again. That it's . . . I dunno, *meant to be,* that Ed would be back home, after two years. He's a doctor. Pediatric rheumatology. He moved for work."

Sam listens carefully.

"But he ignored me. Looked right through me when he saw me. And then I ended up here."

Sam looks through the windshield—that methodical gathering of words in his head. "I did a climb with a bunch of medics last year," he says. "And they may be smart and noble and stuff, but in my experience—they do stupid shit on mountains. Hurt themselves, leave important stuff behind, almost die trying to get the perfect shot for Instagram. I was ready to push one of them *off*. Tell the cops he wore bad shoes or something."

I laugh. A warm, belly-clenching laugh.

"So maybe it applies to parties too," he says, looking over at me. "Ignoring you: stupid shit."

Warmth spreads across my skin like the sun just rose.

"Seriously. Ed the Ped sounds like a shit *head*," says Sam, as if it's a fact. "Not that you're asking me."

"I am," I say.

CHAPTER SEVEN

I'm shaken awake, a warm hand on my shoulder, and for a moment I forget. It's still dark outside, but the snow has stopped, and the stark white lights of hundreds of headlights outside makes it feel like someone's flicked the house lights on. The show: *over.*

"Sorry," says Sam croakily. "The road's reopening. Cop just knocked."

"God, did I—did I fall asleep?"

"For just an hour, I guess."

"Did you?"

He looks pale, and his dark hair is ruffled on the top of his head, as if he might have. "I napped a little, I think."

I sit up, push the hair from my face. Sam has already doubled his blanket over in a rectangle on the armrest. I do the same, folding mine into one thick bundle now and resting a hand on top. And it's now that the weirdness of everything hits me again, like a slap in the face. I slept in a stranger's car. I slept wrapped in another stranger's blanket. I ate biscuits handed to me by a man in a ski mask on the M4. I left home almost *twelve bloody hours ago.* If I were to suddenly discover this was all a fever dream, I think I'd believe it. It would make the most sense.

"What do you think we should do with these? The blankets."

Sam gives a shrug, runs his hands through his dark, wavy hair. "Donate them? Keep them?"

"I'll take them with me. You're not going to want to be lumbered with them at the airport, are you? That's if you're going straight to the airport?"

"I am," Sam says simply.

Something sits between us in the car now, and I don't know what it is. Perhaps it's because it's early and I've been asleep, but the car suddenly feels cold, and my skin is prickled with a layer of goose bumps. The warm, snuggled easiness has gone, and everything feels a bit rigid—*awkward*. Like when the lights come on at the end of a film at the cinema and you feel a pang of vulnerability—the worry of how your sleepy face looks to the strangers streaming by you to the exit, skin cold from too much air-con, the inevitable start of the fun-hangover. And despite myself, I really wish it was last night again. Eight hours. Eight tiny hours is all they were. And already I miss them. Ridiculous. I am *ridiculous*.

Sam straightens in his seat, arching his back. He relaxes then looks over at me. The car is deathly silent. No radio. No more drifting outside voices of other drivers, of other in-car stereos. No more calming hum of the heater.

"I suppose I'd better go, then," I say.

Sam nods reluctantly, but says nothing, and I start gathering up things to take with me—the blankets, my handbag, my koala umbrella, my scarf—

"Do you want some help? I can walk you over." He gives a small smile at the notion of the last few words. The swelling balloon of tension between us deflates a little, and I breathe a bit easier.

"If you don't mind."

Sam and I get out of the car, our coats zipped and buttoned to the top. It's bitter cold outside and the ground at our feet glistens like smashed glass from the salt that the crisis group must have put down from those big cardboard tubes they were holding. Sam holds my things as I try to unlock my car.

"Why won't it—" I struggle with the key. "God, bloody thing usually locks us in, not *out*—"

"Let me try."

Sam passes me back my stuff and jangles the keys in the lock, teeth nibbling his pink lips as he does, his hair dangling over his eyes. I want to tell him to stay in touch. I want to put my arms around him. *God,* what am I even *thinking?*

"There." Sam straightens and pulls open the

car door. I look up at him, the remnants of our evening piled high in my arms. "Thank you."

He gives a singular deep nod.

"And thank you for the phone charger. And the company. And . . . everything."

Sam smiles—a smile that makes that prod-mark of a dimple appear in his cheek. "Ditto," he says. Then his lips part, and I think he's going to say something else, but he doesn't. *Go on, ask for my number.* An email address, an Instagram handle. *Something.* We could be friends. We could keep in touch, keep each other updated. A second chance at that pen pal in Portland. Yes, he lives in Oregon and barely comes over to see the family he alluded to visiting "once in a blue moon," but we can't just leave it at this, can we?

"We better go," says Sam as an engine from a car behind us rumbles to life.

"Y-yeah. OK. Right." I smile—fake and awkward, more like a strain, but he buys it, I think, doesn't sense my disappointment. And he starts to walk away, as I stand there by my open car door, engines chugging around me, blankets and belongings bundled under my arm like it's 1999 and I'm on my way back from a sleepover. Then he stops and turns, shoes crunching on the ice: "Noelle?"

My heart lifts in my chest, as if suddenly suspended.

"Yes?"

"Drive safe."

And that is the last thing Sam says to me.

When I get into my car, when I chuck the bundle of crap on my passenger seat, as I start the engine, when the car starts to smell of singed dust from my ancient heaters, as I turn up the radio, I wait. For him to jump out of the car, to tell me to wind down my window, to pass me a number—something scrawled on that old crossword page. But it doesn't come. And although I really want to be the one to ask, something inside me tells me not to. And really, what would be the point of staying in touch? All those miles. Another person to miss. He probably meets a lot of people, a lot of strangers, and his friendliness, his easy-to-be-aroundness is probably part of the job. It's why people recommend him. "Oh, you need Sam," they probably say, "he's cool and calm and *such a nice guy*. Also, if you're in the business for nice strong arms that could wrestle away a mountain lion in nothing but rags then throw you over his shoulder for no reason whatsoever, then *whew,* he's definitely your guy . . ."

When the traffic begins to move, Sam and I are alongside one another for a while. Me in my car, him in his, the hire car he'll soon drop at the airport to be parked and lost in a meaningless fleet of others. A few times I look over, study his face through the glass—the straight line of his nose, the dark stubble of his jaw, the smile lines by his brown eyes. I squirrel it away in my memory.

The roads clear, traffic speeds up, and I watch Sam until his car is a speck in the distance, and like those eight perfect hours, he is gone.

CHAPTER EIGHT

FIVE WEEKS LATER

Charlie taps the wooden shop countertop with a hand twice, like an impatient drunk in a bar. "Hey, babe!" she calls out. "How are we getting on back there with those tomatoes?" She turns to me, her eyes dreamy, flicks of neon-pink liquid liner at the corners. "I swear to God, these tomatoes, Noelle. Had them last week. Felt like my life had changed—literally. Something . . . *opened* inside of me. Fruit can do that to you, you know."

"Is that right?"

"And some veg too. With the right asparagus . . ." Charlie winks. "Mark my words." And I would, if I had a clue what they meant.

She leans across the counter, craning her neck to see out the back of the shop. "Theo?" she shouts again. "Oi." Theo doesn't reply. A customer filling a glass bottle with thick, treacly olive oil from a glass keg looks over at us, eyes unblinking like a disapproving teacher, and I desperately want to laugh.

I love Wednesdays. I know some people find routines stifling or monotonous or boring.

You're a total robot, Elle, Dilly would say. But to me—I don't know. Routines mean knowing what to expect. Routines mean having something to look forward to. And every Wednesday looks the same. Ian drops by for breakfast with Mum, meaning I can get up and out early, just me, a few dog walkers, the glow of a new sun, the sound of birdsong and my own footsteps. I drop by the tiny little supermarket in town that always does their price reductions far too late and has yesterday's flowers at pennies, and pick up what I can find (today, two bunches of alstroemeria, the color of strawberry milk). I drop by Adly's flat—a London banker I clean for once a fortnight, who hardly ever comes back to his clinical square of a studio flat, and then it's on to clean my friend Charlie and her husband Theo's two-bed maisonette above Buff, their plastic-free grocers and deli. Their flat is the total opposite to Adly's. All rugs and cushions and weird wooden artifacts that I'm sure, after dusting and considering them every week for two years, are mostly sculptures of genitals. I clean, I organize, I arrange flowers in the windows, and at twelve, Charlie glides in on her lunch break and constructs an organic lunch from Theo's salad bar that she tells me will "momentarily open her third eye." We stand then, like we are now, on the shiny, wooden shop floor and talk, as Theo scuttles about in the storeroom and serves customers, and most of the time with

Petal, their three-month-old baby, on his chest in a sling, her tiny starfish hands clenched. Nothing much really ever happens on Wednesdays. They're simple really, but they're dependable—safe little markers to remind me that I've made it another week, and how lucky I am that I have. Plus, Theo and Charlie are two of the happiest people I know, and regardless of your mood, it rubs off on you, like perfume.

"Right." Theo appears behind the counter, a baby monitor in one hand, Charlie's lime-green bento box in the other. Today he's without little Petal and the baby sling he hand-sewed from an old duvet cover. "That's the last of them, my love."

"King of my heart," Charlie says, holding her hands in a balled fist at her chest.

"Queen of mine," he replies, and he leans to adjust her headband, kissing the tip of her nose through his thick brown beard. Charlie and Theo are really in love—that sort of brazen, public in-love that would usually make me want to dunk my head into a bowl of steaming hot custard. But it suits them, Charlie and Theo, in their totally unapologetic, hippie—and admittedly, sometimes utterly bizarre—little world.

"Petal's down for her second nap." He looks at the baby monitor, her fluffy little head a fuzzy ball on the dark screen. "It helps, I think, the baby massage."

Charlie smiles. "You are the father to end all fathers," she says. "I used to think it was Peter Andre. But frankly, you'd shit all over him."

Theo chuckles. "Do you want to come up, kiss her goodbye?"

"Better not," says Charlie, eyes sliding to the baby monitor on the counter. "She looks flat-out; I might wake her. Plus, I've got an appointment in ten."

"Ah." Theo nods, pushing his hands into the thick square pocket of his apron. "Well, you just keep telling all those weird musos that visit the studio to come and get their lunch here. Had a whole rock band come in last week, Noelle, from Char's studio. They cleared me out. Canadian. They were really taken with my okra."

I laugh. "But I thought rock stars were supposed to snort cocaine off bare arses and throw TVs at people. Not fawn over *vegetables*."

"Mm," says Charlie, nodding, a sun-blushed tomato between her fingers, the short nails painted grapefruit pink. "They definitely do that as well. Singer's a total letch with a face like a plate, but—" Charlie shrugs. "What can I say? The geezers know good veg. *And* once they posted their ink on their Instagram, I got like five thousand followers overnight. Total pricks. But very useful pricks. Anyway—" She snaps the lid on her bento box and jerks her head. "Walk me to work, Noelle?"

The shop bell jingles like an old bicycle above our heads as we leave Theo's shop and step out into the warm spring sunshine. An all-windows-down car booms with bass-y dance music as it zooms by, rumbling exhaust and thick gray smoke.

"Half past twelve," says Charlie, glancing at the watch on her wrist before linking her arm through mine. "You're living *wildly* today, Noelle Butterby."

"Because I bought a tenner's worth of organic dates?"

Charlie laughs and squeezes my arm. "Because it's twelve thirty and you're walking in the direction that takes us into dangerous Ed McDweeby-Donnell territory."

I shrug, although of course I know this—might as well have a wall chart up in my bedroom marking his movements with pins and alternate routes mapped out to *avoid* his predicted movements. Since the time capsule event, Charlie has seen Ed in town twice—albeit from a distance—and both times at about half past twelve on a weekday, near the train station. Ever since then, I've avoided that part of town, walking the long way to my car.

"I know," I say to Charlie. "But I point-blank refuse to avoid him any longer. This is my town, right? He left, not me. And even if he is back for good, *he* should feel weird about seeing *me*."

The words sound convincing coming out of my mouth, but I'm not sure my heart is quite sold just yet. I figure it'll follow eventually, get bored of being the odd one out.

"That's my girl," says Charlie. "And remember what I said. When you *do* eventually see him, just smile, give a wave, say, 'Oh, you all right?' and walk on by as if you've seven thousand better things to be doing today. You know, like, *see ya, gotta roll, too busy to chat.* Oh—quick." Charlie yanks me toward the crossing. "Green dude."

Spring has arrived all of a sudden, as if it's never been away. Sleepy bees, the chivey smell of cut grass, and the gullibility that you might just be able to get away with not wearing a jacket (until the sun is swallowed whole by a cloud). I'm grateful that it's late April, the sun bleaching away old stains, and the fresh spring breeze blowing away the cobwebs, ready for all things new. Those few weeks that followed the reunion seemed to drag and stagnate, like the endless, relentless gray skies outside. I called the college every day for the first week, to see if they'd found Daisy's camera. I gave up when I got a sigh from the man on the other end of the line, the second I spoke my name.

"I really do think you need to wait until the rescheduled event," he said, sounding bored. "In the unlikely event it's already been unburied, we have your details." And I'd said sorry, and I still don't really know what for. Because I'm not sorry for wanting something that belonged to my best friend, or for wanting to see the last photos she ever took of us all. And I'm not sorry to want to post new pictures of Daisy to her mum, Mingmei, who has lived for fifteen years with the same ones. I couldn't bring myself to send her letter last week—the one I'd written to Daisy fifteen years ago, waffling about all the places we'd go. A letter talking about all the things her daughter could've done would be easier to read, I'm sure, if there'd been photos of her inside, too, bursting with life and smiles, as Daisy always was.

And then of course, there was all the day-dreaming about Sam. God, the bloody *day-dreaming* and the replaying. I thought about him so much at first that I started to forget what he looked like—as if I'd worn the memory away, like the print of an old newspaper. It's simmered down a lot—and thank God—but I still think about him, of course (including one *Oscar-worthy* dream that starred me, Sam, and an outside mountaintop shower last week that sounded like a Regency novella when I typed it out to Charlie in WhatsApp the next morning). But the routine of normal life and the new spring sun has really helped the snow of March feel like another lifetime ago. And I'm relieved. No normal Homo sapien wants to spend their nights trying to mimic someone's deep, sexy laugh out loud, and asking, "dearest Google, is it classed as stalking if it's only thoughts and occasionally punching 'Sam Oregon Mount Hood Alpine Guide Hot Instagram' into your little search bar and hoping to find an account?"

Charlie leans her head against my shoulder, her ice-blond hair tickling my chin. "I keep reading Daisy's letter to you," she says with a sigh. "I must've read it like, twenty times."

I nod. "You and me both, Char."

"I love the way she wrote. The way she talks about your soul mate, the *pizza dough*. And the red thread—what's that about again? I remember something. Vaguely. Didn't she actually give us red threads once?"

I smile. "She did. For Valentine's."

Charlie sighs again, spreads a hand across her chest.

"It's a belief—a Chinese proverb," I tell Charlie. "That a red thread connects two people who are destined to meet. It can tangle, but never break."

"God," breathes Charlie, "she was so bloody romantic, wasn't she? So . . . I dunno. Magic. She'd have been a novelist. A poet. She'd have—made mountains move, that's for sure."

"She would have," I say, and an unexpected lump bobs in my throat.

"Felt a bit gutted," says Charlie, "that I didn't go to college with you both."

"Really?"

"Yeah," she says sadly.

Daisy and I met Charlie when we were sixteen and started working evenings as waitresses for a local caterer who did weddings and posh birthday parties. Charlie was two years older than us and the cool girl we so desperately wanted to be, with her ever-changing hair and fishnet tights and hot pants combos. She was a *shitty* waitress—seriously, the worst—and did nothing but snog groomsmen and eat half-finished plates left by guests, and we did nothing but cover for her. We officially fell in love with her the day she bribed a chef to store dinner rolls in his boxer shorts, which after an hour, she reclaimed and served to a wedding guest who'd groped her arse without consent.

"Arse-baked rolls," she'd smirked at us, and she'd left before the dessert course, when her latest musician boyfriend had picked her up in his rusty old minivan, cigarette smoke billowing from the windows like a bonfire on wheels.

"I just keep thinking about what Daisy might've said to me, if I had a letter," says Charlie. "What do you think she'd have said, Elle?"

I smile to myself, but a small bubble of sadness inflates in my chest. I tortured myself for such a long time, back then, about what Charlie might've secretly thought of me, for letting Daisy get in the car. I asked her once, and she was horrified, of course, said she'd have let her go too, and it helped. But I've wondered over and over if she just said it to make me happy. Because Charlie's good at that. Fiercely unrelenting in her support for people she loves, regardless of what they do. I truly think if I suddenly announced I was taking up nude basketball, there she'd be, in the stands, my name printed on the back of a jersey, cheering me on.

"I think she'd have told you to go and snog all the rock stars," I say to her. "To get backstage at Warped Tour. To keep being Charlie Wilde. Charlie Wilde by name—"

"Wilde by nature," Charlie finishes my sentence, and we both laugh. We come to Wilde Heart, the narrow, glass shop front of Charlie's tattoo studio—she's had her shop six years now, a venture she ran with, like she always does, without a single shred of fear or self-doubt. "So." She unloops her arm from mine and puts her hand on the glass door, its wooden frame painted bubble gum pink. "You track down the American from Ohio yet?" Clouds drift over the sun, a cool breeze bristling the ends of her blunt bob.

"Oregon." I laugh. "And no, you know I haven't." I don't tell Charlie that I've tried. That I keep putting random things into Google, that I actually found where Sam works—the website for the summit programs he mentioned, on Mount Hood. I was led there by a mention of a "Sam" in

a blog by another guide, detailing "A Day in the Life of." That's all I can find.

"Private investigator," says Charlie now, and I laugh again and say, "Yeah, because that isn't creepy at *all*."

"He might be trying to find you too."

"I doubt it."

"I had my first sexual awakening with an American," she says. "On MSN. His name was Justin."

"I thought your first sexual awakening was with H from Steps."

"Oh shit, yeah," she says. "Can't forget H. OK, so I had my *second* sexual awakening with an American on MSN. First was H. In that video, *It's the Way You Make Me Feel*. Holy shit, dude. The ruffles. The forlorn look of a Regency man who'd ruin your life."

"Sure."

"And your *gusset,*" Charlie says, and we both burst into laughter. She holds her arms out for a hug, and I put mine around her. Charlie always smells like pear drops and bubble gum, a contrast to the deep, fermented orange skins smell that wafts over from the greengrocer's next door.

"Elle," she says, pulling back and looking at me. "Do you think I'm still her?"

I pause. *"Who?"*

Charlie looks at me sadly. "Charlie Wilde."

"Well, you're Charlie *Christopoulos* now. You got married, remember? That Greek bloke back there. With the life-changing tomatoes and good bread."

I laugh. Charlie doesn't.

"No, I mean—have I changed? Like, totally?"

I hold her shoulders. "No," I say. "And also, *yes*. Like all of us have. Because that's normal, right, that we all grow up, all change? But course. You'll always be Charlie Wilde to me."

She smiles at that, a look of victory on her face, and kisses my cheek. "Bye, Noelle," she says, then she strides off into her shop, the loud music inside flowing out into the street, then fading again as the door closes behind her.

I walk for ten minutes or so, stopping at the bakery for the nice bread Mum likes, for some things she wanted me to pick up from Superdrug. But it's like they say—well, like Charlie and Theo say, and those weird law of attraction videos they watch on YouTube. The more you think about something, the more you pay mind to it, whether it's something you want or don't want, the more it seems to crop up. And as the bleep of the green man sounds and I walk across the road, I see him. Ed. Standing outside the coffee shop next to the train station, on the phone, a bag slung over his shoulder, his mouth moving quickly.

And it's too late. He sees me, holds a hand up in a wave, and I can't stop, can't turn around. I have no choice but to keep walking with the flurry of people crossing—crossing to *his* side of the road,

78

right into his path. Reaching the pavement, I plan on doing what Charlie said—a quick smile, a wave, an "Oh. You all right?" as I keep on going, too busy to stop, but he's hanging the phone up, dropping it to his side and walking toward me, and we meet a few strides from the curb.

"Nellie," he says. "Hey."

It's strange seeing someone you used to see so often that they just became part of the scenery of your life. Even when it's been over seven hundred days without a single word from them, they slot right back in. You remember instantly the things you thought you forgot. The sharp lines of their cheekbones, the wide mouth you've kissed a thousand times, the two tiny moles, like two paint flecks on their jaw. A part of me wants to throw my arms around Ed, as I look at him now, to snuggle up with him, catch up with him, talk about the thousands of days of memories only we share. To hear him say, "We were idiots, Nell. Why did we do what we did? Why did I leave without you?" Another part of me wants to run the fuck away too, of course, pretend my little world is totally undisrupted—as it always is.

"Hi," I say. "You all right?"

"Yeah, good. It's good to see you. How've you been?" He smiles, the sun catching in his eyes. Light always makes Ed's eyes look the deepest olive green.

"Fine, fine. On my way back from work so . . ." My stomach churns. I can't believe I'm looking at him. Ed. *My Ed* for so long.

"I've just finished," he says. "Working over at the hospital. Ten-hour shift that ticked over into twelve, then thirteen. You know how it is, Nell." He grins at me knowingly.

"Cool, so, you're back, then?"

Ed nods. "Yeah! There was a new opportunity—in a rheums wing, but working with adults at the moment. My brother recommended me, and it just seemed meant to be, you know? The US was amazing, but—I dunno. I needed to get away for a bit. And I missed home." He looks at me then and I feel warmth spread across my chest, like sunlight. But almost in tandem, my hackles rise, thinking of the way he ignored me at the reunion, turned as if he didn't even know me. That I was nobody.

"So, did you pick up your envelope?"

He stares. "What?"

"Your envelope," I carry on. "From the reunion. The time capsule thing."

"Oh. Yeah. Yeah, I did." He scratches the back of his neck and cocks his head then, gives me that sideways wince. The "ah, shit" wince he's given me a thousand times before, across the kitchen table, or from his pillow to mine, when he'd screwed up, or I'd cooked something bad for dinner that I'd spent seven hours marinating.

"Nell, this—" Sideways wince. "Sorry, this tastes . . . awful." I almost smile right here on the pavement imagining us both melting into laughter at our little round dining table, before sliding our dinners into the food waste bin and calling Masala Hut for our usual takeaway.

"Look, I'm sorry. I just—I wasn't really expecting to see you."

"Wasn't expecting to see me?"

"No, no, I knew you'd go, obviously, of course I did. I think I just thought I'd probably missed you and then . . . there you were. I was just a bit thrown." He laughs then, flashing that cheeky grin I obsessed over in college to Daisy, who shared biology class with him. "I don't get it, Noelle," Daisy would say. "You and Charlie and your cheeky chappy thing. I mean, he's nice, and funny and everything, but don't you want someone better? Taller? I want a tortured poet. Someone like Lee, that boy on the plumbing course. He's like that, I can tell. *Total* troubled Byron vibes."

"Nell, I'm sorry," says Ed. "What can I say? I was a bit of a twat."

I nod. "A bit. A *lot*."

"OK, fine. A lot."

That's what's unfair about breakups. They're nearly always one-sided. One person has made their mind up way before the other. They've done the grieving, they've done the boxing away of feelings, and you—well, your feelings are still wandering around, like lost kittens, trying to find their home. That's how this feels. My wandering, homeless feelings have emerged from their little dark corners. Because he's back. The person that tossed them out in the cold in the first place. And for twelve years, Ed was my home.

"Sorry, I really need to get going."

" 'Course." Ed nods and takes a step forward, like he considers hugging me, but instead he puts his hands in his pockets, shoulders square. "Maybe we can—grab coffee or something?"

I hesitate. "Bye, Ed" is all I say, and I turn away. Because this has lasted longer than I ever planned it to in my mind and I want to quit while I'm ahead. Before he mentions something to ruin it. Oregon, and everything I missed by not going with him. The woman with the auburn curls and perfect eyebrows that was beside him in his Twitter picture for a few months that I'd zoom in on and pick apart with Charlie. "She looks cruel," Charlie would say, well and truly scraping the barrel. "And I bet she has really bad breath too. You know. Not-eaten-for-hours, sour, horse-poo breath. She looks the type."

I don't wait for Ed to say goodbye, I don't give him the chance to. I walk away, heart banging in my chest, as if it had started running long before I did.

CHAPTER NINE

Today I have opened the website for the summit program Sam works on three times. Some days it seems totally sweet and harmless, the idea of sending an email. Other times it feels like I might as well be outside his house in a false beard and sunglasses, wearing a hedge and holding an SLR camera. There are sixteen of them, half-written in my drafts folder. I've yet to send a single one, of course, but sometimes, when he flits into my mind, I'm tempted to press send. I think of him now, too, as I tie these daffodils together with brown hessian twine, the odd plum-colored tulip nestled in the spray, and remember the conversation we had about flowers during those eight hours in his car.

"So, would you say your hobby is your job?" I'd asked Sam beneath my blanket that night, and he'd said, "I guess it is, yeah. And what about you?"

"I wish," I'd told him, then I'd shown him photos on my Instagram page of the posies and bouquets I make for my clients' reception desks and windows; finishing touches for when the rooms are clean and tidy: a burst of fresh color, the scent of the season on the other side of the glass. "I buy my flowers from the supermarket at the end of the day, mostly," I'd told him, "the flowers nobody wants." And Sam had smiled and said, "So, that officially makes you the flower rescuer, then."

A tingle of something trickles down my spine at the sound of his voice in my head. Maybe that's what I loved about those hours in the car with Sam. He asked me questions, he listened, and nothing was off the table. I didn't have to worry about my words inadvertently hurting anyone. Not that talking about my weird and unexpected love of flowers hurts anyone, but it's loaded, how much I wish I could do something more with them in my life. It started as something I did on a whim—planting bulbs in pots in our tiny concrete courtyard garden the summer after Daisy died. I think it helped, having something to nurture, something to look in on every day. Something that started as nothing then burst into life and color. If I didn't care for the seeds, or the bulbs, if I wasn't here anymore, they'd die, or wouldn't have the chance to become anything at all. From then on, they became an unexpected comfort. And I'd be lying if I said I didn't wish they could be a bigger part of my life. To sign up for six-month-long floristry workshops, go to college, try my hand at an actual wedding bouquet that is carried down an aisle instead of put in a vase in the living room and posted online. But if I said any of that to Mum, she'd internalize it. See it as everything I'd do if it wasn't for having to be here for her.

"Going to make a chamomile, I think." Mum comes into the kitchen now, her gray furry mule slippers scraping against the lino, her hand gripping the slate-gray countertop to support her. "Took me a bloody age to get off to sleep last night—*oh*. They're pretty, darling. Who're they for?"

"Jetson's," I say. "They're all on a team-building day tomorrow, so I'm going to clean there in the morning. Candice loves daffodils."

"The receptionist girl?"

I nod.

Mum smiles, the creases by her eyes like doodles of bare branches. "They don't deserve you," she says. "They hire a cleaner and get a bloody angel."

"They expect it now," I say. "They get excited to see what I bring."

I leave out the part about Candice and Steve asking to book me as their wedding florist months ago, and how it took absolutely *everything* inside of me to turn it down. But they're getting married in Edinburgh, which is three hundred and eighty-six miles away (I, of course, counted and counted again, to be sure) and it just isn't doable. Without Ian next door, and with Dilly on tour with his band and living in the back of some sweaty old van, I don't have anyone to keep checking in for a day or two. One day I hope it'll be different. But until then, making up little bouquets at my kitchen table will have to do. Big things, I hope, might happen someday, but it's the little things that are important, isn't it? They keep us grounded. The little things are the things we miss the most when normality is turned on its head.

Mum yawns, the kettle boiling and clicking off, steam rising under the kitchen cupboards like a mushroom cloud. "Dilly said he should be popping home next week," she says, "for a few days. Says he's made quite a bit doing the circuit up north."

"Let's hope so," I say. "Last time Dilly said that, that club owner paid him in meat. Not sure the council accepts pork chops and beef sausages as payment for council tax these days."

Mum laughs, moving a dainty hand flat to her stomach as she waits for the bag to brew in her cup. Sometimes I look at Mum and I can hardly believe her stomach was where I began. Mum is small—*petite,* is what the clothes shops call it. When she was a performer—a singer, and a brilliant one at that—I'd watch her on the stage of holiday parks as a kid, in awe. Everything she wore hung and clung perfectly, and her neat, pixie features under the stage lights made her look like some sort of fifties Hollywood star. Dilly is the same as Mum. Pretty-featured and lean, despite the fact he eats as if he has a stomach hiding in every limb and consumes entire rotisserie chickens while the rest of us manage a sandwich. I'm not like either of them. I take after Dad. I never really knew him, but I've seen photos, have the odd, fuzzy memory of him from when Dilly was a baby. He's tall like me. Curly haired, like me. When I was a kid, I'd dream of suddenly hearing from him, like they do in movies, that he'd have a perfect reason for his absence and it would all suddenly make sense and a perfect fix would be revealed. I'd imagine both of us walking along, our wild curls bouncing in unison. But you learn as you get older and wiser that some people just aren't meant to be in your life. It just doesn't work, even if on paper, in theory, it should. It just *is* the way it is. Mum has always been enough for Dilly and me, anyway. A whole village in one small person. Well, that's who she *was,* anyway, until the stroke.

"Money's really tight, Noelle." Mum's words pierce my thoughts.

"What? How do you mean?"

Money is always tight for us. We've always had to budget, to tick off the bills as they're paid on the list on the fridge, to plan ahead for anything we want to buy that isn't essential. It's all we've ever known.

"Just—well, I didn't realize that Dilly's credit

card bill still has six fifty on it," says Mum. "And the monthly payments are almost double what I thought."

What? And I want to say it, let it blurt from my mouth like I usually do, but I don't with Mum. Because I skirt around her like she is brittle glass, as if the slightest tremor can crack her. And I see now, being close to her, that her usually pink, religiously moisturized skin is gray. She looks tired.

"He said he'd send money back," Mum carries on. "From the gigging."

"And he hasn't."

"I'm sure he'll bring some with him, Noelle," says Mum, her eyes wide and eager, as if to sell it to me. Dilly. Her baby. So like her, in looks, in dreams, in ambition, in musical flair. "But it's just—until then." *And in case he doesn't,* I think.

"I'll speak to him," I say. And I want to say so much more. Because every day I hope Mum will say the words, admit she needs help—counseling, the group therapy a doctor suggested once— admit she misses who she used to be, before she shrunk herself so small. But I don't. Because I understand more than anyone. And things could be so much worse. *I'm here.* I have my family. I have this home. And that is lucky. Luckier than so many. Luckier than where I could've ended up, back then.

"We'll be OK," I say, and I think I convince her. I'm just not sure I've convinced myself.

Text message: Hey Nell. Was nice seeing you the other day. Let me know if you wanna grab that coffee :) You can catch me on my new number. 07882 171 7712 x

CHAPTER TEN

Dilly doesn't come home much. He pretty much lives on the road, playing guitar and singing backup in his band, Five Catastrophes. And while Dilly has the responsibility and common sense of a shelled walnut, I'm always relieved when he comes home for a bit. I don't have to rush back from work. I can go to the market on a Tuesday, browse the weird, vintage clothes stall on the corner. I can visit Charlie in her studio, take lunch in for us, both of us eating it sitting on the leather, hydraulic tattoo chairs. When Dilly is home, my time is—however fleeting—*mine*. Except for today, that is. I planned to meet Candice at a tearoom next to Jetson's to talk about her wedding, help her plan the flowers. I planned to spend a birthday voucher I've had since last February. But then Dilly texted: **Could you come back sooner rather than later?** and then he'd sent a long meandering voice note that started "Do you mind popping back and taking a look at Mum's ankle?" and I'd cut it off before he went on and tossed the phone in my bag. A walnut. That's what happens when you leave a walnut in charge.

I find Mum sitting in the living room with her

leg up on the sofa, a bag of frozen sweet corn around her right leg and a tray of frozen sausages on her foot. Dilly is on the armchair, his hands splayed and holding the edges as if he's just finished counseling her, his white-blond hair sticking up like frosting on the top of his head.

"W-what is going on?"

"We're just doing some meditation," says Dilly. "Help with pain levels."

"Pain levels?"

"Did you not listen to my voice note?" he asks.

Mum is taking deep breaths through her nose and whimpering every time she exhales, but she is rigid, as if there is concrete poured into her joints.

"Yes—well, no, not all of it, it was like a bloody podcast, Dilly, just tell me *what's happened!*"

"Oh, Noelle." Mum opens her eyes and looks at me, like a scolded puppy. "I fell."

My heart drops to my arse. *"Fell?* Where did you fall?"

Mum starts to cry and holds her face in her hands, tears sliding between her fingers. "I was up the ladder," she explains, her voice shaky. "Trying to get into the loft. I've got so many records up there, so many things I don't use anymore, microphones and all sorts, and I thought—well, Ian is always banging on about eBay, and seeing as we were talking about money the other night, I . . ." My heart aches then, like there's a fist wrapped around it, squeezing.

"Oh, Mum. Why on earth did you attempt to climb a bloody ladder—Dilly, where were *you?*"

"I was in the bath," he says with a shrug. "Watching *Gilmore Girls.*"

"I was just lucky I didn't fall down the bloody stairs," Mum carries on. "I fell onto the landing. But my leg got caught in a rung and . . . oh, Noelle, it's really, really hurting."

I rush over to the sofa and carefully peel back the bag of frozen sausages on Mum's skinny ankle. There's a patchwork of purple and blue that seems to be getting darker just as I sit, staring at it.

"Is it bad? I can't look."

Dilly leans over and winces. "It's uh, yeah. That's fine, I reckon."

"Fine? Dill, it's black and purple."

Dilly cocks a single sad eyebrow at me as if to say, "Well, *you* can be the one to tell her we've got to go to the doctor, then, 'cause I'm not."

"I think maybe we need to try and get someone out to look at this, Mum."

Mum goes white almost instantaneously. She hates hospitals. She was in one for four weeks after her stroke, and begged me to break her out daily, as if she were being imprisoned and not cared for. "You come in here with something as simple as a bloody gallbladder problem and come out with MRSA. And that's in a coffin, and with

'My Way' playing on the sodding organ. Don't look at *me,* that's just what Sheila says. Her, in bed four. She used to be a dental nurse."

Mum sniffs, straightens in her seat, and shakes her head, as if shaking off the worry like raindrops. "No. It's a bruise," she says. "I'll be fine." She stretches over to take a look, but I can tell by the way her round eyes widen that she's alarmed at the sight of it, growing, like a marbled island across her skin. "Just get me some painkillers, and maybe call round to Gary at twenty-one. See if he's got ice packs or something in the freezer. These sausages are beginning to defrost. You'll have to cook them, though, Noelle. Don't waste them. Do a nice casserole. A nice sausage toad."

I flit around the kitchen, gathering everything I can find for an injured ankle—ibuprofen, Deep Heat cream from 2003, KitKats for the shock—and Dilly manifests ten minutes later with multiple ice packs he's sourced from Gary's freezer (and an addition of a fine sparkling piece of bullshit plucked freshly from his own arse).

"That was a bit embarrassing." He laughs. "Talk about awkward. *Ol' Gary.* He was a bit starstruck."

"What?"

"Well, he's not seen me since we performed on Radio Rock Gloucester. I dunno, his face when he opened the door and saw me. He was sort of . . . starry-eyed. I suppose that's how I was in Waterstones. When I met Brian May."

I want to tell him that there's as much chance of Gary (who practices hooligan chants before the football season) listening to Radio Rock Gloucester as there is of Mum and her leg exploring Asia with nothing but a compass and harpoon, but I'm trying to find the heating pads, pulling open every kitchen cupboard, as if they'd ever be nestled in with the chocolate Hobnobs and cans of Big Soup.

"Do you think we should call 111?" I ask Dilly. "For medical advice."

Dilly reappears in the doorway after delivering the ice packs. "Nah. I reckon the ice will sort it. Plus, she hates the fuss."

"Do you suggest we just leave it, then?"

He doesn't respond, and instead, starts tapping away on his iPhone, swiping through photos of multiple swollen ankles and calves on Google Images, and disappearing into the living room.

"Dilly?" I call out. "Dilly, do you have that hot-water bottle you got for Christmas?"

"What?" Dilly pokes his head around the door, phone flat to his ear.

"Hot-water bottle?"

"Don't have one of those. Oh—hello, mate, how's it going? Nah, just chilling with the fam, what're you up to? It's 'The Storm,' Mum. Yeah, Dwayne, but he goes by 'The Storm' now—"

I sigh, hold on to the counter, look around our poky little kitchen that in this moment feels so empty and so suffocating all at once. I wish there was someone else here, someone I could talk to, to lean on. When I was with Ed, he witnessed so many times like this. He'd sit calmly at the kitchen table, his analytical brain looking for and compiling a solution as chaos ensued around him. "The GP could prescribe Sertraline," he'd say, or, "You could employ a carer, Nell." If he were here now, he'd be doing the same. And then we'd secretly laugh together at Dwayne's new stage name. Dilly's bandmates always change their stage names. They've been everything from cutlery to different types of sediment.

"Elle?" calls Dilly. "Where're these heat pads? No, no, Storm, I'm still here, mate."

Dilly is horrendous in a crisis. He melts down. Purely because he's been protected from them all his life by Mum. Dilly was born with a hole in his heart. He's fine now—it closed up over time, something doctors always hoped would happen. But sometimes I think Mum gives her best self to Dilly, so not to put any strain on his heart. My heart can take it, I suppose she thinks, and I wonder how often the pair of them think, "Noelle'll sort it. Noelle'll deal with it." And I wonder what would happen if I said, "No. Noelle *won't* actually. Noelle is sick of dealing with it." But I don't. Because I love Dilly. Because I love

95

Mum. And isn't that why we do anything at all? However directly or indirectly. Love.

"Noelle?" Mum calls now. "Noelle, darling, are you there?"

"Yes," I call back. "Yes, I'm right here."

It seems incomprehensible to me that not even an hour ago I was asleep in my bed, and now, I'm in a silent hospital waiting room in a pair of tracksuit bottoms, a coat, and an old tatty pajama top which is printed with the big, rounded, and somewhat inappropriate-for-hospital-emergency-rooms face of a Moomin.

Mum's leg swelled up in the night, and by the early hours, she was in agony. Dilly was still up, having got back from the pub at midnight, drunk and smelling like beer and kebab shop burgers. He'd met up with a guy he dates on and off called Matt, who works there, behind the bar.

"I got home and was taking a wazz," he'd said, "and I could hear her, as I come out, crying in her bedroom." Then he'd woken me up. And Mum asked—she actually asked—for us to call her an ambulance, and relief and worry washed over me like a wave. But then she'd started freaking out. The panic, the hyperventilating, the anger, the nasty words. "Why on *earth* did you call an ambulance? *Why?* They'll make me go in, Noelle. *They'll make me go in.*" I calmly told her it would be fine, pretended the words she threw at me bounced off like rubber bullets, but I took deep breaths when I got into my ice-cold car, stopped myself from crying. I'm doing my best, I wanted to say, that's all I'm trying to do.

Dilly looked haunted at the front door, biting the cotton of his sleeve, the lights of the ambulance painting blue ominous stripes across his pale face. I'd told him to stay at home. He'd be no use to anyone, rile us up, both me and Mum. Plus, he was drunk. The last thing I needed was him throwing up in a hospital bin and trying to keep a Lucozade down.

The ambulance arrived and left quickly, and I followed in the car. Mum was taken off, checked over by nurses who took her blood pressure and temperature, before she was sent down for an emergency X-ray. She shook the whole time, holding an oxygen mask over her face, her eyes wide like dinner plates, her face stone, despite my fake, encouraging smiles from the plastic orange waiting room chair. She's been gone for half an hour now, and I don't even know how anyone is going to know where to find me. They plonked me here, on these benches outside a silent rheumatology wing once I followed Mum in her wheelchair as far as I could; and before I could ask what I should do, where I should wait, they wheeled Mum off to the top of the corridor and into an elevator. The corridor is silent now, save for the whir of two vending machines and the traipsing of doctors and nurses back and forth, squeaky shoes on polished floors. I think of Ed. Of him walking these corridors as a kid, the night Daisy died, and of him walking them now, as an adult. A doctor. This, his workplace, somewhere he comes to make a living, while others' lives fall apart.

The clock on the wall ticks 2:45 a.m.

That's the thing about the middle of the night and its loneliness and bad memories. It makes you clamor for comfort and safety. And it's why I texted Ed in the car park, as I steeled myself to go inside. This is the hospital we came to when they called us about Daisy. I remember everything about it—the car parking space, the overpowering rosewater perfume of the nurse who greeted us, the agony in Daisy's mum's face, the man with the huge red umbrella who blocked the entranceway, how the color felt too bright for my world where everything was fading to gray . . .

I'd opened Ed's message in the car, as rain spat against the glass from the black sky. Then I'd saved his number in my phone, pasting over the old number that I'd never had the heart to delete.

Mum's in hospital, I'd texted him. **I'm here on my own. Are you working now? Noelle.**

While a part of me hopes he never sees it, another part of me—a slightly larger part, that sits in my chest, an open chasm, would give

98

anything to see him push through the two double doors now, scrubs on, cheeky grin. A familiar face. The face of someone who knew me. Who *knows* me. Knows us—Mum, Dilly, and me— and our little clockwork life that was part of his for twelve years.

An elevator bell sounds, and for a moment I think it's Mum, but it's a group of nurses and a frail, tiny woman who barely looks alive, being wheeled silently on a bed. Red polished fingernails peep from beneath the crisp, white sheets. I wonder if she had any idea those fingers would be resting on a stretcher, while strangers push her down a corridor, wires snaking from her skin, as she painted them. And I understand why Mum hates hospitals, why so many people do. No other place has that feeling of otherworldliness, and that heavy static air it always has, of lives ending and changing and beginning, all at once. And I suddenly feel alone. And I suppose that's because I *am* alone. With all of it.

I bring my coffee to my lips, just for something to do with my shaking hands, when the double doors open—a sound like something stuck, unsticking. And it takes only a second for him to stop in his tracks, at the same second my heart does the same behind my ribs, as if someone pulled the power cord.

It's—*no*. No. Way.

Sam.

American Sam from the motorway. Right in front of me. Tall. Real. Here.

He freezes, his mouth gawping open, the same as mine, a takeaway coffee cup still in his hand.

"Oh my God." Each tiny-sounding word catches in my throat.

"Noelle," he says. "Noelle, are you—God, are you OK?"

And it's then, finally, that I cry.

CHAPTER ELEVEN

I think from the sight of me, Sam assumed there was something far more wrong than there actually is.

"It's my mum," I'd sniveled, and then I'd launched into a violent, mad-sounding sob, completely out of nowhere and completely to my surprise. I can't remember the last time I cried in front of anyone—well, besides when I cried in front of the entire M4 and most notably, Sam, but in my defense, I didn't actually *realize* I had. But it was too late. Once I started, I couldn't stop, and Sam gently put his arms around me. I cried into his sweater, his chest hard and warm beneath the dark fabric. He smelled exactly like he smelled on the motorway that night. Showers. Cedar-y aftershave. Fresh laundry. "I'm sorry," I'd said, drawing back. "I'm so sorry. I'm a mess—a bloody wreck. And you! I mean, are you OK? I haven't even—"

"I'm fine," he'd said calmly. "It's my dad. He has some stuff going on, but he's OK."

We sat down eventually, and Sam handed me a tissue from a packet in his jeans, as I waffled about Mum, about the X-ray, about not knowing where she is.

"You're organized," I said thickly, and he'd laughed and said, "You saw me produce a first-aid kit from my bag on a motorway, and *tissues* surprise you?"

The tears that I dabbed away were for Mum, yes, but that's not what they were entirely. That worry wasn't enough to cause a waterfall of spontaneous, snotty, embarrassing sobs. It was the loneliness, I think. That huge yawn of loneliness I'd felt in that moment on the bench in the waiting room that felt so gaping and black and barren that I felt like I might be swallowed whole, never to be seen again. Then Sam appeared, like he did on that snowy motorway, just when I needed someone the most.

"Do you think it's broken?" Sam asks now, and I explain to him what happened, now that the tears have stopped, as we sit on the plastic hard-backed chairs, a vending machine whirring and clinking beside us, its blue light turning Sam's white Converse shoes light blue. I tell him about Mum and the ladder. About Dilly waking me, and the ambulance, even the part about texting Ed, and he listens. He tells me he broke his leg in high school, that he's dealt with climbers with broken *everything* and up mountains, miles from help, and everything was fine, and now you'd never know, and it just feels so nice because his brown eyes have not left my face and he's listening as if everything depends on the words spilling from my mouth. It's like we're in the car. It's like we've picked up where we left off.

"What?" Sam says, a smile at the corner of his mouth. I realize I've stopped talking and I'm just looking at him.

"Just—you're here. Don't you think this is so . . . *mad?*"

"*Mad.*" Sam laughs. "Seems to be our thing."

Butterflies then. Completely out of nowhere, a burst, set free.

"And you're back for your dad?" I ask. "Is he all right?"

Sam pauses, looks down at his hands, clasped in his lap. "Back for Dad, but also work. I was in Wales. I've been in Wales for a week, actually. Got a new job over there. But then I got the call. He fell. *Again.* But he's doing OK."

"I'm sorry."

Sam shrugs. "It is what it is," he says simply, and says nothing else.

"And so, what, you live in Wales now?"

Sam nods, pushes a hand through his dark hair. "For a little while. It was sort of why I was back last month. Setting things up. You know, when you and I . . . met."

I feel something open in my chest when he says those words, looks at me from under those black lashes. Plus: *Wales.* That's not far at all. An hour or two on the train, perhaps. We could stay in touch. We could be friends. We could be . . . *no.*

103

No, stop it, Noelle. No need to go bollocks deep. You do not want to be that woman in a hedge with the beard and funny glasses.

"That's exciting," I say. "New job. Closer to your dad."

Sam gives a mournful smile, as if he doesn't think it's exciting at all. "I guess so," he says. "I mean, the Wales job is good. It's over in Snowdon, which is cool. I just wasn't expecting to be here so soon. Back here, I mean."

"Well, I'm sort of glad you are," I say, and Sam doesn't say anything, he just gives a small smile.

We sit in silence for a while, side by side in the quiet, shiny-floored waiting room. I can't believe he's here. I can't believe we've bumped into each other again. I think of the website, the emails I wanted to send, and I'm tempted to tell him, for a moment, but I don't. The clatter of a bed being pushed down the corridor echoes, and shortly, it appears being pushed by three nurses. One of them smiles at us as they pass.

"I hate hospitals," I whisper out of the side of my mouth.

"Me too," says Sam.

"And they're even worse in the middle of the night. I'm no good in the middle of the night."

Sam makes a sound—like a deep, bemused half chuckle in his throat, and motions with a hand up to the clock on the wall. It's one of those clocks that sat in every classroom at school. White, circular, rounded black numbers. "Three-fifteen," he says, then he leans, nudges my arm gently with his. "I seem to remember we did OK with three-fifteen in the car. Eating those crisis group cookies. I think you told me the story about Dilly's drummer and the dominatrix at about three-fifteen."

I laugh quietly, the sound echoing around the silent waiting room, like giggles in a church. "I love that you're here," I say quietly. "I mean, of course I don't *love* that you're here, because being here means something bad's happened, but—it's so nice to see you again."

"Ditto" is all Sam says. Then he leans and touches his arm to mine again but stays there longer this time. "Noelle *not*-Gallagher."

We both buy two more plastic tasting machine coffees, then sit together and talk some more, about Sam's flight, about the weather, about the traffic jam. Sam tells me he told a friend about the back-of-a-lorry cheese sandwiches, and about the driver with the banjo, and I wonder if he talked about me, about the weirdly perfect time we had, just like I did with Charlie—in absolute microscopic Holmes and Watson detail.

The vending machine clicks and hums, and the low ring of a hospital phone sounds in the distance. Silence falls between us, and I notice my old friends the stars are back, racing under my skin.

"Have I missed anything else?" I ask. "In what, four, five weeks. Climbed any good rocks lately?"

"Of course," Sam says.

"I still think you're slightly insane, by the way."

"So I'm never getting you up a rock face, then?"

He flashes a playful smile and my stomach flips over. God, he's handsome. Really handsome, in a sort of classic way. Dark eyes, square jaw, straight nose. "You're all about noses and chins," said Dilly once. "You have a type, and it's always about strong noses and chins. So predictable. Live a little. Try a rounded face from time to time, Noelle. A chin that couldn't cut pie."

"And how about you?" Sam asks. "Have I missed any Post-it action?" I like his voice. The accent, of course, but it's deep and croaks at the end of some of the words in that sexy, raspy, rumbling sort of way. I tried to mimic it once, to Charlie, who said I sounded like the voice from the *Saw* films.

"Yes," I say. "Steve and Candice are getting married. Did I tell you that? Yup. The Post-its were only the start of their love story."

"Holy shit, really?"

"I *know*—I mean, I'd be lying if there wasn't a part of me that was slightly jealous—"

"Well, same—"

"Mr. Attwood?"

We look up, almost in unison. A woman in a blue nurse's tunic stands in the doorway, pale, tired eyes, a rosy smile. "The doctor's arrived."

Sam clears his throat, places his large hands on his thighs. "Thank you, Nurse."

She nods then turns on her heel, the door swinging closed behind her.

Sam nods at me. "I better, um . . . Look, I hope your mom is OK, Noelle," he says gently. Then he touches my hand, a brush, so briefly, and there is no jumping away this time, from either of us, but the jolt through my body is the exact same. Electric. Sparks. Aura-exploding energy, or whatever Charlie and Theo say it is. He stands.

"Should we—" I jump up. "Maybe we should . . . I dunno." It's not every day that this happens, is it? That two strangers from two totally different countries, separate *continents,* bump into each other twice in mere weeks. Maybe I *am* meant to know Sam. Maybe bumping into him is a sign, like Charlie and Theo said. "Do you want to keep in touch?" Fuck it. I've said it now. It's out there. Can't take it back.

Sam doesn't reply right away, and heat works its way up my back like I'm suddenly standing too close to an open flame. *I wish I hadn't asked.* Me and the Moomin on my pajama top stare at him, waiting.

"W-we could swap emails or numbers or

something?" I carry on. "But of course, no pressure if . . . well, you must be busy and stuff and . . . climbing and . . ." Oh God. Shut up, me. *Close the bloody cupboard.*

Sam swallows, scratches the back of his neck. "Yeah," he says. "Of course. Sure. But I actually—don't have my phone with me . . ."

"Here." I lean over a low oval wooden table of leaflets and information booklets fanned next to the vending machine and take the first random pamphlet my hand finds—a leaflet calling for blood donations. I pull a pen from my bag and scrawl my mobile number on it. "There we go," I say, handing it over. "Old-fashioned way. Like Steve and Candice." Crayfish Face times *one hundred* at those last words.

"Cool," he says, smiling, folding it over in his hand. "Thanks. Take care, Noelle."

And just like when I got home from that freezing night in March, it's like he was never there at all.

CHAPTER TWELVE

I wake to the sound of a shutter going up, the warmth of a familiar hand on mine.

"Nellie?"

My eyes snap open, and almost instantly they start to water under the harsh, bright fluorescents. There are three more people on the waiting room chairs now, all bright-eyed and awake, smelling of toothpaste and perfume. The fresh faces of people who had a good night's sleep and got up, washed and dressed, ready for their appointments. And it takes a second or two for me to gather my bearings, to realize that Ed is here, stooping over me, scrubs on, his caramel waves arranged in that rough pushed-off-his-forehead quiff I used to love looping my fingers through as he slowly woke up beside me in the mornings. At the sight of him, my heart collapses to my stomach.

"I got your message," he says brightly. "Came in a little earlier."

I sit up. My neck's so stiff from napping on this chair, I'm surprised when it doesn't creak like an old garden gate. "Do you know where Mum is? She went for an X-ray, but I've not heard anything. I—I fell asleep."

"I just got here," he says. "But I can find out."

I sit up, my head rushing, starting to thump, right behind the eyes. Ed is already over at the little window, and a receptionist is nodding at him, her hand hovering over the phone, the bangles on her wrists jangling, like keys. I run my hands through my mad curls, try to tame them, because without seeing them, I know they've all come together in a mass that looks like a Halloween mad scientist wig.

"Receptionist's gonna call down to A&E," he says, striding back to me. He crouches, a hand landing on my arm, his shoes squeaking on the shiny floor. "See what happened after the X-ray. Hopefully she isn't still waiting."

I nod. He stares at me, and I stare back at him, magnetized. *Ed.* My Ed for so long that I almost forgot there was ever a time without him. I'd always taken it for granted that we were together. Other people broke up, not us. Not Ed and Noelle. We were the ones discussing other people's breakups in the comfort of our safe little indestructible bubble. "Did you hear? Such a shame. I really thought they'd go the distance, you know?" we'd say, while feeling secretly smug that we were the ones who'd done it— been through the mill of life and were still strong and together. I didn't for a minute stop to think anyone would ever be discussing us one day. We just *were*. There was no part of me that ever expected us to *not* be.

"I shouldn't have texted you," I say.

"Don't be daft."

"No, I really shouldn't have."

"Seriously, Nellie." He looks at me, and silence puffs its way up between us again, an invisible cloud. And as much as I've said words to the opposite, I am glad I texted him, and I'm glad he's here. Because if we were still together, if things were different, this is where he'd be, the way he always was. Sleeping on my floor for fourteen nights straight after Daisy died, crying with me, holding my hand, shushing me to sleep, listening as I relentlessly, torturously replayed that night in words, going over and over what I could've done, and what might've been. Then as the years went on, cooking my favorite breakfasts to cheer me up on hormonal, PMS-fueled Saturday mornings ("a Nutella nightmare," he'd say with a grin, placing chocolate-drenched waffles in front of me). Excitedly showing me websites of night schools and workshops in Oregon, streets away from the hospital he'd be working in. "Look, Nell. Floristry workshops, business courses . . . and see, there're loads of shops and restaurants nearby, for you to get a job while you're studying, so we can still save." All that hope he had for us both—to tick the boxes his brothers and their wives seemed to be ticking with their eyes closed. Dream jobs. Savings accounts. Mortgages—lighting his eyes up. I remember the way it disappeared, too, as if I'd blown it out, like candles on a cake, when I told him I had to stay.

"What's the time?" I ask Ed now. A man a few seats away from me coughs into a pale blue handkerchief and a baby starts crying, although I can't see one.

"Seven thirty," says Ed. "I start at nine. Although, now I'm here, there's no way I'm going to get away with sitting chilling till then." He gives me a wide, cheeky smile. "Come on. Let's get you some breakfast."

Ed McDonnell saved my life.

I know if I were to mention this to someone, say it out loud, they would either (a) assume I was ill, or in some sort of freak accident, and he was all doctor-y and heroic and literally saved my flailing heart, or (b) assume I'm one of those gooey, twee sort of people who collect sickly Pinterest quotes and say things like "you saved my life, the day I met you." But I don't mean it in either of those ways. I mean it literally. Because Ed did save my life. Without Ed, I wouldn't be alive. Because fifteen years ago, on January ninth, Ed stopped me from getting into a car that would've killed me. Into a car that killed my best friend, and soon after, Lee, the boy she fancied, from the plumbing course. The one she'd whimsically daydream about, collecting

112

his secret smiles and flirty looks in her diary (and texts to Charlie and me.) And regardless of how inadvertent, how *by chance,* every day that I have lived since then feels as if it's owed in some small way to Ed. I'm here because of Ed. And I kept living, after Daisy, because Ed gave me reason to. So when I'm thinking about him too much, when I'm scrolling his Twitter page, squashing cereal straight from the packet into my mouth while zooming in on that photo he had up of the pretty auburn-haired woman with the good eyebrows and bad breath, and when I reach out and know, against my better judgment, that I shouldn't, I give myself a little pass. A little, "Well, yes, you really shouldn't be lying awake at midnight torturing yourself with images of Ed in an open white shirt, hair blowing in the wind, and whoever that pile of auburn waves is draped across his lap, but who can blame you, Noelle Butterby? It's Ed. The man saved your life." And I know many would advise against this, sitting opposite him in this bustling hospital canteen that smells like crispy bacon and filter coffee. But I can't help it. There's a huge part of me that's more than happy to be sitting in front of him. It feels safe. It feels like home.

"It's shit you had to deal with this alone last night, Nell," says Ed gently. "But at least it's nothing major." Mum has a fracture and was taken up to a ward at five a.m. They tried to find me, but couldn't; they also tried to call me, but my phone has no signal and they never do, I find, in hospitals. She's in Marx ward, just upstairs from where I was sitting with Sam, and I can visit after nine. "So, where's Dilly? On the road?"

"At home, till Tuesday," I tell him. "I didn't really want him coming, to be honest. I think he would've done my head in. Plus, he'd been out, came home drunk and stinking of burgers."

Ed shakes his head and laughs. "Everything changes and nothing changes, eh? At least if he's at home, Ian next door won't freak out when he knocks and nobody answers. Do you remember when we went to the cinema—"

I giggle, lips at the warm ceramic of my coffee mug, because I know the story before he's said it.

"—and your mum was in the bath and he pulled that community copper off the road to investigate and your mum thought someone was dead when they eventually got her to come to the door?"

We both laugh, then Ed throws a quick glance to his side, at the busy cafeteria, and bites his lip as if he shouldn't be.

"Ian's moved, actually," I say. "Not far, over in Kingswood. Met someone. At the squash club. *Pam.*"

Ed's green eyes widen and he brings a mocking hand up to grasp at his chest. "You're *kidding me.* Tell me he at least confessed his undying love for your mum before he went?"

114

"Nope," I say.

"What? But the man worships her."

"Ah, but she knows. Because he already sort of had told her, you know? Without saying it, all the little things he used to do for her. And I know Mum misses him. I just wish—oh, I dunno what I wish." I sip my coffee, the tingles of caffeine like sparks of electricity, slowly firing my brain up. "I wish they'd get together, I suppose."

Ed nods wordlessly. "Yeah," he says. "I guess he didn't want to wait around though. You can't blame him for that."

I smart at that, shame blooming hotly across my cheeks. Is that how Ed felt when the job offer in America came up? When I stalled. When I knew I couldn't go with him, had to stay to look after Mum, and I'd danced around it, avoided the subject as if it was even possible to, until he had no choice but to ask me outright. *"So, are you coming with me, Nell?"* Ugh. He called me a doormat. He called me "truly pathetic" for letting my mum rule my life at thirty. But then we both threw them—harsh, sharp knives of words, as if it would help, as if hurting each other would shock us into changing into what the other wanted, or something. We were both guilty.

"So come on," Ed says, patting the table with his hand, "talk to me. How's Dill's band? What are their latest stage names? The Broom? The *Blender?*"

I clear my throat, smile. "Dwayne's latest one is 'The Storm.' "

Ed gulps down a mouthful of coffee and laughs, his hand flying up to his mouth as if to stop him from spraying it everywhere. "The *Storm*," he repeats. "Seriously? More like *The Bit of Wind*."

"The Light Breeze."

Ed laughs. "The Very Small Almost Unnoticeable Gust of Wind that Doesn't Even Disturb the Empty Recycling Bins."

Being with Ed, I realize how much his voice has been living inside my head for the last two years—that teasing, sarcastic tone, with the tiny Cheshire twang he's never been able to lose despite it being somewhere he hasn't lived since he was sixteen. I suppose when you share twelve years with someone—almost a third of your life to date, and most of your adult years—you grow up together, you *grow* together. Your thoughts and their words and your anecdotes and their views and jokes, all sort of weave together, until you're one, and you have no idea where you end and they begin. I knew he'd understand why I left Dilly at home. I knew he'd laugh at Dwayne's new stage name.

"And how're your parents?" I ask, and I see pinkness, just slightly, spread across his cheeks. Ed's parents were always nice, but I don't think they ever fully approved of me. A family of doctors and vets and university professors never quite warmed, I don't think, to me, someone who wanted to travel—and who then didn't go any further than Sainsbury's most days and spent her life cleaning other people's houses and checking in on her mum. *"So, what's the plan?"* Ed's mum, Helen, would say to me often, as if I were in a sticky situation and not just, you know, living my life.

"They're good," Ed says. "No, really good." He cycles through, about his dad retiring after forty years, about his mum stopping lecturing and obsessing over organizing his dad's seventieth instead, about his brothers. National Parks in Borneo. Private practices. Awards.

"Wow," I say, and I think of how typical an Ed response that is. Factual. Career and achievement focused. No information on how they actually *are.*

We drink our coffee in silence, and I pull off a piece of the bacon roll, put it in my mouth, let it disintegrate. I don't feel like eating. The exhaustion, the churning adrenaline of ambulances and hospitals and all things middle-of-the-night. I feel—and almost definitely look—as though I've been found during a river dredge.

"It was weird seeing you," I say. "In the street."

Ed nods, reluctantly, looks down at the mug in his hand. "Yeah, I know. It's been a long time."

"Two years and two months."

"You're counting," he says, with a sad smile. "It doesn't feel like that long. Does it?"

I shake my head. "Sometimes it feels like forever and yesterday all at once," I want to say, but I don't, and a silence drifts over our little round table like a cloud.

We finish our coffees and walk back through the hospital. It seems to have woken up fully now, bustling with people and telephones and the rattle of wheeled-along hospital beds, and I pull my cardigan around myself, as we walk, to hide the big Moomin on my stomach peeping out at everyone like a spy.

A doctor passes us in the corridor, takes Ed's arm, slaps him on the back.

"Ay, it's the runaway." He grins. "Didn't fancy Virginia, then? We should catch up. Few drinks?"

"Sure." Ed laughs, nods, slaps him back in that over-the-top masculine sort of way, and the doctor strolls off, shoes squeaking on the hard floor.

"Virginia?"

"Fuck knows," he whispers. "Probably meant Oregon."

Ed grabs a sheet of visiting times from the receptionist and hands it to me. The first visiting slot is at nine. I'll go and see Mum, and then I'll go home, get some sleep. I need it. I feel wobbly, like I've had too much of Charlie's mad home-brewed beer.

"How do you think Bel's going to handle being in a ward?" Ed asks, as I scan the paper in my hand.

"Fine," I say.

"Yeah? What, really?"

"She's getting better," I lie, "doing more."

"Really? Well, that's good."

And I'm not sure why I say it. I suppose to show him things have changed, to give the impression that things are different now, that *I* am different, no longer that person he stared at as he pulled a suitcase from the top of the wardrobe and called me—what was it? *Shackled.* "You're shackled to other people's problems," he'd said angrily, "and what makes me so pissed off, Nell, is that you have absolutely no motivation to change it. Do you? And I *try.* I try to understand why you insist upon shouldering it all. But—" And that was when he said it. "It's becoming pathetic now, Nell. *You're* becoming pathetic, and in turn, so am I." I cried then. And eventually, so did Ed, the pair of us sitting on the edge of his bed, a suitcase, empty between us.

We say goodbye at the elevator, and as the doors slide closed, he says, "Be good, Nellie," as he always did, and as he flashes me the wide smile he's given me a thousand times before, I see an image of him in my mind: seventeen and handsome, throwing that lopsided smile across college corridors, Daisy rolling her eyes, me melting to girl-syrup beside her. And as I walk away, I'm almost grateful for the interruption to the cauldron of thoughts and feelings and emotions bubbling in my brain. It feels like they're all there: happiness, excitement, fear, and worry and all their counterparts, all simmering away, a confused soup.

"Excuse me? Miss Butterby?"

I turn. It's the receptionist Ed spoke to.

"A doctor would like to speak to you. Just in here," she says kindly. "In private."

Doctor Henry sits in a tiny room with milky blue walls and a fluorescent light that flickers above our heads like in the locked room of a horror movie.

"So, Mrs. Belinda Butterby, your mother," she says, looking down at papers in her lap. Her smart paisley trousers are covered in navy-blue swirls, like milky ways.

"Yes."

"And you are Noelle Butterby. Address: number eight, Levison Drive."

"Yes. That's me."

She dips her head once in a stiff nod. "It's nothing alarming," she says. "We just have some concerns for your mother and would like to discuss them with you. How is her health generally? She keeps up with her hospital checkups?"

I nod.

"And she is generally well? I know she had the liver trouble but that's been rectified with a change of statin medication, yes?"

I nod again.

"OK." She laces her fingers together. "Miss Butterby, the paramedic mentioned the panic your mother displayed in leaving home, and we witnessed the same when she was admitted into a ward. Is there anything we should know? So we can help?"

I pause. There's a right and wrong answer here, or at least there would be if Mum were sitting beside me now. "What does she say?" I ask.

The doctor hesitates, leans back in her chair. She has dark, curly hair and smooth, brown skin. She's about my age, perhaps a little older, and something about her calm manner and slow breaths makes me want to tell her everything, spill it all in front of her, watch her gather it all up, fix it, put it all together. Although some people in her position have already tried. "Your mother says she suffers occasionally with panic attacks."

"Yes," I say. "Yes, she does. She's—since the stroke, she's lost confidence and she goes out less and less and—"

"You live with her?"

"Yes."

"Just you two?"

"And my younger brother, but he's away a lot."

Doctor Henry nods, sits back in her chair. "Do you think she needs help with her mental health? Her anxiety?"

I've tried. I've tried so many times. I've called Mum's GP, I've self-referred her for CBT therapy with a local NHS mental health scheme, I've found forums for her to join, online courses. I even spoke to Tom, Ed's brother, when we were together, and he was a junior in A&E, and he'd given me a list of things to try. Physio, he said curtly. Counseling.

"I've tried," I tell Doctor Henry. "She— she doesn't think she needs the help. Because she's fine if she's at home. She has her routine at home: she cooks, she bakes, she cleans, and every day she sees people. Me. Our neighbor Ian. My brother . . ."

"And you—you're her carer?"

"Well, I'm not her carer really, I . . ." I trail off, and the doctor waits until she realizes I'm not going to say any more, and she nods and takes a big breath.

"We can talk to her about beta blockers which may help—"

"She won't take them. She doesn't think she needs them. It's her confidence, as I said, since it happened. She was so busy all the time before. She was a singer—worked in clubs, at holiday parks, in local shows. She was a workaholic, really. And then it happened and . . . she's lost herself, a bit."

"I see," she says, nodding. "I understand." She leans over her desk, then, and hands me two leaflets. "Your mother is asleep. You may visit, but she let us give her a sleeping pill at least, so she might be sleeping for some time."

"OK. Thank you."

She looks down at her notes. "And you are feeling OK?"

"Me?"

"Yes . . ." She looks down at her notes again, as if to double-check my name. "Noelle. How are you? You're coping?"

"Yes. Yeah, I'm *fine*—"

"And your mental health?"

My heart stops its galloping—a rabbit in headlights.

"I can see on our notes that you—"

"I'm fine," I cut in. "I'm fine now."

The doctor lingers on the page in her hand for a moment then looks back up at me. "All right. OK, then," she says, and I find myself breathing a long, hot sigh of relief. She doesn't want to talk anymore. I can go home. Mum can go home. Everything can go back to normal.

"There is a support line here," she says, stretching out a hand and running a lidded Biro across the leaflet in my hand. "For you. For your mum. For various things."

"Thank you."

The doctor smiles gently. "Great."

Doctor Henry follows me out and whisks off in the other direction, someone else to fix, to survey, to observe, and I walk down the corridor that I saw Sam disappear down hours ago. Was it even real? Was any of it? It's bright outside now. Through the large, square windows, the sky is a brilliant tropical blue, and a fresh spring breeze laps through the crack at the top of it. When I saw Sam, the night was black, the air was freezing cold, the corridors silent. It feels like a different place altogether.

I get to the end of the corridor; push through the sticky doors I saw Sam arrive through. And that's when I see it. A leaflet balled up on a bench. I almost don't want to reach out and pick it up, but of course, I do. And I don't want to open it up, either, but of course I do that too. Because there it is. My three a.m. old-fashioned "like Candice and Steve" scrawl. My phone number on a blood donation leaflet, written down for Sam. Who screwed it up and dumped it on a bench, like rubbish.

CHAPTER THIRTEEN

O h, Elle, I can't actually *believe* he was at the hospital."

"I know."

"I mean, out of all the bloody places you could both be, at the *same time*."

"I know!"

"What do you think this means?" Charlie says without so much as a glance over her shoulder, and I know she isn't addressing me. She's addressing Theo, who is refilling a big container of glistening stuffed olives behind the glass deli counter I lean against, Petal snuffling on his chest in a black sling with silver loops at one shoulder, like a toga.

"I think it means a lot," says Theo calmly. "They're on the same plane. They have the same energy. They're in complete alignment. They're being pushed together like magnets."

I laugh, my hands around a mug of herbal tea Theo made me, one that seems to be floating with what looks like bits of garden waste I don't dare inquire about. "I don't know about that—"

"Oh, come *on,*" says Charlie. "Don't give me that, Noelle Butterby, you know it means something." Charlie crunches an organic sourdough crouton then stares at me, eyes crinkling at the corners, as if staring into my very soul. "You're marrying this man."

I laugh again, louder this time. "Ah, well, see, I'm very sorry to report to you both that I don't think that's going to happen."

"I'm afraid it is."

"He threw my number away," I say, throwing the words into the middle of the room like a bomb. "*Yuuuup.* That's right, my friends. Like balled-up bog roll he'd wiped his arse on."

Charlie stops chewing then, a rainbow of salad speared on her fork. *"What?"*

"I gave him my number at the hospital. On a leaflet. I wrote it down. And he chucked it away."

"How do you even know that?"

"Found it. Screwed up, chucked on a bench."

Charlie freezes, her brow creasing beneath her blunt fringe. Her earrings, two plastic slices of lime, swing beside her rosy cheeks. She turns and looks at Theo, as if for the answer to the conundrum, but he says nothing.

"Ah," I say, stealing a crouton. "Still think I'm marrying him now?" I crunch it between my teeth.

It's been a week since the hospital and it already feels like it didn't happen—like it was something I imagined, like a weird, tired, delirious three a.m. fever dream. Mum going in an ambulance. That coffee I had with Ed in my

ridiculous Moomin pajama top. Seeing Sam—
actually seeing him—in the middle of the night
in a place the pair of us probably least expected.
My number screwed up on a leaflet and chucked
on a hospital bench.

"But why would he throw it away?" asks
Charlie. "Like—why? I don't get it."

"Fear," says Theo, sliding the glass deli
counter's door closed. "Most adverse reactions
to things are because of fear."

"Or a girlfriend?" I offer. "A *wife?*"

"Oh, who cares about that?"

"Him, Charlie. Maybe he's, you know, a decent
person."

"But you—you got on so well, Noelle," Charlie
groans, lagging behind us on the conversation
trail. "You could just be friends. You didn't give
him your number and proposition him, for God's
sake." Charlie looks at me. "Did you?"

"No." I laugh.

"Well, I know you, and sometimes you say
batshit things, especially when you're tired. Or
drunk."

"Or nervous," adds Theo.

"Well, I *didn't.* I just said we should stay in
touch."

"Well, there you go." Charlie straightens like
she's solved it, like *that's that* and the leaflet is
now safely out of the bin, folded neatly, and in
Sam's back pocket where it should be. "Staying

in touch, so mild-sounding. So benign and *friendly*." She looks at Theo as if he's an oracle and not a Greek deli owner. "What's he got to be afraid of?"

"Well, a number of things," says Theo measuredly.

"Maybe he got the vibe," I say. "That I was sort of checking out his nice jaw, and his broad shoulders, and imagining just a bit what he might look like up a mountain in nothing but bear skins . . ."

Theo shakes his head. "Nah, we don't pick up on things like that," he says, a hand resting on Petal's little curved back. "No, I think it's fear. It feels like fear, sounds like fear . . ."

"I don't suppose we'll ever know." I shrug. "Plus, it wasn't all bad, I—" And I stop the second I feel the words working their way up my throat. I want to tell them about Ed, of course I do. I tell them everything. But I haven't told anyone, yet, that I've seen him, because I know they won't approve. Mum might, she always loved him. But everyone else in my life has filed him under various permanent labels, including "spineless, dirty little dweeb" (Charlie) and "Knob-Ed" (Dilly), and "Stupid, Little Cretin. Am I allowed to say cretin?" (Ian). Because there's some sort of law, isn't there, when you break up with someone? They're forever remembered and defined by their behavior when you broke up, and anything after. Everything they did before that is null and void. Even the happy memories. Even all the love you gave each other. Means sod all if they walk out on you during what was supposed to be a very adult, grown-up goodbye in Pizza Hut and leave you crying into a bowl of ice cream you piled with an embarrassing amount of jelly tots from the ice-cream factory. That's how it really ended. No tear-filled farewell at the airport, no sobbing in his bed, wrapped in his old hoodie. Just a "let's meet for pizza and say goodbye" lunch that turned into a "go fuck yourself" lunch when Mum called my phone three times in a row, when Ed sighed, and when I thought he was having a dig about his move without me when he ordered a "barbecue Americano" pizza. He walked out. I ate too much. I vomited when I got home. Not quite the heartbreaking, romance-movie good-bye I'd imagined us having after twelve years together.

"It was just nice to have someone there," I say to Charlie and Theo instead, "even if it was fleeting." Petal starts to cry, tiny hiccupping mews. Theo shushes her through his bristly beard, kisses the top of her head.

"I reckon he'll be back," he says, swaying, his hand circling Petal's back. "I reckon there'll be more. Things happen in threes. And destiny—"

"Destiny," I say with a laugh, although I'm

not sure the laugh was real enough to convince anyone, because destiny is exactly what I was thinking about when I saw Sam push through those double doors. Those stars beneath my skin. That *something* I sensed. And then I felt like an idiot when I saw that leaflet balled up. A stupid, gullible, stars-in-her-eyes twat.

"Destiny can't be deterred," finishes Theo.

"Exactly," says Charlie with a quick smile as she straightens, snapping her bento box closed. "Anyway. I need to go."

"Already?" says Theo, over the growing sound of Petal's crying.

"I'm packed out with appointments, Boo." Charlie whisks her beige chunky-knit cardigan on. "Got one in five minutes. Bloke coming for the outline of a back tattoo, and then another in for a sleeve. Proper intricate and pain-in-the-arse."

"Oh. I thought you said—" starts Theo. "Never mind." And I can't help but notice something in Theo's eyes as he looks down at Petal's fluffy little head. Disappointment, maybe. A glimmer of worry.

"I'll be home at five," says Charlie to Theo, but pressing her cool, powdery cheek to mine.

"Bye, Elle. Text you later about the cinema." And she's gone, the bell above the shop door jangling, the posters stuck to the glass of the door curling at the edges from the breeze.

Theo looks at me sadly, and there's silence for a moment.

"I'd better go. Mum wants me to take a trip into town, go to the market for some stuff. And I want to get some hydrangeas. Saw this amazing arrangement on Instagram and I want to try it out."

"I like *your* amazing arrangements on Instagram. I loved the daffodil one you put up a couple of weeks back. Beautiful."

I smile. "Thanks, Theo. You two are always my first likes."

"Your biggest fans," he says proudly, with a nod. "And I told you about Mum's coffee kiosk in the station, didn't I? That it's available. Up for rent. I said to Char . . . Could be a flower stall."

I look at him. "I *wish,* Theo."

"Ask the universe and you'll receive." He grins, then he pulls his lips into a grimace, like he's gearing himself up to say something. "Noelle," he says, "does er—does Charlie seem OK to you?"

"Erm." I hesitate, glance at the invisible trail Charlie made beside me when she left. "Yes," I say. "I think so. Why?"

Petal groans on his chest, little fists breaking free from the sling, skimming Theo's beard. "She just—I dunno, I can't help but think there's something going on. She doesn't seem herself at home. We don't . . . talk, like we used to. I mean,

131

I try, but she just says she's fine. But—oh, I don't know. I just wonder if there's something she isn't telling me."

"Really?"

Theo gives an almost shameful shrug, and I remember for a moment how happy Charlie was when they first met, and how she'd described him after their first date. "He's so calm and gentle, Noelle," she said. "He reminds me of like—*Jesus* or something. Or like Ben Affleck if Ben Affleck was Greek and converted to Buddhism or something. You know?"

"She's always rushing off, rushing out," Theo carries on. "And she said today she didn't have a lot on, but you saw her. She dashed out of here all of a sudden like there was a bloody fire. I worry there's something she isn't telling me. I *feel* that's what it is."

"Maybe it's tiredness. For you both," I say, carefully, but Charlie from a few weeks ago, outside her shop, blinks into my mind. *"Am I still her? Am I still Charlie Wilde?"*

"I don't know too much about babies," I carry on, "but you have a newborn, Theo. Everything is so new and everything's changed, and—well, you wouldn't be the first husband in the world who felt disconnected from his wife two months after they've had their first baby. Right?"

Theo hesitates, then gives a stiff nod. "You're right," he says. "Maybe it is tiredness. Tiredness

132

makes you paranoid, doesn't it? A bit distant?"

"Definitely," I say. "Plus sleep deprivation is used as a torture tactic. If that helps."

Theo laughs, his bushy eyebrows meeting in the middle. "It does, Noelle. Very weirdly, it does."

I walk to my car and half expect (and half hope) to see Ed as I pass the train station on my way, and can't help but let my mind wander. Say if we did just need the break? It doesn't exactly sound unrealistic, does it, to say, "my boyfriend went and worked abroad for two years and we broke up, but when he came back, we realized how much we missed each other and that was it. The rest, as they say, is history!" Cue: cheesy *Hello!* magazine style photo of Ed and me, laughing in a sunlit apple orchard, me in one of those floppy summer hats. *No.* No, come on, it was just once. One coffee. One twenty-minute coffee. But after seeing him at the hospital, I can hardly believe I was so nervous to see him. It was—*nice.* Like putting on an old comfortable cardigan or something. Something you lost that fit perfectly, that you then find again, and it fits just the same, wraps perfectly around you, and you wonder why you've left it so long. The thought of Sam niggles at me though, every single time I think of the hospital, and it twists in my chest. Embarrassment, I think. Total bloody cringe. *Why* did he throw my number away? And why did I have to go and be all "ha, ha, let's do a Steve and Candice who wrote to each other! And then fell in love! And then got engaged! Who me? No, I'm not intense at all, Sam, not intense in the slightest!"

I get to my car, slot the key in the door. It jams. Last time this happened, Sam wriggled it, unlocked it for me on the frozen road, gave me that small smile . . . then—I freeze, my hand full of keys. *Is that* . . . it is. I can see her on the other side of the street. Charlie. In her car, driving in the complete opposite direction, away from the tattoo studio she so desperately needed to get to five minutes ago.

CHAPTER FOURTEEN

When I get home from work today, I'm met by a full house and the smell of hot tea and freshly sliced cucumber. The sound of the strumming of a bass guitar emanates through the floorboards and Ian sits eating a triangular half of a ham sandwich at the kitchen table, reading out loud about veganism. It reminds me of what it used to be like a few years ago. When Dilly was at home, when Ian lived next door, when there was always someone whisking in, whisking out, the kettle working itself to the bone.

"I just couldn't do it, Ian," Mum is saying, as Ian stares down at his iPad. "I couldn't give up my crumpets and butter."

"Mm." Ian nods. "Although I'm not quite sure all crumpets fall under the animal product umbrella, Belinda."

"Oh," says Mum, her new hospital-prescribed crutch leaning against the kitchen counter. "But then what about bacon—*oh,* Noelle, hello darling. We're just having a cuppa and a sandwich. Do you want a sandwich? Ian got some lovely ham, didn't you? From that meat man on the corner."

"Colin," he says. "The owner of Meat Man Plc. And good afternoon, Noelle."

"Hiya. And I will actually," I say, taking a seat at the table, shrugging off my denim jacket, draping it over the back of the chair. "But are you sure you're OK to do it? Your leg—"

"No, no," Mum says. "It's good to move it, they say, or it gets all stiff, and Christ knows, I have enough trouble as it is. I don't want to be going back, all seized up, God knows what they'd do with me then . . ."

Since the hospital, Ian has been coming around more and more, and I've loved it so much, having him here again. The other day, he even stayed until nine and helped Mum up to bed for me, and I watched the pair of them slowly taking the narrow steps of our little two-up-two-down, Ian's arm lovingly holding Mum, and felt a tug at my heart. Ed's right. Ian *does* love Mum. And I often wonder whether Mum has no idea, or if she has in fact *every* idea but is too frightened to look it in the eye—this person who loves her for everything she is—not everything she was, or the idea of who she could become. When Ian sat us down and told us about Pam, I thought she'd tell him—because I really do think that she loves him too. Except she didn't. She clapped her hands together, she beamed like a quiz-show host, she strangled a tea towel in her hand as if it were the neck of a mortal enemy, then told him how happy she was for him. Then she denied that the flood of tears she cried while watching *Coronation*

Street later that night, and the six slices of toast she stress-ate while she did, were for any reason but the excellent script writing and "can't a woman eat bloody *toast* in her own home without being psychoanalyzed?"

"He's a trained botanist, would you believe," Ian continues now, placing a crust of bread on the plate in front of him. "But working with meat—he said it was one of the only things he felt he could do. Once he got out of prison."

"Sorry—*who?*"

"Colin."

I look blankly at him, and Mum says, "The man we got the ham from."

"Meat Man Plc," adds Ian.

Ian knows everyone and everything in this little town. He's lived here his whole life. Even worked here, at a local secondary school as a geography teacher before he retired early and then filled his time with the Neighborhood Watch forums and watching YouTube tutorials on anything from pruning cucumber plants to asserting yourself when making a complaint in a luxury hotel, despite not having actually stayed in a hotel for twenty-two years. I honestly never thought he'd move from next door—leave his little pride and joy of an immaculate everything-in-its-place house. I didn't think he'd leave Mum, either, of course. But then what is it Ed said? You can't wait around forever. And maybe

137

Pam turned up just as he'd given up waiting.

"I don't know what he was in prison for," Ian continues, as the low buzz of bass guitar upstairs comes to an abrupt stop. "But I said to Belinda, your mum"—Ian always says this, as if I need reminding of who my mother is—"if I was a betting man, I would put a small sum of money on burglary. Looks the sort, you know. Eyes far too close together."

Mum nods seriously, buttering two slices of bread at the counter, as the clomp of feet pummel the stairs. "Oh, that's true, that is," she says.

"I don't think it is." I laugh. "I mean, if you think about it, Dilly's eyes are actually—"

"Uh? What's this about my pork pies?" Dilly arrives in the doorway, his drummer, Dwayne, following dutifully behind him, a black woolly hat pulled down to his eyelids. "Oh, and is that ham? We'll take one of those, won't we, mate? The Storm loves a sandwich."

And as if on the set of an advert, to my surprise and apparently nobody else's, Dwayne says, "Ham from Meat Man Plc? Good stuff, that. I'll happily take one."

The two of them barrel into the room, plonk themselves on a kitchen chair each, and Mum frantically butters bread. Dilly and Dwayne (or The Storm, since he's gone "method" slash *mad*) have been in what must be close to a hundred bands together now, since secondary school.

Five Catastrophes is their latest project. And surprisingly, they're good. *Really* good. I suppose that's what years of absolute obsession, practice, and crying during rock concerts does. Dilly once fasted for thirty-six hours, "like Gandhi," he'd said, but for the cause of Iron Maiden.

"Oh," says Mum. "Noelle, Ian has something to ask you. Don't you, Ian?"

Dilly takes the plate from Mum before I can even raise a hand to take it myself. Then he smirks and slides it over to me, his eyebrows wiggling "gotcha" at me across the table. But suddenly I don't want it. I know that face of Mum's—the eager eyes, the big gaps between blinks.

"Ah yes. Of course." Ian interlaces his fingers like a newsreader. "Are you familiar with Farthing Heights, Noelle?"

"No," I say at the same time Dwayne says through a mouthful of bread, "Great book."

"No," says Ian. "No, that's *Wuthering Heights*. No, see, Farthing Heights is the estate on the way to Newham Park, and I play squash with a man called George who says his neighbor, Frank, is looking for a cleaner for his flat there. And of course, I thought of you."

Mum's eyes are fixed on me. I nod, my hands at the plate in front of me, but my heart sinks like a stone in a tank at those final words. Because I'm already working a lot, and when I'm not working,

139

I'm running errands for Mum, and since Mum's leg, doing so much more of the housework. I wanted to start a video course I've found online, about making table arrangements, but I've barely found the time. I wanted to meet with Candice at a wedding fair last week, but couldn't fit it in. Charlie and I were also meant to go to the cinema last week to see an old black-and-white film at the Tivoli, but we ended up canceling because I'd gotten home too late from Jetson's. My own time—it's running from me, at the moment, like a downhill stream.

"And I'm not exactly sure what's happened, Noelle," Ian carries on, "but this man needs to move, and before he moves, he requires a cleaner to aid him in clearing his home. He's elderly."

"You're used to the elderly, aren't you, darling?" says Mum hopefully. "What with Betty, the old lady you sometimes clean for. She's good with them, aren't you?"

Dilly laughs to himself, mouth jammed with sandwich. *"Good with them,"* he says under his breath.

"I said I know just the woman," Ian says excitedly. "I said, you won't find a more trust-worthy and more diligent cleaner, even if you searched the whole of England."

"Oh." I smile weakly. "Thanks, Ian. And I'm . . . it's not that I'm not happy that you thought of me—"

"Of *course*."

"But my time is so . . . I mean, I only really have Tuesday afternoons and Sundays free at the moment."

"Yes." Ian considers these words and nods slowly, his round little head bobbing like a balloon in the breeze. "Hm. Yes. I can't say I don't understand that, Noelle. Well. Never mind."

Mum doesn't say anything, but she turns, twists the tap, starts filling the sink with water. And I can feel it swelling in the air, like a thick cloud, threatening to burst and pour down upon us all. The worry. The expectation. The unspoken words of "But we're struggling with money. But I'm up at night worrying, and I'm not sleeping, and there's a job, Noelle. A job that pays money." And I wish she'd look at Dilly like this. But she won't, because he's Dilly. Dilly, her baby, Dilly the bloody walnut, and she wouldn't want to worry him. Plus, he's following his dream. The touring, the music. What am I doing? Besides fannying about with cut-price flowers and scaring away mountaineers in waiting rooms.

"Did they say when they needed a cleaner by?" I ask eventually.

Ian looks up from his iPad, surprised. "Oh. Yes. *As soon as humanly possible,* George said." He chuckles to himself.

"Tell him I might be interested," I say, as

Dwayne and Dilly tear into their sandwiches like hyenas, both scrolling on their phones.

"I'll inquire with George again tomorrow." Ian taps away on his iPad. "There we are. I've even set an alarm. This reminder, which is linked also to my smart watch, will tell me to speak to him just as we're having our post-match elevenses."

Mum smiles at him. "Clever," she says. "And the sandwiches are all right, are they, boys?"

"Stellar, Mum." Dilly chews. "Mad to think he was in the nick, that butcher."

"Burgled a pub," adds Dwayne, and at that Ian yelps, as if he's just got four corners in bingo. "Burglary!" he exclaims. "I can't believe I just did that. I was right, Belinda. Right on the *nose*."

CHAPTER FIFTEEN

It takes me a while to find the correct entrance to the block of flats in Farthing Heights, and by the time I find the right one, I'm flustered and sweaty, and nervous I've blown this casual *job interview* that I didn't even want in the first place. Frank's son is home and waiting for me, apparently, at his dad's flat on the seventh floor, and for what feels like an age, I stand in the lift on the ground floor waiting for the doors to close. It's like they know. "I thought you wanted to spend your spare time on that floristry course you saw on that online university," the doors say. "I'll remain open, you know, just to give you a chance to walk away." I don't move. They close. The lift starts slowly drifting upward.

Ed and I viewed a flat in a block a little like this about seven years ago, when he got back from uni. Ed had side-eyed me as the estate agent looked at his watch and the elevator light above our heads flickered, wordlessly saying, "Let's hope the flat is better than this lift, eh, Nell?" And God, it really hadn't been. There was a shower over the toilet; a terrace that wasn't a terrace, but a window that you could climb out of onto a tiny square of flat asbestos-looking roof; and every room smelled like raw potatoes, especially the bedroom, which had a huge mirror on the ceiling. We'd stifled giggles the whole way around, which we released as soon as the estate agent drove off.

"I know the carpet stain isn't appetizing," Ed had imitated the estate agent on the way home, his hand squeezing mine, *"but a good rug and Bob's your uncle!* No, mate, sorry. Bob is not my bloody uncle, if my uncle is that absolute pile of shit." We found somewhere better a few weeks later. Cleaner, more modern, but still tiny, and everything—absolutely *everything*—felt possible the day we put the deposit down. A year. That's all we got, until I moved back home. I pull out my phone as the lift continues to glide upward. Should I text him back? He'd sent one straight after the coffee. **Nice seeing you Nell, hope your mum is ok** is all it'd said. But I hadn't responded. I've typed out numerous replies since—a couple every day. But then deleted them and closed the window. I stare at his name on my screen. I put my phone back in my bag.

When the elevator doors clatter open, I'm greeted by the smell of garlic and the piney smell of a newly mopped floor, and Frank's flat directly across the corridor, just as Ian had said. 178A. There is silence. No television mumbling, no music playing. Daisy lived in a flat similar to this in a block a few streets away, and there were always sounds to be heard when I approached her door. The clatter of pots and pans where her mum would be cooking, the tinny music of Daisy's bedroom, the mumble of Saturday evening game shows when Daisy's dad was home from work. But here, there is nothing. I knock on the door, the wood hard beneath my knuckles.

For a moment, I don't think anyone's in. Then I hear the clatter of a latch on the other side of the door. It opens in one swoop.

"Sam."

"Noelle."

CHAPTER SIXTEEN

H oly. *Shit.*
My hands fly up to my face. That's the first thing I do. Well, besides gasp so loudly, I sound like I'm in some sort of cartoon. Then in unison, Sam and I burst out laughing. I even snort, which makes us laugh even more.

"Were you expecting—"

"No," he says.

"Wow, this is—"

"Crazy." Sam laughs, hand at his chin. "What are you doing here?"

I stare at him, my eyes sliding toward the brass, rust-blistered numbers on the door. "Um. 178A. Right?" And I see that it registers in his face then, just as I say, "Frank?"

"Oh. *Oh.* Of course."

"Yup. It's me. The cleaner," I say. "At your service. And—Frank must be your—?"

"My dad." Sam nods, a deep duck of his head. "This is his place."

Then it clicks into place, like two puzzle pieces conjoining. The hospital. The sick dad. Of course. Then *the leaflet* bursts into my mind like an unwelcome guest at a party, screwed in that ball on the bench, and like a shield, I cross my arms over my chest. Yes, that's right, I feel like saying, I remember you saying about your dad before you swiftly wiped your arse with my phone number.

"Do you want to come on in?"

"I suppose I'd better."

Sam steps aside to let me pass over the threshold onto the thin, bottle-green carpet. Despite myself, my heart is racing, as if it's going to shake itself free and go bouncing all around my body. How has this happened . . . *again?* Destiny, Theo had said, *like magnets.* Is that what it is? Some weird magnetic force at work? God, if I carry on with this stuff, I might as well open a reiki retreat of my own. But seeing him in a hospital waiting room in the middle of the night, seeing him today—more than just a coincidence, Charlie and Theo would insist. But . . . why? What would be the point? He isn't interested in even being my friend, sending the odd text or email, "keeping in touch." It's almost torturous, then, a big joke, that this keeps happening. Especially since the man clearly didn't *want* it to happen a third time. He literally threw my phone number away to ensure it didn't. Which turns this from beautifully serendipitous, to plainly and simply, as Dilly would definitely say: awks as fuck.

Sam takes me through the large but musty flat, and I follow. There are boxes and objects piled high, a hodgepodge of papers, and towers of books, like those teetering stone cairns on rocky beaches. We stop in the doorway of the living room, side by side. Our upper arms touch, and there goes my heart again, like a crazed horse, and I wish so much that it would just *chill.*

"So," he says, "I, uh, I know this is crazy—"

"You can say that again, Samuel."

Sam hesitates, hand at his chin, but avoids my gaze. "I, uh—I meant the apartment."

"Oh. *Oh.* Yeah, I suppose it is a bit."

There's painful, awkward silence again until Sam clears his throat and steps into the cluttered living room—it's a square space filled with more books and papers in piles, and a round dining table with barely an inch of sandy wood showing, thanks to the crowds of objects balancing on top of it, like a garage sale. "So, the old man. He needs to move. Somewhere ground floor. Safer. Somewhere he can navigate if the elevators are out."

"And how is he, your dad? Since the hospital?"

Sam nods, looking around the room more than he looks at me. "He's—well, he's getting there. He had a bad fall. He's not great on his feet. Severe arthritis that took a turn for the worst last year. I don't know, he's sort of . . . difficult. But you know, that has shit to do with the arthritis. He's always been difficult."

"Well, that sounds hard."

Sam shrugs his broad shoulders. "We're not really close so—"

"Really?"

"Yeah. Classic neglectful, shitty father problems."

"Oh."

"Yeah."

God, this *is* awkward. Hard work I suppose is the phrase, like wading through treacle, and so much so, that I keep checking my teeth aren't clamped together, that I'm not visibly cringing like that emoji with the white teeth. Every hour in that car on the motorway, the walk along the hard shoulder (our Quebec park, in that moment), the hospital waiting room— none of it felt like this. Painfully, could-cut- the-atmosphere-with-a-knife-or-perhaps-the- chin-of-one-of-my-predictable-crushes awkward. I certainly wouldn't have stayed a moment longer than I needed to in that car, if it'd felt like this. I'd have tried to charge my phone using the light of the bloody *moon* if it had. But it didn't. Those hours were—*alive.* Buzzing. Electric. But this feels different. All rigid and standoffish and stiff, as if we're in a room full of invisible trip wires.

"I'll show you the kitchen," Sam says flatly, and I nod, follow him through the stale-smelling living room.

Perhaps he thought I was too keen. Maybe he was just being nice, making the most out of a bad situation on the motorway. Maybe he's married. Or maybe he's a secret prick. And if any of those are true, of *course* he'd throw my number away. And maybe this is what this is, this standoffishness—a way to tell me that *OK, the car was lovely and everything, and we had a really nice evening together, especially nice because we knew it was what it was—a few weird, freezing, stranded hours and we'd never see each other again. But I have a hot, smart, worldly girlfriend and a hot, smart, worldly job and I really don't want a new friend, and certainly not one who blushes when I breathe in her direction. I have plenty of those in my full, busy, traveling, mountaineering, bear-skin wearing, prick-ish life.* And I get it, I suppose. The car—it was almost unreal. A pocket away from reality. But the hospital, and this. This is real life.

We stand silently in the kitchen. A boiler ticks and then rumbles on the wall, and a small, white fridge under the counter buzzes.

"So," I say, breaking through the awkward silence, "you want it decluttered? Cleared, so you can pack for the move. And then cleaned, ready for new owners."

"Exactly," says Sam. "It's a big job, and there's a lot of personal stuff, and I figured the house clearance guys would probably just come in and take it all, and I mean, he's a jackass. But he deserves his stuff."

I gaze around the kitchen. Large really, for a two-bed flat, but cramped with *things* and over-stuffed drawers. A hoarder's home, but definitely not as bad as the ones you see on TV. It just looks like nobody has spring cleaned for twenty years, that there are jars of food in the cupboards that could be used to resurrect the seventies.

"Do you want a tour?" he asks. "No pressure if you're thinking this is not a job for you or—"

"No. No, a tour seems a good idea."

I stay a while with Sam, in Frank's stuffy flat. There are two bedrooms, and a tiny olive-colored bathroom, and a balcony too. You can see the sandy buildings of Bath city center in the distance and I'm not sure I've ever seen it from this high up. Under the blue spring sky, it looks idyllic. Grand. Historic. Sam is quiet as he takes me around, but he tells me his parents split before he was born, that his stepsister and his mum live over in Oregon, and he isn't close to Frank, because Frank didn't really ever try—didn't really care, as Sam put it. "But he has no one else," he says. "So, it's down to me."

Despite myself, my heart blooms in my chest like a flower opening when he says that. "You're a good person," I want to say, "and no wonder I felt like you really *got it* about Mum, in the car, because you know how it feels," but I don't. Because it feels like there's an invisible electric

151

fence between us now, that if I was to get too close, step too far, I'd be thrown backward. He's guarded. And maybe he's wishing the cleaner wasn't me. That I hadn't exploded my way into his life again, however serendipitously, however random.

"Do you stay with him, when you come over?" I ask.

Sam shakes his head. "I try to keep my distance. Hotels and stuff. Now I'm over in Wales, I just drive back. I tried once or twice to come here, to live here with him when I was in my teens. Longest I managed was four months. It wasn't an easy place to live with him. And I've lived *all over.*"

"Icy mountains," I add, and there's a tiny shadow of a smile on his face.

After the tour, we end up back at the front door, and I'm surprised when he opens it and steps aside, as if to prompt me to leave, and quickly.

"There's no pressure," says Sam, "to take the job." His hand holds on to the door and I clutch the buttons of my cardigan, as if they're life buoys for us both. A mahogany clock with a ship on the face ticks noisily on the hallway wall.

And I don't want to take it. Not really. But we could use the money—*really* use the money. But despite myself, despite the awkwardness and my best judgment, I want to do it. For Sam. I don't feel I can walk away, say no.

"I'm happy to take it on."

Sam gives a reluctant smile, brings a hand to his square jaw. "Cool," he says. "Shall we say . . . start the week after next?"

I nod. "I can do Tuesday afternoons?"

"That should be OK," Sam says, pulling out his phone. "Let's get your—" Then he looks at me as if he realizes what he's said. "Number."

"Noelle!"

I'm walking away from Farthing Heights into the warm May sunshine, when he calls my name. I know it's him before I even turn, but when I do, Sam is on the concrete, tall and broad, brown eyes squinting against the sun. It feels like summer today—blue skies, apple-green grass, bursts of color in gardens the color of feather boas—and I can't help but notice the golden tan on Sam's bare arms out here in daylight.

"You walk fast," he says breathlessly.

"Sorry. Is everything OK? Do you need to change my start date or—"

"No." Sam shakes his head and walks closer, closing the big gray space between us on the street. "No, that's . . . Tuesday's fine. It's . . . it's your phone number—"

Ah. He'd grimaced as I'd punched it into his phone on the doorstep, and then a neighbor had come out of 178B and asked how Sam's dad was, and I'd made my excuses and left. I'd been so

153

thankful to be saved by the bell, I could've kissed her for interrupting us.

"I didn't take your number," says Sam now, guiltily, a breeze ruffling his soft, dark hair. "At the hospital."

"I know."

"And I wanted to keep it, Noelle," he says softly, "I did," and his shoulders relax as he says the words, as if it's a load he's finally set down. At the same time, I feel my body tense. "I wanted to call you, text you. I couldn't believe that I'd seen you again. I mean, I'd hoped I would, somehow, and God knows how . . ." My heart races looking up at him, at the burnt-sugar eyes, the thick black lashes. He always looks so good. He's one of those people who doesn't even have to try. Like today. Just jeans and a T-shirt, muscular arms snug against the seams of the sleeves. "Tell me how tall and strong he is again?" Charlie had asked a few weeks back, and I'd told her that I predicted Sam could carry me like I was nothing but a bread roll. Not like Aaron, that date I went on just after Ed, to try and feel better. We'd sat on his living room floor watching films, and when he tried to lift me in a sudden act of passion he'd likely seen on a Netflix period drama, he acted like he was trying to single-handedly shift a shipping container.

"And when I do see you," carries on Sam. His

brow furrows as if trying to work something out. "I don't know, I—it's hard to explain."

My heart bangs inside my chest. He feels it too. He must. He must feel that weird *something* too. Maybe it is destiny. Maybe *I am* meant to know Sam. Maybe he is meant to know—

"But Noelle. I'm with someone."

I stare at him.

"I wasn't," he jumps in, "for quite a while. But we're . . . trying. To fix things. And I don't know if it's the right thing, but . . . we've been together since we were nineteen and . . . ." He gives a shrug and looks down at me. "It just didn't feel right taking your phone number."

And despite the sinking feeling I have in my chest, despite the ache he's seemed to prompt in my stomach, I feel weirdly lifted. Because he is a good person. *That* is why he threw my number away. It wasn't that he didn't want to see me, to stay in touch, or he thought I was some weird bush-dwelling stalker with a mustache disguise. He has a girlfriend. Sam has a girlfriend.

"I get it," I say. "I mean, you know I do. I talked your ear off about Ed in the car."

"Ed the ped," says Sam with a small wistful smile.

"Exactly."

"It's similar I guess, with me and Jenna. We met when we were students. In Amsterdam. Both Americans, both traveling. I'd lost someone

155

close to me, and I was in a bad way. And then we met. And—" He suddenly shakes his head, as if snapping himself out of a trance, and laughs. "I don't know what I'm trying to say here—"

"You feel like you owe something to all those years," I say.

"*Yeah*. Yeah, I guess that's it." Sam gives a nod and tucks his hands in his pockets and looks at me and laughs.

"What?"

He shakes his head, gives me a flash of a grin, dimples and white teeth, that annoyingly melts my kneecaps. "Nothing. Just—you know more about me than some people I've worked with for a decade."

"Bump into each other, have an emotional breakdown, use each other as confessionals," I say. "It's just what we do."

iMessage to Ed McDonnell: Hey, thanks again for being there at the hospital the other morning. Mum's home, doing well! I wondered if you wanted to grab a coffee. I could meet you after a shift? Nell x

CHAPTER SEVENTEEN

Ed and I sit beside each other on a bench outside the train station, two warm, creamy takeaway coffees in our hands. I'd bought them from Theo's parents' cute little wooden coffee kiosk as I waited for Ed's train to get in. They've owned it for years, but now they want to retire, spend more time in Athens with their family. Theo's mum, Yolanda, told me all about the trouble they're having with letting agencies, about renting it out, about how she doesn't enjoy it anymore, and as she stirred milk into the drinks and took another order, I'd daydreamed for a just a moment about what it really would be like to have it as mine, as Theo suggested. A flower stall of my own. *Imagine.* It was almost too painful to, and I was grateful when Ed's train got in and Yolanda passed me the drinks, then leaned to squash a kiss onto both of my cheeks.

We've been sitting here, outside the station in the warm, honey rays of the sun, and we've barely taken a breath. We've covered small talk—the weather, how hot the sun is, his work. Then we went on to Mum's leg, then Dilly, then Charlie, and it's like we can't stop. So many gaps to fill, so many empty spaces on a calendar

157

to account for. Ed and I always "got on," so I don't know why I expected it to be awkward, really, or stifled. In college, that's how it started. Nonstop chats at the bus stop, about music, about movies, about whether we'd go on to university after college, when we turned eighteen, as Daisy fiddled with her phone and I obsessed over things he'd said and the way he smiled, as she smirked and rolled her eyes. And I've missed this. I really have. I've missed this familiar, easy conversation about the world we both shared for so long.

"Charlie with a baby," says Ed. "In my mind she's still sleeping with guys in rock bands and trying to talk me into trying out tantra. Did I tell you my brother Tom's having a baby?"

"Seriously?"

"Yup. Due in October. Layla's taken early mat-leave. Can't exactly operate on people when you're vomming. Hyperemesis gravidarum."

"What?"

"Severe nausea and sickness. She's really suffering."

"God. Sounds like a bloody *spell*. Poor Layla."

"Mum's fussing. Keeps on going round there. Every McDonnell is waiting for the baby call." Ed smiles brightly.

Something hot pangs inside of me. *Jealousy?* Maybe. And it's not that Layla wasn't sweet. She was, she even used to call me her sister-in-law, and I'd loved the sound of it at the time. But maybe it's seeing a tiny glimpse of what might've been, if things had been different. But then, would Ed's parents ever have treated me like they did Layla? Fussing, caring, waiting by the phone? I always felt like half a person when I'd sit round their dinner table. Doctors. Vets. Bloody brothers off on casual trips to Borneo to save lions and sloths. The last time my brother went anywhere, it was Hull, and that was to stay in his friend's nan's caravan for the weekend and he'd got off with a guy that dressed up as a pug for the kids at the holiday park. I always wondered how Ed's parents took it when we split up. Glee, probably, that Ed and I never married and never got the thirty grand all married McDonnell couples get. They'd sooner save that for when Ed met a medic or that bloody professional ballet dancer Ed's mum always forced him to speak to at weddings and parties. "Ed, did you know Felicity is here? She's just got back from Prague, she looks lovely," and I always had to wrestle down the urge to say, "Yes, and did you know *I* was here, you know, his girlfriend of ten years?"

"Shall we take a wander?" Ed asks me now, and we both get to our feet. *Shall we take a wander?* There's that old, snuggly cardigan again, my arms slipping straight in. How many times in my life have I heard that sentence? Holidays together and lazy Saturday mornings in town, coming out of a café for breakfast, sunshine on cobbles, the day ahead of us.

Ed and I leave the station and walk through town, the blue sky smudged with pearly clouds, the sound of distant church bells carried on the breeze. My phone vibrates in my bag. Mum. Her third missed call. She's had a letter from the hospital. They want to check her leg, see how the fracture is healing, and she does *not* want to go. "Ring them, Noelle," she said desperately as I left for work this morning, as if she'd been sent a ransom note and not an NHS letter. "Tell them I'm fine. You won't forget, will you, darling?"

Ed's eyes slide down to the phone in my hand. "You OK?"

"Fine." I quickly type out a text instead. **Everything ok? Will ring hosp asap.** She's obviously forgotten that I'm meeting Ed, although meeting a friend is what I told her.

"Your mum?"

I put my phone back in my bag. "It's fine," I say. "Can we go via the flowers?"

Ed rolls his eyes, but smiles warmly. "Do I have a choice?" he says, and we turn to enter the bustling heart of the market of our little town. "You gonna load me down again?"

" 'Course," I say. "It's tradition."

Ed chuckles, ruffles the caramel curls on his head. "True."

I keep thinking about what Sam said about

Jenna, and about owing the years. Jenna is Sam's Ed. And I don't know what this is exactly, with Ed, just that it feels nice. That blanket around my shoulders, that cardigan I can snuggle into. Safe and worn in and familiar.

"Did you ever do the course? The part-time floristry one? At the florist in the city?" asks Ed, as we wander through the market stalls. The deep smell of sticky toffee hits us in a sweet, warm gust as we pass a sweets stall, sunshine bouncing from the lines of glass jars in shards.

"No, I haven't yet."

"Why not?" Ed's questions are always like this. Short, to the point, black and white, no added fluff. We argued over his directness, probably more than we argued over anything else. Ed is blunt. Straight to the point, to the heart of the matter. It's probably why he was always going to make a good doctor. But his bluntness often felt like heartlessness. "Why not get her a carer?" he'd say about Mum, as if she was just a problem to be fixed, like booking a plumber for a leak. "Why is it that you feel like it's *you* that has to stay?" and "What do you actually want from your life? Well? It's a simple question, Nell."

"I haven't got around to it yet," I say. "Work's busy, I barely have a minute to myself . . ."

"Because of your mum?" He holds his hands up then, showing his palms, a silver band on his middle finger. "I'm not prying, Nell. I'm just asking. I know how much you wanted to do it."

"I know. But I still do a lot with flowers," I say, like I'm trying to sell myself to him or something. Impress him. Pass some sort of test. "I make posies, bouquets and stuff. I post them on Instagram. I've got a few thousand followers now."

Ed glances at me, his mouth a straight, impressed line. "Really?"

"I did request you. As a friend. Last night."

"Oh, did you? I'm hardly on it. Insta-newb. That's me."

We wander through the market. Clothes stalls, soap stalls, a huge white truck with an open shutter selling meat, the man behind the counter shouting something in such a musical way, I have no idea what he's saying and can't imagine anyone else does. I look at Ed out of the corner of my eye. He looks exactly the same as he always has to me. Even if I think back to teenage Ed, I feel like he's barely changed. In looks and in character and ambition—it's unwaning, like him, I suppose. He always wanted so much from life. He wanted it all for me too. "This hospital in Portland, Nell, it's incredible," he'd said to me the night everything changed—the night we officially began to split right down the middle, a hairline crack. "They have an opening. Elias, my uni buddy, he's over there, and he called me." Then it was *you could do this* and *we could do*

162

that and—"we could even come back after a year or two; I could do my intercalation year—" and I remember saying, "Ed, this is—a lot. This is miles away."

And I remember the websites he'd shown me then. Courses. Workshops. Houses to rent. A plan he'd made, with a space for me. But a space I didn't quite fit into—a size too small, or too big. I didn't sleep the night he came home with the job offer. I watched him sleep beside me in the dark instead, and I think I started to grieve then, for us. I knew he would go regardless. I knew those were the last nights I'd sleep beside him. Because I couldn't leave. Mum wouldn't be OK, suddenly not needing me, and she'd never have left me when I needed her. Twelve weeks later, Ed got on a plane, and I'd sat in the garden watching plane after plane fly over, wondering which one was his, and in which one in an alternative universe I was sitting beside him.

Ed budges up next to me, touching his shoulder to mine. "This is nice, Nell," he says, fingertips brushing mine at my side. "It's really nice to be back."

"It is," I say.

A cloud slides over the sun, casting us in gray shadows, the June breeze pricking the tops of my arms with goose bumps.

Ed laughs. "Yeah, not sure I've missed the unpredictable British weather, though, to be fair."

"Was it good? In Portland?"

Ed's eyes light up at the question, and like someone just squeezed the flames between their fingertips, it's gone. "The weather?" he asks.

"Everything."

He hesitates, weighing up the two options. To divulge, or to not. Then he just says, "It was cool, Noelle."

We wander more on the cobbles through stalls selling clothes, selling wind chimes, and punnets and punnets of plump summer strawberries. And before I've even realized, we're outside Charlie's tattoo studio, its candyfloss pink wooden sign jutting out from the sandstone brick. *Shit balls.* I hope she doesn't see. But then—I sort of hope she does. I'd rather her just see us than have to explain, because she'll ask me. "What's it all about, then? Do you want to get back together?" and I don't know the answer to either of those questions.

"She in?" asks Ed casually.

"Yes," I say, "and no, we're not going to say hi. She's packed out today. Saturdays are her busiest day."

Ed laughs and then gives a shrug. "Does she still wanna whip my arse, then?"

"Absolutely yes," I say, and he looks down at his shoes as we start to walk by, as if a little wounded. I peer inside—half expecting to see Charlie looking at me from the inside, mouthing,

What the actual fuck, Elle? But . . . she isn't in there. It's a tiny little shop; you can see right in, watch Charlie and Clemmie, her assistant, at work. And I can see Clemmie inside, chatting on the phone, her thick purple hair in a high ponytail, swooping black eyeliner flicks by her eyes. But no Charlie. Weird. Where is she, then? Maybe she's in the loo. But where are all the customers she said she had today? So many she couldn't help Theo in the shop, so many she couldn't look after Petal and had to work an extra day. I think about the day that she was driving in the opposite direction, and about what Theo said about being worried about her. An affair? *No.* No, how can I even think that? Only a *traitor* would think that about their closest, kindest friend.

"And do you still want to? Noelle?"

"What? Sorry I just—Charlie isn't in there. And she said she would be, and well, she isn't so—"

"Right." Ed gives a shrug. "So?"

"She's been—Theo said she's been . . . weird lately." And I know what he's thinking as he looks to his side at me, his eyes hooded, bored. He's thinking he wishes I'd concentrate on worrying about *my life* instead of other people's lives. He'd say it all the time, when Mum would blow up my phone with missed calls, when Dilly wouldn't come home until late and I'd wait up on the porch, in my dressing gown. "Why can't you see that you have a life to live of your own,

Nell?" he'd say, frustrated, and I'd tell him I was living it. *Wasn't I?* Then "For who?" he'd ask, and there would always, always be an argument. I'd accuse him of trying to change me. He'd shout at me about being stagnant. I'd cry, tell him I'm sorry I'm not a McDonnell. He'd apologize, tell me he just wanted more for me. That he wanted me to remember it was Daisy who lost her life that night in the car with Lee, not me.

"Charlie's fine, Nell," says Ed now, pushing his hands in his pockets. "Stop fretting."

"I'm not."

"You are." He smiles knowingly, and I look at him then, properly, the face I know every contour of, and I feel this longing, like a reaching hand from my chest to his. Ed. My Ed. I know his favorite fabric softener, the way he hates buttering toast straight from the toaster because the butter melts, and I know the names of all the motivational speakers he likes to listen to in the shower. I know him, and he knows me. Even the ugly, dark parts I try to stuff deep in the back, pretend they aren't there. I want to reach out and hold him. *I'm still me. You're still you.*

"How was America?" I ask him, stopping suddenly on the pavement. He stops too.

"Er, I already said? It was cool."

"No, Ed," I say. "How was it *really?*"

A sudden breeze whips through the air, and something topples and smashes onto the cobbles from a nearby stall selling handmade stoneware—little milk jugs and rustic, stone-colored mugs. A group of builders opposite whoop and cheer.

Ed watches, takes his time looking back at me. "What do you mean?" he asks.

"You know what I mean. What did you *do* every day?" I carry on. "Like . . . did you still eat a takeaway for dinner every Friday? Did you miss watching *EastEnders*? Did anywhere serve bacon sandwiches like Chancer's? Did you meet any friends? God, I don't know. Just—tell me things. Everything. All of it." I've missed him. I've missed two whole entire years of memories and experiences and *stuff*—there's a blank space between us of things I don't know, that he doesn't know. We knew what each other had done every day down to the minute for twelve years. And now we know nothing.

"You know you're asking me to gloat, don't you?" says Ed with a rueful smile.

"So be it. I want to know what I've missed. I want to know what it was like." Because I was almost there, right beside you, I think. Those memories would've also been mine.

Rain starts to spit from the sky and we both look up at it.

"All right," says Ed slowly. "Let's grab some lunch, then head back to mine."

CHAPTER EIGHTEEN

Hi, this is Noelle Butterby. I'm calling again about the—"

"The camera?"

"Yes. Yes, God, I bet you're sick of hearing from me, but the guy I spoke to last week said the head of history was back from annual leave yesterday so—"

"No, no, that's quite all right. But I'm afraid we still haven't come across it. I'm sorry."

"I just—I know it would mean a lot to a lot of people—"

"I know, but it's like I said to your friend last week, it probably is in the other vessel—"

"My friend?"

"Yes. He called asking about a disposable camera. One that might have been unclaimed, I just assumed it was something to do with you—"

"What was his name?"

"Um. I don't know; he didn't leave a name, I don't think. It was just a casual inquiry."

"But it was a guy?"

"Yes. A man. He said he was an ex-student."

Sam's dad, Frank, won't speak a word. I was expecting rude remarks, I was expecting grumbling and tutting and short answers, and perhaps having *too* much to say every time I picked up an item or opened a bin bag. But what I wasn't expecting was him completely blanking me as if I were an unwelcome ghost haunting his little flat who he's been advised to ignore by a priest. *"Ignore this strange and troubled soul and she will get bored and eventually pass on to the other side, Frank. I'm afraid it's the only way."*

I said hello when I arrived, and I offered to make him a drink. Silence on both occasions. I was almost tempted to go up and prod his wrinkly face, check he wasn't some sort of waxwork.

A woman called Gloria opened the door when I first got here—a carer with one of those smiley faces I would have definitely described as infectious had she actually had any sort of effect on Frank other than making him look even more like a man hopeful for death.

"You are Noelle," she said in a strong Irish accent. "Come on into the happy house." And she'd laughed and whispered out of the side of her mouth, "I hope to get a smile from him by the time I retire. What do you think? Possible?"

She sorted Frank's breakfast and helped him into his dining chair to eat it, then back into his armchair. I could hear him grumbling about it being "bloody pointless," but Gloria explained he'd seize up if he spent all day in one armchair.

"Nonsense," he'd snapped. And when I'd

smiled, passing the doorway with a full box of cardboard recycling, he'd stared at me with as much contempt as you'd give a passing door-to-door salesman and/or criminal. Then I'd dropped half of it, and he'd inhaled so deeply, it's a miracle I wasn't sucked up his nostrils along with the sideboard.

And now, it's just us. Me and Waxwork Frank. A match made in the fiery pits of hell.

"Frank?" I call from the kitchen, peering my head around the door, but he doesn't respond because *of course the fucker doesn't.*

He's in his chair, watching a daytime TV show as if there is a gun to his temple forcing him to, and I'm hesitating in the kitchen doorway after spending fifteen minutes more than the three hours I'm being paid for in the spare bedroom filling bin bags, emptying cardboard boxes of old newspapers, and a suitcase bursting with papers I showed to Frank before he shouted, "No! Don't touch that!" and I'd dropped it like it was a bomb. I've overrun because it's in disarray, this flat. In every nook and in every little crevice is just more stuff. It's like Mary Poppins's magic bag, but full of crap instead of fancy lamps and funky umbrellas. But I've also overrun because I can't stop thinking about what the woman at the college said on the phone. I'm totally distracted, my brain doing all sorts of laps and relays around itself, coming up with hundreds of stories that belong in library shelves and not in real life.

"Your life is not a Nicholas Sparks novel, Noelle," Dilly would remind me now if he knew I'd even lain awake considering *Lee* being the male student asking for the camera, when in fact Lee is sadly very much dead. And yes, there's nothing to say it's the same camera, but I dunno—I think it is. An "unclaimed camera." Of course they'd assume Daisy's camera would be unclaimed—that's the language they'd probably use if they were referring to an item belonging to someone who isn't here anymore, and something that, without me being there to collect it, would definitely just sit there. I'd asked Ed, who looked at me as if I'd finally crossed the border into madness.

"Nope, wasn't me Nellie," he'd said with a shrug. I'd met him straight from the train station again with a takeaway coffee the day of the call. It's become a bit of a routine. A coffee straight off the train after his shift, walking through town together, meandering through the market, Ed tugging at my arm to join him in his flat above a cycle shop, and sometimes I do, depending on how many calls Mum has made, whether Ian's at home. It's a temporary let—someone his dad knows, who's traveling, and every time I visit, I feel like I'm in someone else's home, with someone else's things.

"Look, I don't mean this coldly," Ed had carried

on, "but maybe you need to let this camera go." I'd stiffened at how dismissive, how *Ed* he was, but also because something passed over his face. Pity. Worry. *Something.* Or maybe I'm paranoid, because why would he lie? Why would he even want some old camera?

"It's just photos, Nell," he'd said.

"*Her* photos," I'd added, and "one of us," I'd thought but didn't say. One she took of Ed and me, Ed's arm around me, the floodlit college field behind me. "My future's in that photo," I'd thought as Daisy's thumb had wound back the film. "I know it. I just know it. And I'll prove it when we eventually come back here and take it out of the ground. Together."

"Frank?" I call again from the doorway.

Frank doesn't look up, his eyes on the TV, his lips parted, his eyes slits as if it's an effort to keep them open. Sam must look like his mum. I see not a single likeness between Frank and Sam. Perhaps the nose, but at a push. The straight line of the bridge of their noses is the same. But everything else—they're chalk and cheese. Polar opposites. In looks and in nature, and as far as I can tell, absolutely everything. I wonder how they met, Frank and Sam's mum. Sam's dad is nine years older than Sam's mum, I know that much, but I wonder if she wore lipstick, in case she bumped into him. I wonder if he made excuses to brush past her, to be close, and if she analyzed it afterward, the looks, the touches. I can't imagine it. I can't imagine him even *smiling,* let alone touching anything (well, besides souls with a cold stare).

"Cup of tea before I go?" I try again.

"No," he says, in more of a grunt than a word, and I nod pointlessly as the washing machine ironically sings a happy, tinkly tune behind me to signal that its wash load has finished. "I'll just, uh, hang this out on the balcony, then, shall I?"

No response.

"OK, brilliant," I say, "I'll do that. It's lovely and sunny, so it shouldn't take too long. Gloria can fetch it in. Or Sam. *Is* Sam coming today?" And I know I shouldn't, but I really hope he is. Sam and I haven't spoken since that day on the concrete, outside. Well. Besides one text. **I'll be there Tuesday before nine**, I'd sent, and he'd texted back, **Great** with a smiley face. Not even Charlie and I could pick apart and analyze that bland, boring exchange.

The balcony is seven floors up, and although I'm not exactly afraid of heights, my knees wobble as if on a rickety bridge, as I start hanging laundry on a clothesline. It's not natural to be this high up, really, is it? I was never afraid of flying, though. I love flying. Mum loved it too. We'd go on holiday once a year up until I was about sixteen. Spain. Crete. Cyprus. Portugal. She'd save and save, her whole year revolving

173

around that one week she could whisk Dilly and me away. I remember the little rucksacks she'd pack us for the plane—puzzle books and sweets and a packet of pencils—and how she'd lift them out of the trunk in the dark, bleary-eyed but excited for our little adventure. It wasn't always like this. Mum was sun-kissed and zesty and hungry for the world once. And then the stroke—and slow and fast, all at once, she retreated. Little sparks inside her slowly going out. It can happen to any of us. Turn back the clock about nine years, and that person was me. The version of Noelle Butterby Doctor Henry was inquiring after. The one who lost herself, for a bit, when everyone else was at university, starting their lives.

"Stay tuned for a fantastic competition . . ." a distant TV chatters from a nearby flat. *". . . and later, we will be showing you how to cook not one, but two perfect summer dishes . . ."*
You can see for miles up here. Stretches of houses and buildings, but just on the horizon, hills and lush green trees and blue sky. There's a particular specific smell up here. The smell of other people's houses; evidence of other people's lives. Freshly cut grass of someone's garden, the smell of frying onions from another flat. I grip the balcony rail and close my eyes. Daisy and I used to do this on her balcony, or at night at a sleepover, the night silent through the

174

open window except for the distant whoosh of motorway traffic far in the distance.

"Where are you, Elle?" she'd ask sleepily, and I'd always make her go first, because she had the best ideas—the best imagination. It's why she took art. It's why she wrote the best short stories and poems in English Lit.

"Oh, I'm in Italy with you," she'd say, closing her eyes. "We're celebrating. I just sold this movie script and they're saying I'm the new Nora Ephron, so I have a shitload of money to spend. We'll pick up some hot, tortured poets at some dive bar tonight. They'll *romance* us." She would always giggle, as if with glee at the glory of her own little stories. "Come on, Elle, close your eyes. Use your imagination. What do you see?"

Her happy, lively voice swirls through my mind now, girlish and giggly. I hate that Daisy is stuck in time. I hate that she will forever be eighteen. That she'll never know twenty-two, thirty-two, *seventy-two*. That she'll never fall in love, or see New York, or Amsterdam. *Amsterdam.* The first place we promised we'd go when we left college and saved up. "Jump on a bargain flight," Daisy would say, and I'd feel almost sick to my stomach with longing.

"Where are you, Elle?" her voice asks me now.

And I think. Hands gripping the balcony, I think, and I try. Where would I go if I could go anywhere? But nothing comes. Nothing at all. And I wonder, for just a moment, if I'm stuck too.

"Hey."

My eyes snap open and I turn around. Sam stands at the balcony door, tall, handsome, his lips a soft smile.

"Taking in the view?" he says easily.

"A bit." I clear my throat, straighten. "My legs are having a bit of a barn dance, though."

"Barn dance," he says. "Interesting." He comes to stand beside me, then leans to rest his tanned forearms on the bar of the balcony and looks ahead, like me. He smells amazing. Of showers and suntan lotion and that cedary aftershave. Something flutters in my chest, madly, like a trapped moth.

"See, you've got to trick your brain," he says. "As long as you have something under your feet, you've just gotta convince yourself that you're on the ground."

"Right," I say. "Sort of hard to do when, you know, the cars down there look like Hot Wheels toys and you're closer to birds than people."

Sam laughs. "Takes practice," he says. "Is that why your eyes were closed?"

"Ah. Not quite. It was something I used to do. With my friend, when we were kids. She had a balcony just like this and we'd . . . close our eyes, pretend we were somewhere else. Somewhere we

176

wanted to be someday. Say what we could see. I know, it's silly—"

"No it's not," says Sam. Then he leans closer and says quietly, as if asking me something secret, "And what did you see?" And I feel it. Despite myself, there's an electrical churn in my stomach. Like I just started a downward plummet on a roller coaster.

I clear my throat. "Um. A-a pasty," I lie. "A um, huge, golden pasty." Sam's eyebrows knit together a fraction, as if shocked by the sudden change of tone, but he laughs.

"You sure it wasn't oysters?" he says.

CHAPTER NINETEEN

Two Wednesdays ago, as I arranged giant yellow sunflowers in the window of Charlie and Theo's living room, Theo sidled up to me and asked me quietly if I'd look in on Charlie on Saturday.

"I'm not going to be here," he said worriedly. "My brother Andreas and I are going to meet some new suppliers, in Normandy. And Charlie'll be on her own from Friday to Sunday. She hasn't been alone with the baby overnight and—well, I'm a bit worried. I wondered if you could—"

"Go and see her?"

"Would you? She stresses, I think, when she's alone with her. I don't want to arrange a baby-sitter for her, but perhaps you could just be passing—"

I nodded. "Got it," I'd told him, but there was a small part of me that was reluctant to. Of course I'd do it. I'd do anything for Theo, and anything for Charlie. (Well. Besides go on a date with Jet with the torso from the reiki retreat.) But I feel reluctant because I don't want her to feel I'm checking in on her. I'd texted her after I'd seen she wasn't in her tattoo studio and she'd seemed quite taken aback. **I was probably out**

for lunch? she'd replied, and when I'd asked if she was OK, she'd said, **fine**, and I'd felt like I'd overstepped somehow, said too much. That she felt I didn't trust her.

"I can text you, when I've spoken to her and I know they're awake," Theo had said, and he did, half an hour ago. But Charlie isn't answering the door. And I know she must be inside because I can see the wheel of the stroller through the sliver of glass next to the front door. I can't imagine she'd go anywhere without it. Plus, the windows upstairs are open. But there's no answer—no movement. I know the code to the little secure spare key safe. But that's overstepping, isn't it, letting myself in? Ed's voice chimes in, in my brain, as if whispering into my ear. "Stop fretting over other people's lives and worry about yours, Nell." I shake it away.

I knock again.

Nothing. But I keep hearing a mewing—a baby crying? *It is.* That's Petal, her distant wails sailing through the open windows.

"Charlie?" I call pointlessly. *"Charlie?"*

I take out my phone, hover a thumb over Charlie's name. She's probably in the shower. Yes, that makes sense. Or maybe she can't hear the phone over the crying. Petal does have one powerful set of pipes on her, for such a small, doughy little person. I go to press call, but the screen changes in my hand, and Mum's name

179

bursts onto the screen. *Argh.* I cancel it, and call Charlie instead. It rings off as Mum texts me. **Could you get shower gel?** the first message says. Then, **What time will you be home?** and then, **Roughly**?

I knock frantically. "Charlie? *Charlie?*"

The crying continues.

Sticky, July heat zips up my back beneath my jacket which I only wore because rain was forecast, but it's so warm. My cold hands sweat, my heart beats faster and faster. Mum texting. The sound of Petal wailing. No sign of Charlie. The relentless hot sun on the back of my head. It's too much all of a sudden, and as my heart bangs and bangs, my hand, as if it has a mind of its own dives into my bag and pulls out my keys. I hold the square key ring in my hand, close my eyes, run a finger along one of its hard resin sides and breathe in as I do. I trace a finger along the next side and hold my breath, and running my finger on the next, I exhale. *In, hold, out.* It's just a baby crying, just text messages. Nothing awful is happening. Nothing awful is *going* to happen. I'm here. Feet on ground. Heart beating.

After a moment, I open my eyes but keep the keys in my hand, which shakes. It was stupid, I'd thought, when a nurse taught me that breathing technique. I was twenty-two and shaking like a leaf. "Whenever you feel the panic coming on, find a square," she'd said. "A window, a poster, even a wall. Inhale as you trace your eyes along one side, hold your breath along the next, then exhale tracing the next side, and just keep going around that square, *in, hold, out.* No matter where you are, you can usually always find a square." The key ring has always been my square. I'd found it on the ground in town when I was seventeen—a sprig of heather set in clear resin. It was a day or two before the time capsule was buried, and I remember because I contemplated having it as "my item." It's been years since I've had to pull it out to calm myself, and of course, now the worry creeps in, like fog. Why now? Am I going backward? No. *No. Charlie.* I need to get hold of Charlie.

I knock on the door again now, knuckles stinging with how hard, and my tired heart slows.

"Charlie?" I curl my hand into a crescent on the frosted glass sliver, rest my forehead against it to see inside. Is that—is that a leg? No. No, it can't be. It is. *It is.*

I glance at the key box. I punch in the code Theo told me ages ago, in case of emergencies (Charlie's birthday with an extra nine), and release the key. I turn it in the door and push it open. Immediately I'm hit with the sound of Petal's hysterical screams.

Charlie looks up at me from the floor. Her

skinny pink knees up to her chin, her face tear streaked and gray. "Oh my God, Charlie, what's happened?"

She looks at me, wide-eyed, her lips quivering.

I crouch to the ground, my shoes squeaking on the polished wooden floor. "Charlie? Charlie, talk to me."

"I can't," she says, her voice wobbling.

"Take some deep breaths—"

"I can't do it, Noelle," she says. "I can't. I don't think I can do this. I don't love her. I don't love my baby."

Charlie looks at me over her black-rimmed glasses, the rings under her eyes the color of bruises, the whites of her eyes a map of pink veins. Petal is still on my chest, a warm weight, and I lean down to smell her spiky tuft of hair. Petal *always* smells like soft towels and vanilla beans. Babies just do, don't they, without even trying? I look up at Charlie from the floor, cross-legged. She's in a ball, in the corner of her sofa, a blanket up to her chin, odd socks poking out of the bottom. She looks frail and small and totally defeated.

"I don't know what to do, Noelle," she says thickly. "I *dread* coming home to her." Charlie puts the tips of her fingers under her glasses and rubs at her swollen eyes. "God, what a fucking terrible thing to say."

"It's not."

"All day, I feel like I'm fighting this battle. I get up in the morning and my first thought is 'I can do this, of course I can, I'm a parent, I'm her *mum*.' And then she cries and instantly I think I can't. I can't do this. And I lie there sometimes, just listening to her, waiting for Theo because he's always so good with her and—I just seem to make her worse—"

"Oh, Charlie, you don't make her worse."

"It feels like that, Elle."

Petal snuffles on my chest. The flat is a mess, the coffee table strewn with muslin cloths and bottles and colic drops and pacifiers. An iPad still plays, quietly, with the sound of white noise. An artistic representation of a parent who's tried everything.

"Charlie, you're exhausted. Tiredness is torture; it's enough to make anyone feel like this—"

"But what about everyone else, Noelle?" Charlie cuts in, her large, tired eyes wide behind her glasses. "I see them. Every day, I see them pushing their strollers along and they look—fine. Like, totally *fine*. And they just cope. They just get on with it. They post beaming selfies of them and their kids on Instagram and they look so fucking happy."

I reach out and put a hand on her cold, bony knee. "Charlie, nobody ever broadcasts the bad bits of their lives. You don't ever sign onto

Facebook or Instagram and see a photo of—I don't know, someone shouting at their husband because he's been a tosser. You just see the flowers he bought her as an apology and some sickly bloody hashtag—"

"I spoke to this woman in the supermarket," Charlie barges in again, "and I said I was tired and finding it hard, and she said, 'Ah, you wouldn't change it though, would you?' and I had to of course say no. But I wanted to say yes. I wanted to say, 'Actually, Brenda, I would.' I want to go back sometimes. And I do, Noelle. I don't want to be Charlie of right now. I want to be Charlie of *then*." Charlie bursts into sobs.

"Oh, Char." I shift forward, put my arm on her back as she hides behind a tissue, hiccupping with tears. I stay like that for a while, one hand on Petal, her tiny strawberry-sized heart beating beneath my fingertips, and one hand on Charlie, shuddering beneath my hand.

"I'm so sorry, Noelle," says Charlie.

"*No,* don't be sorry. Please don't be sorry."

Charlie looks at me then, doe-eyed, like someone about to confess to something. "Noelle, I can't stop thinking about Daisy. About what you said, about what you think she'd have expected of me—"

"Oh, don't listen to me—"

"But what have I even done?" She shrugs, looks around the messy flat, a thick stripe of sunlight streaming through a crack in the heavy drapes like a stage spotlight, lighting the three of us up. "My life has started. I'm *in it*. It's not something I'm waiting for anymore. I'm here. And whatever I wanted for my life, was it this? I doubt it, Noelle, I really do—"

"Charlie, you've had a baby—"

"Who hates me. And all I do all day is—oh God, it's so dull. I just . . . clock watch. Until I can go to work. Until Theo can take her. And everything in my mind is taken up by her, and I'm not even with her all day. How awful is that? I change nappies and I'm worried. I hold her, and I'm worried. Has she had enough milk, is she going to be sick in her sleep and choke, or has she taken a fucking *shit*. All I talk and think about is shit sometimes. Shit shit shit."

Petal wriggles, and I stand, start to sway like I see Theo do behind Buff's counter. "Have you spoken to Theo?"

"No," she says. "*No,* I can't. How can I? I've started seeing someone." My heart stops. "A counselor," she adds, and it starts beating again, relieved. Of course. Of course she wouldn't have a bloody affair. "Once a week. I go during work time so Theo doesn't know." So that's where she's been going, and probably why she wasn't in the shop, and where she was driving to the other day. "But he'll want me to go to the GP and I'm—I'm worried they'll put me on meds and

185

the meds will numb me. I already feel so numb, Noelle. And I'm scared. Of being that mother who needs pills to get through what's supposed to be one of the best things that ever happened to her. I'm a shit mother."

"No, Charlie. No." I shake my head, cross the floor, and crouch on the carpet. "Charlie, you're crying because you care about her. And that makes you a good parent. *The best.* You're just exhausted. Plus, you can't prepare for this, nobody knows how to do this at first."

"But Theo does."

"But it's like anything—it's like . . . *bowling.* You know?" I say, nodding eagerly, dying for her to get on board with my weird analogy. "Two people who have never bowled before. You stick them in front of a lane, chuck them some balls, and you'll find one of them's like you—strikes within minutes. Bowling prodigy. They can't explain how, they just find it easy. And then you get people like me. Who chuck it and hit one pin and end up sitting on the side with a tray of nachos because it's all too fucking hard. Some people find things easier, and some people find things harder. There's no right or wrong. Look at Mum. Look at—me."

Charlie gives a watery smile, then bursts into tears again. I hug her, and Charlie puts her arms around me tightly, as if holding on for dear life. Sandwiched between us, Petal sleeps obliviously and Charlie's tears dot her little head like rain-drops.

"I can't tell Theo," sniffs Charlie. "That I can't be this mum he thought I'd be. That I'm no good at this."

I shake my head. "You don't need to do or say anything right now. You need rest. Look, why don't I take Petal out for a bit? Tell me what I need, when she's due her next feed, and we'll—I dunno, we'll go on a bit of an adventure or something. I've got things to get for Mum. Plus I can take her to the park, show her the flowers, the ducks—"

"No. No, I can't—"

"I insist on it. Have a bath, *sleep*. I'll let myself in later."

Charlie hesitates, unblinking, looking from me to her daughter, to the sun beckoning through the drapes. Then she swallows, swipes away a stray tear. "She's due a feed in two hours. But can you wind her after every ounce or so? If you don't give her the colic drops and burp her a lot, she gets so windy and her stomach hurts her."

"Of course."

"And if she gets too hungry she gets so angry, she can't feed—"

"Oh, *same*," I say, and Charlie laughs through her tears, reaches up and touches Petal's little fluffy head. "She'll be fine, Charlie. And so will you. Trust me. Auntie Noelle's got this."

187

CHAPTER TWENTY

I'm not entirely sure I've got this, I'll be honest. I feel like someone dragged me off the street and put me in charge of a small, unpredictable creature before fleeing. But after a little bit of a screaming performance outside a shoe shop (Petal, thankfully, and not me), I bobbed her on my chest in front of a basket full of cut-price flip-flops and with a dummy and strange shushing noises that made me sound part-vacuum, Petal managed to settle, and is now sleeping soundly in her stroller. The weather's turned in the last hour, a surprising chill in the July air every time the sun goes in, so Charlie wrapped her up gently and meticulously in a cellular blanket, like a little takeaway fajita, and I wished so much she could see what I see. Someone who cares so much about their child, they're just so frightened of getting it wrong.

It's nice pushing Petal along, soothing almost, and I cover so much more distance than I would if I were walking alone—through town, and around the park, and now, back through town, a bag of fresh roses in the basket underneath, from my favorite florist. I stopped to take a photo in the park as Petal slept—huge masses, like clouds, of cornflower-blue hydrangeas, their petals like resting butterflies. I uploaded it to my Instagram, something I've been neglecting lately since taking the extra work at Sam's dad's, and seeing Ed (who still hasn't accepted my request, the tech-granddad), and added the caption: "Some say hydrangeas symbolize gratitude. Be thankful for the little things, always." It got ten likes almost instantly, and I felt like a classic internet fraud, the sort I mentioned to Charlie. Because I'm trying today, to feel grateful, to feel lucky to be here, but I can't seem to grasp it. Something Charlie said keeps nagging at me, like someone pulling at my sleeve. *"My life has started. I'm in it. It's not something I'm waiting for anymore. I'm here. And whatever I wanted for my life, was it this?"*

Was it this? Was this what I saw for myself? And what *is* it that I wanted? Am I still waiting?

We pass a full bus stop, and an elderly woman in a coat the color of figs looks into the stroller, then at me, and smiles, and for a moment, I allow myself to zoom out, like a camera. View myself from a distance, pushing a baby along the old, cobbled streets of my little West Country town. I wonder if Noelle Butterby of fifteen years ago would see this scene in a crystal ball and assume the baby was hers. Mine and Ed's. We'd talk about it sometimes, like we talked about everything in the future, as if we'd suddenly be different people when we got there. A house, careers, savings, two children, maybe three. A checklist, really, and I watched Ed's brothers as they ticked each box, but Ed and I seemed to lag behind. All the things on our checklist seemed to be waiting for us in the future, a future that never seemed any closer, even as time passed and should've brought it clearer into view. I'm not sure why. Was it me? Was I the only one holding us back? Ugh. Probably. That's what my instinct says—that little voice on my shoulder. Ed's a doctor. Ed went to Oregon. He's living far more than I am. A fat raindrop plops onto my forehead, like a finger prodding me to stop making myself feel like shit.

Petal and I walk until we're under the charcoal-bricked viaduct bridge as rain begins to spit from the skies, like sparks. A glimmer of memory flickers into my brain of Daisy and me standing here sheltering from a sudden torrential down-pour after shopping in town for eyeshadow and bras.

"Lee is so cool," Daisy had said, the straw of her milkshake at her lips. "Like, you know those truly cool people who are totally autonomous? That's Lee. He knows who he is and doesn't care what people think. I love that."

"Well, when can I meet him?" I'd said, and she'd beamed. Pretty and sparkling as she always was.

"Soon," she said. "He'll be at the time capsule thing, and he mentioned maybe giving me a ride, so obviously we have to make sure I'm looking totally *off the charts* for when I'm zooming off in his sexy little car."

"Obviously."

"How are you and Ed getting there? Train? Oh, maybe you can jump in with me and *Lee*. Me and Lee. Sounds right, doesn't it? Daisy and Lee."

I shake away the memory, because sometimes I can't bear to think further than that. It's an old, broken record, an old, well-trodden path, one that I know every step of and can so easily fall onto with the slightest nudge. How I might've been able to save Daisy's life if I'd known. If I'd insisted she come home with me and Ed on the train, she'd still be here. If I'd gotten in the car with her, maybe I could've stopped Lee speeding or doing whatever it was that made what happened, happen. But if I'd gotten in, I would've died. Was I meant to get in? Was I meant to not?

A train shoots overhead and Petal stirs, and I'm grateful to the noise drowning out the chatter in my brain, plonking me straight back in the present. I could go home with her. Mum would love to have a baby in the house, I'm sure. But then it's quite a walk in the rain and I don't want Petal to get cold. I could go into Neo's, but their steampunk coffee machines are loud and the music is always brash, and I wouldn't want Petal to wake before her feed and screw up Charlie's routine.

The rain falls harder and I hover under the bridge. I unfold the rain cover from the basket underneath and secure it over the stroller. The breeze whips it up into my face, and Petal sleeps on.

"You just lie there, oh queen," I say under my breath. "No, don't mind Auntie Noelle in the wind like a knob head, struggling with this—*thing*. God, how does this even fix on?"

"Noelle?" I instantly recognize the voice and look up, and my body reacts before my stressed little brain has even registered that he's here.

"Hey!" Sam jogs toward me, the fast-falling rain making him squint. My heart speeds up as if from a sudden jolt from jump leads, and there's my stomach again, swirling like I'm nervous, like I'm seven and it's Christmas Eve or something. *Ridiculous.* What about Ed? What about *Jenna?* But it's pointless. It happens completely involuntarily every time I see him. Against my bloody will. Against all better knowledge and judgment.

"Hiya," I say. "Fancy bumping into you, eh?"

"I know, right?" He grins broadly. "It's all we do." He's wearing a gray hoodie, dark tracksuit shorts, and a sports bag, the thick black strap across his chest. *"Cor,"* Charlie would say. (And so would I, of course, if it wasn't totally socially inappropriate.) *"Hit me up, Captain America."*

"I didn't think you were back until tomorrow."

He ducks under the bridge with us, rain from overflowing guttering above the station slapping the tarmac. "Change of plan. I got in last night." He looks down at the stroller and smiles, damp hair falling over his eyes. "This yours?"

"Yeah, forgot to mention it!"

Sam laughs.

"This is Petal. My friend Charlie's daughter. She's not been sleeping, so I thought I'd take her out for a walk. Give Charlie a bit of a break."

"Your good deed of the day." He smiles. "Do you wanna get out of here? You got plans or—"

"I was just considering whether to go home, or to a café, actually, but the coffee shop's really noisy and—well, I'm out of ideas. The baby whisperer, I am definitely not."

Sam laughs. "Well, let's walk," he says. "We'll find somewhere."

Sam and I sit in the launderette with two coffees from Neo's a few doors down with its cork walls, bearded baristas, and neon lights twisted and bent into wanky motivational quotes on the wall. We are the only ones here. The air smells like laundry detergent and the coppery metallic scent of loose change, and we sit side by side on a narrow wooden bench, only the two of us here, the windows steamed up. We'd tried to get a seat in a quieter café, but there were no free tables, and when we'd rushed by the launderette, the pair of us getting showered with rain, Sam had stopped and I had been completely wooed by the condensation on the glass and fairy lights around the frames, promising a warm, snug shelter. We'd gone in and sat down on the wooden bench, our skin quickly thawing, and the rhythmic whirring of the machines seemed to settle Petal too.

"I really like launderettes," I say now, looking around. The walls are tiled halfway up in squares of duck-egg blue, and weird out-of-place framed paintings hang on the wall, of beach towns and boats in a harbor. "I like the nostalgia of them, I think. The smells, the sounds. I don't know. It's comforting."

"I've never really thought about it," says Sam quietly, looking over his shoulder at the line of machines, a uniform line of white plastic baskets on top of each one. "I guess I like the old-fashioned feel of it. You know, it's kind of cool having somewhere that isn't always manned. It's a reminder that people can maybe still sort of be trusted, or something."

I sip at my coffee, a raindrop helter-skeltering down a curl at my chin, and dripping onto my thigh.

"No?" he says, taking in my face.

"I don't know." I give a heavy shrug. "Feeling

a bit jaded today. Do you ever get those days? Where you feel like a grumpy old man?"

"You mean like Frank?" Sam chuckles, looks down at the cup in his hand. His long legs spread, his forearms resting on his thighs. He dips his head, in one nod. "But yeah. I guess we're all allowed to feel a bit jaded sometimes, right? Anything you wanna share with the room?" He gives a coy smile.

And I tell Sam about Charlie, about finding her this morning the way I did. I tell him about the panic that almost overtook me, the deep breaths I took with my bloody ancient keychain, and I tell him about what Charlie said, about life and being *in it,* and my mouth moves so quickly, the words pouring out of me like the endless rain outside. Sam listens quietly, stoic in that cards-close-to-chest way of his.

"It's just—what Charlie said. I keep thinking about it. Like—I worry I've wasted time."

Sam looks down at his coffee, then at me. "Wasted how?"

"I was a bit like my mum," I say, and hearing myself say it out loud feels like a breath I've finally released, one I had no idea I was holding on to. "For a while. For a year or so. It hit me out of nowhere, but looking back, it was a perfect storm, really. Ed was at university, my friend had died a few years before, and I found out my dad—he lives in Australia, we don't have anything to do with him. Well, I found out he'd got remarried. And I think it all just caught up with me. I was in hospital for a while." Heat creeps up my skin as I say it—shame, I think, deep shame, that something that seemed to be confined to my mind, that seemed to be *thoughts,* landed me somewhere with beds and doctors in white coats. And I really wish I didn't feel it but I do. Sam though, he barely reacts. He just listens, a fixed, calm gaze. "But Mum looked after me and . . . to be honest, that's why I understand. Why I don't push her. I couldn't have been pushed out of anxiety, out of depression. Nothing worked for me, other than time." And there's a part of me that believes the stress of that probably caused the stroke, I want to say, but I can't bring myself to. I haven't said that out loud for a long time. It used to frustrate Ed, and he'd bombard me with cold medical facts which I think he thought would help, but of course didn't.

"Everyone wastes time," says Sam calmly. "And it sounds like you've had a lot of stuff to fit in a small amount of it."

"Maybe. Or maybe I'm stagnant."

"Nah." Sam stretches, pushes back his shoulders. "You don't look stagnant to me, Gallagher. Not from where I'm sitting." He smiles at me, so warmly, so reassuringly, and it makes my cheeks glow, like someone just turned the heating up.

"Thanks," I say, and I turn away, hide my probably bright salmon-pink face as I sip my coffee. I love being with him. I do. *I really do.* Every time I'm near him, I want to stop the hands of all the world's clocks. I never want to leave.

A washing machine whirs and a group of shoed feet outside thunder past. Kids running from the rain, I expect.

"I was taught that trick, by the way," says Sam. "The um—the square one." He draws a square with a finger in the air, tracing one of the dryers. "With the breathing."

"Really?"

"Yup." He bows his head. "I would've been like . . . eighteen, nineteen maybe? Tried living with my dad for a while, and—God, it was the worst idea I ever had. Everything went wrong, things were hard at home, and I went for a run and had a panic attack, went home thinking I was dying or something. I was sure of it. I always thought I was dying back then." Sam chuckles darkly to himself. "So, Frank whisked me off to the doctor and a nurse told me—"

"A nurse told *me* too. I bet it was the same one."

Sam laughs, then his face softens. "One little panic," he says, "doesn't mean you're going backward. If that's what you're thinking."

"I was. I thought it might be a sign or something, of things to come."

"Nah. Signs are bullshit. I don't believe in *signs*."

I don't say anything, but I sit and run over his words in my mind. *Do I?* Do I believe in them? I look for them everywhere, I think, without noticing I do. Signs that things might change—get better, or worse. Signs about Sam—why he's in my life, why we keep bumping into each other. Signs that Ed likes me, is glad to be home, still fancies me, missed me. Signs that he's lying to me about Daisy and the camera—the way I thought I saw something in his eyes. Is that looking for signs? Or is that . . . I don't know. Gut feeling?

"So, you don't believe in signs," I say. "But what about gut instinct? What does your wild mountaineering brain think of that? Ever smell a mountain bear at thirty feet?"

Sam takes the coffee away from his lips and laughs. "Yeah. Yeah, I do. The gut instinct, not so much the bear." He smiles, his cheeks pink from the rain. "But yeah. I believe when you just *know* something."

"Me too," I say.

"Why, do you know something?" I look over at him, his gorgeous brown eyes, his pink lips, and I feel such a tug toward him that I almost tell him, almost say, *What is this that's happening to me, Sam? Why does looking at you feel like looking at the fucking sun?*

"Come on, spill." Sam smirks, ducking his head closer to mine, dark hair falling over his eyes. "What do you know, Noelle?"

I swallow. "Nothing much," I say in a tiny voice.

But I feel like I *know* a lot in this moment. I know I'm meant to know Sam. I have no idea why, there's no logic or reason—just that I'm meant to. In the same way I know there's something about Daisy's camera, too, and that look on Ed's face. I just don't know what.

Petal snuffles in her buggy and I'm grateful for the distraction. I jiggle the brake with my foot, and the juddering settles her again.

"She's cute," says Sam, as if despite himself.

"She is." I gaze at Petal in the buggy, tiny fists at the side of her chubby face. "A whole perfect, clean slate of a life ahead of her to live how she wants to."

"I know, right?"

"Says you," I say. "The man who tries to cheat it."

"What? Cheat death?"

"*Yes*. You said yourself, people die every year up on mountains and yet you just—fuck it and do it anyway."

"Say yes and panic later." Sam laughs, then looks down into the caramel liquid of his coffee cup. "Maybe it's not cheating death, though. Maybe I'm just . . . looking it in the eye. Telling it I'm not scared of it."

"But why would any normal person want to do that?"

Sam cocks his head to one side, a wordless "well," then blows a long breath out between his lips. "My cousin died when I was young. And you know, he was—wild, I guess? Took too many drugs, drank too much. But we lost him. Way too young. Took his own life."

"I'm sorry. That's awful."

Sam exhales, nods weakly. "Something about that makes you feel like it can all be over in a second, so what's the point in fearing it." Then he pauses, ducks his head, and says with a small smile, "Plus. Who says I'm normal?" and I know, with that joke, he doesn't want to give away any more. And I get it. More than anyone, I understand.

Rain pummels the glass of the launderette, raindrops making trails down the glass between the mosaic of pamphlets and ads. We talk, and Sam tells me he's got "a crazy" few weeks coming up, and I'm reminded how busy his life is compared to this tiny pocket of time in the cozy launderette. Work, a charity event in Scotland, and flying home to Oregon. "I'm there about a week," he says. "It's my mom's birthday. She'll be sixty. And then a friend of Jenna and I—he's getting married."

I nod but feel like someone just stuck a huge pin in my mood. *Bang.* "And how're things going with Jenna?"

Sam fidgets, runs a finger under his black watch strap absentmindedly. "It's—OK. Which—I don't know if OK is *OK, you know?* I've known her my whole life and it's so easy for us to just fall back into some sort of routine, of how it always was, but then *how it always was* is how we ended up in this mess, so . . . but she's looking at visas."

"To move here?"

He nods.

"I see," I reply, because I don't know what *else* to say, and he knocks back his coffee as if it's something stronger.

Someone outside bursts into laughter and there's the sound of a police siren—a whole world going on outside—and I suddenly feel all filled up with tears and confusion and emotions I don't recognize, with nowhere to go.

"And how's Ed the Ped?" Sam asks.

"It's—it's *OK.*" I force a smile and Sam smiles back. Easy to fall into a routine, I think but don't say, for us to crawl in and curl up in the comfortable hollows we left in the past, like indents on an old sofa. Easy for it to be how it always was. And that's how we ended up in the mess we did too.

I check my phone. No text from Ed. Nothing from home, or Charlie. Nobody needing me for anything. So, we sit quietly together, listening to the rain for a while, the sound of a button in one of the dryers tapping like a tambourine, exactly every two seconds. Warm. Safe. Slow. Another Noelle and Sam bubble, away from the rest of the world.

Half an hour later, after Petal's feed—which Sam and I managed between us by unpacking the entirety of the changing bag and barking orders at each other like people on some sort of game show—"No, not that bottle" and "Those are nappy bags, not wipes!" and "Quick! *Quick!*"—we begin packing up and preparing to leave the warm little nook of the launderette. Outside, the rain has stopped, and the skies are blue, and I wheel the stroller back and forth on the lino beneath our feet, as Sam methodically repacks the bag in the way a mountaineer does, I expect. Zipping it up, everything neatly packed and slotted in tightly. Then he holds my keys in his hand and looks down at them, jerking his hand so the keys fan in his palm.

He freezes, looks up at me slowly.

"Noelle, where did you get this?"

"What?"

He's holding my heather key ring—the square. My old, little breathing square. And he's looking at me, his lips parted, but in a quizzical half smile.

"That's my breathing square." I laugh as Sam

looks down at it in his hand, rubs a thumb over the clear resin. "It's heather. Real, I think, in resin."

"I had one of these." Sam looks at me and then laughs—a surprised burst. "Seriously, I had one the *exact* same."

"Really? What, heather—"

"*Yeah!* Heather, clear resin, silver chain." He looks down at it, swallows, and when he looks back up at me, his eyes are glassy.

"I found it," I say. "I was about seventeen and I found it on the street."

"On the *street?*"

"Yeah, not far from here actually. Outside the leisure center, near Greggs of all places, which for me is predictable because . . . *pasties.*" I laugh. Sam doesn't. "Sam, are you OK?"

Sam shakes his head, as if shaking himself out of a trance. His chuckle is unconvincing. "Yeah, totally, I just—mine was exactly like this. My grandma gave it to me when I was like, seven or eight, and—I lost it. It was heather. For protection. She believed in all that crap—"

"*Oh my God.*" I stop pushing the stroller and stare at him. "Do you think it's yours?"

Sam pauses, then laughs. He puts the keys back in the changing bag, slots my phone in the side pocket. "No," he says. "But that would've been a turn up, right?"

"But I mean, it could be!" I say, eagerly. "Did

you lose it over here? When you were visiting your dad?"

"I don't know. Could have. But God, they must've made hundreds—it was cheap. From a museum gift shop." He's hanging the bag on the handle of the stroller now, adjusting the strap, making sure it's secure. "*Thousands* of them, Noelle."

"But it's quite an unusual thing to have, though, isn't it? It's not like it was a Disney key ring, or something completely mass produced."

"Well, this probably is too."

Sam pulls open the launderette door and holds it open. "Come on," he says. "We better go while the rain is holding off." And I can tell he wants me to stop talking about it, for whatever reason, and so I do. But something is fizzing inside me. Imagine. Imagine if that was his. That all along, I've been carrying it around with me, something that Sam once carried around too—

"Noelle? Are you coming?"

"S-sorry. Yeah."

Outside on the pavement, the air smells earthy, the way it does after the sun comes out and warms the rain on the pavement, and Sam looks down at his watch. I suddenly want him to put his arms around me, but he steps away, throws his bag over his shoulder.

"Well, thanks for the coffee, Noelle. And

Petal." He reaches a hand down and strokes a finger down her chubby, peachy cheek. "See you around, OK?" He turns, and I watch him get smaller and smaller over my shoulder as I walk, two magnets pulling away.

CHAPTER TWENTY-ONE

iMessage from Candice: Noelle, would you be able to call me when you get a minute? Total SOS wedding situation! Need your help!

Dilly appears in the doorway, his blond, iced-gem tuft of hair on end, a huge flowing bloodred silk scarf spilling from the back of his skinny jeans' pocket. He's home again, for three nights, and tonight he's playing a local gig in Bath city center, but of course acting as though he's about to go onstage at Wembley Stadium and we are lucky to merely breathe his air.

"Say it," he says, smirking over at me and giving a slow wink.

I stop, twine between my lips, three heavy blooms of baby-blue hydrangeas in my hand. "Mm?"

"Tell me."

Mum looks over her mug of tea at him, her proud eyes twinkling as if he is in fact already on that Wembley stage. "You look gorgeous, darling Dilly," she says. "A true rock star. Isn't he, Noelle?"

"Too good, right?" Dilly shrugs, as if it *bores*

him to be this cool. "I mean, that's what I think, anyway. A total ten out of ten."

"You look ace," I say, and he nods, satisfied. He won't sleep tonight. He never does when he gets home from a gig. The adrenaline, the need to retell us over and over with accents and gestures how certain people reacted when he played a certain guitar solo, when he sang a particular note. "Sometimes I really do feel like Jesus," he'll say, and I will laugh and ask how Jesus fancies cleaning out the food waste bin.

The back door rattles open and then closed, and Dilly poses in the hallway, his skinny, pale elongated arm above his head, his head bowed like Freddie Mercury, and I wait for Ian's faux surprise and admiration.

"My goodness," says Ian, his voice traveling down the hallway. Yup. *There it is.* "Do you know, for a minute I thought that was Roger Daltrey." He appears in the living room doorway, dressed from top to bottom in the color of rich tea biscuits. From his polo shirt to his combat trousers and socks. Beige. Always beige. "Did you hear what I said, Belinda? Hello, Noelle."

"Hiya, Ian," I say, the twine muffling my words.

"Roger Daltrey." Mum grins. "Doesn't he look the part, Ian? You can just see it, can't you? Him, on the ol' you know what—MTV awards."

"Oh yes," says Ian, meandering around the

coffee table and pulling at the knees of his trousers as he sits. He sets an oven timer shaped like a pig down on the table. "Although I'd hazard a guess that NME is far more suited to Dillon. If I know my music, and I won't ever pretend to be an expert, then I'd say a rock group like his wouldn't fit in at MTV at all. It's all manufactured pop music."

"Oh," says Mum woundedly.

"Yeah," says Dilly, lifting his chin, looking at something invisible in the air. "Superficial bullshit. Pretentious posers. That's not us."

"No." I laugh. "Definitely not you." Dilly rolls his eyes. "What's with the timer, Ian?" I ask.

"That'll mean the first coat of the anti-mold emulsion is dry."

"Then you'll nip back and do another coat?" Mum asks.

"Exactly."

"Clever," says Mum, picking up the egg timer as if analyzing a rare fossil, and looking over at me, impressed. "Ever such a domestic man, isn't he, Elle? He reminds me of . . . who's that handsome gay man with the lovely, soothing voice? Very clean-looking. Very wise."

"Me?" Dilly says, angling his guitar case on his shoulder.

"Apart from you."

"Nigel Slater?"

"*Yes,* Noelle! That's it! Oh, he's lovely, he

is, Ian. Very domesticated. Ever so good with all things in the home. He wraps all his food in brown paper. You know, steaks and things? You're like that." Mum looks at me. "Isn't he Noelle? With his cling film?"

"Oh yeah," I say. "Cling film."

Ian looks really pleased with himself, straightens a little in his seat. "Yes," he says. "I do think it's important to ensure all things are wrapped safely in a fridge. Especially when dealing with meats."

I make a mental note to tell Charlie—to type out the chat exchange later on WhatsApp, like a screenplay. She'll get it. She'll piss herself laughing and say, "Oh, God bless Bel and Ian. Fucking love them." And I don't want to just keep texting her to ask how she is—like she's something defective that I have to keep checking in on. She went to the GP yesterday, with Theo. The doctor offered her CBT and suggested trying a course of antidepressants which she started taking this morning. She was so worried to tell Theo about what happened last weekend, but within seconds of talking to him, I knew she was so glad she did. I saw it with my own eyes, the relief trickling into her bloodstream, coloring her cheeks. "I love you" is all Theo said. "I love you so much." I cried on the way home, for Charlie, and I cried out all the tears I'd kept locked in at the launderette. And I still don't really know what they're for. I'm confused. *I am.* I even sat down with a pen and paper last night in bed after sketching out something for Candice, just to try to tease out the tangles in my mind.

Ed was my forever, I wrote. *My world ended when he left. And now he's back. But it feels too easy. There's more to it. Why did he come back?* Then I'd buried my head in my hands and groaned as I wrote *I like Sam* on the page before I punctuated it with a question mark that would fool no man, and slammed the book shut and pulled the duvet over my head. I'm confused. A complete tangle of heart and head and gut and logic and what is probably 50 percent bloody *mountaineering lust.* He followed me on Instagram after the launderette—I'd mentioned the photos I took of the hydrangeas in the park— and I felt like I'd been shot with a dart when the notification came through. *SamAts followed you.* He doesn't update much, and when he has, it's all beautiful landscapes, weird knots, "how to wash your ropes" tutorial (who knew?), and beaten-up GoPro cameras with breezy captions like "this little buddy is still going strong." But there *are* some of him. One of which was taken a few weeks ago. Sam with a group of four others completely suited up—hats and helmets, gloves and smiles, nothing but ocean-blue sky behind them. Of course, I spent ages scrolling his grid, the patchwork collage of Sam Attwood's vast and colorful life. Cataluña, Chulilla, Mount Elbrus in Russia. These beautiful places I've only ever seen on the front of gift biscuit tins—a kaleidoscope of color and nature. Then of course, there was the photo that made me so hot, I felt like I'd rolled obliviously into a bonfire. It was from last year. A huge, sandy, bark-colored rock face, with Sam clinging to it effortlessly, his shirtless back to the camera, the muscles large and defined and suntanned. I'd sent a screenshot to Charlie: **Shitting. Hell.** She had texted back: **I'm deeply aroused.**

"Wow." Ian looks at me over his glasses, shakes me out of my muscle trance. "Those hydrangeas are lovely. Who's the lucky recipient?"

"Candice," I say. "This woman at Jetson's. Her florist has let her down and she's asked me—"

"To do the wedding?" cuts in Mum.

I freeze. "Well. Yes," I say carefully, "but I said I wouldn't be able to and I'd just make her up a bouquet for her to copy. She said she might have to do them herself if she can't find anyone in time, at such short notice—"

"When is it?" Mum asks urgently, the words blending into one.

"September twenty-eighth. In Edinburgh. But I'd have to leave on the twenty-seventh—*they* would. The florist, I mean." I hadn't mentioned it to Mum, when Candice had called me and asked me to fill in for her florist, who'd somehow double-booked. My heart, when she asked me—I couldn't put into words, I don't think, how I felt. Like it was too large for my body all of a sudden. I felt like it was going to fill with air, send us upward, into the clouds. But I said no. How could I leave everything at home, travel hundreds of miles away, do a job I've never, ever done before?

Mum stares at me. "Right," she says.

"Well, you have to do it," says Ian, giving a deep nod, and Mum and I look at him like he's just Morris danced on the table in nothing but his probably beige underpants.

"Well, I'd love to do it, Ian, but—"

"I'll stay with Mum," says Dilly, his hazel eyes on the phone in his hand, his skinny nibbled thumb cycling up the screen. "I'll be back on the, um—yep, here we go, the twenty-seventh. About midday?"

I look at Mum, my lips parted, words jammed in my throat, struggling to arrange themselves into a sentence. "I—well—I don't—I'd need to leave really early. Like, really early. About six."

Mum nods, staring ahead as if psyching herself up for a marathon.

"Honestly, it's too short notice and I've never—"

"No," Mum swoops in. "No, I'll be all right. You—you have to go, Noelle. Ian's right." She looks as if she might cry, and I feel like I might too because—can I really *do this?*

"Mum, I don't have to."

"Noelle, you must." Mum's eyes shine, and she digs her two front teeth into her quivering lip. "You have to."

"And you're definitely sure you'll be here by noon, Dilly?" asks Ian, tentatively. He'll get his iPad out in a minute, his fingertips tapping in a flurry of reminders and count-downs.

"Yeah, should be. We're only over in Newcastle, so should be mint."

Something flutters inside me, wings opening, taking flight. Could I? Could I *really* do flowers for a wedding? An actual wedding with posies and guests and wedding breakfasts and, of course, the token drunken sweaty fight? And in *Edinburgh.* I've always wanted to go to Edinburgh! Oh God, I feel sick. With longing, with nerves, with the *Can I actually pull this off?* and the *Is this avenue open, for someone like me?*

"So—I should say yes?" I ask. "Really?"

Mum looks at me and nods. "Yes," she says tearfully, her words quivering at the edges, like blancmange. "Please say yes, Noelle."

CHAPTER TWENTY-TWO

I said yes. I said yes to Candice."

"Finally! Nell, this is amazing. How much have you charged her? Did you take her through the price list we did?"

"Yes, but we haven't agreed on a final figure or anything yet. I'm still trying to work out the details."

"Like?"

And there he is. Blunt, straight-to-the-heart-of-the-matter Ed. Everything is A to B. Anything in between: *fluff.* We'd met the next day, after we'd agreed—Mum, Ian, Dilly, and I—that I'd say yes to the wedding. And Ed's face changed. Brightened, widened. "This is brilliant, Nell. Now, make sure you charge her a reasonable amount, yeah? Don't undersell yourself." And before I could open my mouth to speak, he was whipping out his phone, opening up his Notes app. "So, how much is labor for this stuff?" he asked as we'd plonked onto the sofa, and two hours later I'd left his flat with a price list and my head banging with information about taxes and profits and savings. It almost sucked the fun right out of it. *Almost.* It'd take a lot to rain on the parade I'm leading at the moment. I'm like an excited conga dancer at the front of the line. I'm all feather boas and whistles.

"You know, you'd have known I was looking out for all this if you were to actually accept my Instagram request. I put a call out on my stories. For recommendations—"

"I told you." Ed laughs. "I don't ever go on it. And recommendations—for what?"

"Like . . . suppliers up in Edinburgh, for a start," I tell Ed now, back on that sofa a few days later. We're seeing more and more of each other lately, and I've seen less and less of Sam. I've barely heard from him since the launderette. It's just been texts about Frank, really. I send him an update, and he replies with **Great!** or **Thanks.** Unlike Ed, he does sometimes watch my Instagram stories, though, and he likes every post, and butterflies tussle inside me every time I open the app now and see a new message. And they die, fall like a flock out of the sky, every time I see it isn't him. I got one yesterday and dove on it like it was catnip, but of course it was someone pretending to be a god-fearing soldier needing a good wife, and I'd blocked, deleted, and cursed myself for being so bloody needy. Because of course, he'll be with Jenna, at the wedding, falling back in effortless bloody love beneath fairy lights and stars. He doesn't have time to be on Instagram, and especially to "react" to a photo of my supplier waffle or hefty sausage sandwich breakfast.

"OK, and what else?" presses Ed.

"And a van or something to hire once I'm up there," I say, "and a hotel for me to stay in and a train there because I doubt my car will make it and—well, I might need help, so I'm trying to find out from Candice if there's a wedding planner up there, or an assistant that might be around, and—"

"Whoa, whoa," says Ed, putting his beer down on the coffee table and plonking himself back next to me on the sofa. "I can help. When is it again?"

"September twenty-eighth, but I'd leave the day before."

Ed nods, scrolling down his phone, his hand raking through his curls. "I'm working," he says, "but I finish at twelve on the twenty-seventh, so I could—meet you up there, maybe? Sleep on the train."

"No, no, that's mad, I can't ask you to do that. You'd be exhausted after a bloody night shift. Don't you remember Dorset? That mini break. You *hallucinated* on the train."

Ed shrugs, laughs. He's been out in the sun, his skin golden, with two smudges of almost-red like war paint on his cheekbones. Too much sunshine from those beers he went out for after work, I bet. "Was a laugh, though, wasn't it? Me thinking Denzel Washington was in the train bog."

I laugh. "And you thought there was a finger in your sandwich, but it was just a roll of wafer-thin ham."

Ed laughs throatily, throws an arm behind me, stretching on the back of the sofa. "See? Fun. And it'll be nice, hanging out in Edinburgh with you. A *hotel*." He smiles then, green eyes glinting.

"To work," I say.

"To work," he mocks. Then he leans and I turn my face, and he kisses my cheek. This keeps happening. He keeps leaning in, and I think I want to—a big part of me wants to—but I turn away, give him my cheek, or make a joke, or talk about bollocks, like some weird article I read on BuzzFeed or the price of eggs in Tesco compared to Waitrose. The other day, we were both sitting on the sofa watching TV and his hand found mine, and I was surprised in that moment, how right it felt for me to take it, squeeze it, feel his fingers slip between mine, rest heavy and familiar in my lap. We've slipped into such a routine that I even told Mum and Charlie about it yesterday.

Mum hadn't been as delighted as I'd expected her to be, and Charlie had looked up from her appointments book and her skin had turned the color of clay.

"Why didn't you tell me?" she'd asked, and she'd retracted, like a little crab, looked down at her lap, hurt. I'd told her everything then, that I was afraid she might tell me it was a bad idea, but that it felt so natural, so comfortable and easy, and I wasn't ready to hear it.

"But are you sure this isn't convenience for him, Elle?" she'd asked. "I mean, it seems it to me. He comes back, and you're here waiting. His old life. It must be nice for him, just to come back and slip back into it." But I told her that it was nice for me too, to slip back into things. Into Ed, my warm blanket, my everything-I-ever-knew. "We were together a long time," I'd said, like Sam and Jenna, I wanted to say but didn't.

Her brow furrowed and eventually, she nodded. "I guess I was just hopeful for Sam. It's like a little love story me and Theo have been watching from afar or something." And I felt my heart fall to my arse then, as the *I like Sam?* scribble drifted through my mind like a plane spelling words in the sky.

"What's happening with your mum?" Ed asks now, leaning and grabbing a handful of peanuts from an ugly paint-splodged bowl on the table. I don't think I like being here, in this flat, and I think it's because it belongs to some fifty-something medic who's currently in Dubai with his twentysomething wife. It feels like a stranger's home. It's all white and chrome and misguided decor choices. Something he looked at and thought, "This says cool and young and hip," when it actually says, "I am a present-day Austin Powers."

"Dilly'll be home with her. He gets home about lunchtime."

"So, she does still need people around then?"

I shrug, but my shoulders stiffen up by my ears, like plaster setting. "*You know* she does."

"Just—you say she's getting better."

"She is," I say. "In some ways. But—"

"You still have to arrange a babysitter." Ed sighs, leans back on the sofa. "Nell, you know how I feel about this, that it shouldn't be up to you to—"

"She isn't well, Ed."

"Then she needs the help."

And we slip straight back there, as easily as we slipped into our routine—like a scratch in a record that the needle can't help but get wedged on. Ed's views on how I live my life, how Mum lives hers. I open my mouth to speak, but no words come out at first. We've had this conversation so many times. It was the source of so many of our arguments, and the subject of Mum and me, it's even more loaded now. It's what came between us in the end. It's why we broke up.

"She has to want the help," I say, carefully, but my words are clipped, with sharp edges.

"And maybe she would if you—you know, *withdrew* yours."

I scoff, lean away from him. "Oh, because that's what we do to people who aren't well, is it? Withdraw the help. This, from a *doctor*—"

"Nell, I'm not saying neglect her." He laughs now, as if I've been ridiculous, as if I've got the wrong end of the stick, and holds my hand. "I'm saying . . . you know what I'm saying."

"I know," I sigh. "But you can't just switch anxiety and panic and *fear* off. I know that. You know I do." You'd have known, too, if you'd come home to visit me back then, I think, tore yourself away from the endless parties and gallons of cheap university beer for longer than a single weekend where you just sighed and looked helplessly at me, like I was a car that wouldn't start.

"But she's had her life, Nell," he says, "and she traveled and did all the things she wanted to do, and—you could've . . ."

"I know," I say again. Yes, Ed, I could've done anything. I could have gone to America with you. We could've had it all. I could've been the Noelle you wanted to start a new life with so desperately, away from here. Then it tumbles from my lips.

"Why *did* you come back?"

Ed cocks his head, gives me that classic, infamous sideways wince, his eyes narrow. "What do you mean?"

"I mean, why would you come back here? You wanted to get away so badly, you wanted a new life somewhere different—"

"I—I got the job offer, Nell."

"Did you meet anyone over there?"

Ed freezes, eyes round and unblinking. That look again. The look he gave me when I asked him about Daisy's camera. Pity, worry . . . something he's holding back. Then he takes a deep breath, the way someone does when preparing to sing, or to say something important. "Nell, I don't want to lie—"

"So you did. You did meet someone."

Ed takes another deep breath and looks at me. "I did."

I freeze—a movie still. A lump gathers in my throat, and I just look at him. It's not like I expected him to never look at anyone else ever again. Of course not. But hearing about it for the first time, knowing he's kissed someone else, touched someone else, used all those funny Ed anecdotes that used to make me cry tears of laughter, that felt like they were only for me, *on someone else*—it stings a little, like vinegar in a wound.

"But nobody worth talking about," he says, then he takes my hand in both of his.

"Really?"

"Nah. Just random dates."

I think of the woman with the auburn curls, how much I obsessed over her. And yet, apparently, she is a nobody worth talking about. I lost so much sleep over her, in the beginning. Sat stewing, with sadness and jealousy so powerful, I practically pulsated with it. "Nell, what is this all about?"

I look at him and shake my head, feel myself deflate like a pierced pool toy. "I don't know. I'm just—I feel confused."

"About?"

Race cars screech like hornets around a track on the TV screen, around and around, faster and faster, at dizzying speed.

"Everything. This. You and me. About what it is."

Ed rubs a thumb along the back of my hand, tracing the bumps of my knuckles. "Why does it need to be anything?" he asks softly. "Why can't we just . . . let it be what it is?"

"And what is that?"

"Catching up. Turning back the clock a bit. That's not a crime, is it?"

"Right."

Ed moves a hand, strokes the side of my cheek. "Aren't you glad I'm here?" he whispers.

And I nod.

"Because I am," he says, and when he leans in to kiss me, I let him this time. I let the warm flesh of his familiar lips press against mine and I melt into it. I have missed him. I have missed this security, the life we had—the life we almost had. And isn't it something we all want, from time to time—to turn back the clock?

CHAPTER TWENTY-THREE

Four weeks pass in a blur. I see Ed a lot for takeaways and walks through town after his shifts, and I enjoy being totally caught up in the wedding whirlwind. I watch YouTube videos about preserving wedding flowers and timings of bouquets, from water to bride; I call the hotel to double-check they definitely have a cool, dark room for me to work in; I contact the flower supplier up in Edinburgh. I even got a call from Candice's hotel's wedding planner and I flushed with fizzy excitement as she talked. *I'm a wedding florist!* I've felt like shouting in random people's faces, as I worked, as I ran my usual boring errands, feeling like I have springs in my shoes. *At this moment, I am designing the flowers for someone's wedding and everyone is treating me as though I am the actual real deal!*

"You *are* the real deal," said Charlie yesterday as she sat at my kitchen table, thumbing the leaves of yet another "dummy run" bouquet. "I mean, look at this. If I tried to make this, it would look like I wiped Petal's arse, then whacked Theo over the head with it. You are good at this, Elle. Beyond good. Believe me." And for the first time in my life, I've let myself believe her. Maybe

I *can* do this. Maybe I can expand my world, a little, chase dreams like loose balloons, like other people do. And I don't know how it would work, but ever since I've said yes to Candice and Steve, everything and anything has felt possible. A spark of something has flickered to life deep down in my gut, and it won't go out.

"You can do your own flowers." Charlie had grinned then. "When you and Sam get married."

"I am not marrying Sam," I'd replied, and she'd leaned over and kissed my cheek.

"Tell that to Theo. He is convinced," and I couldn't help but grin back at her. My Charlie, smiling, cheeks like red, rosy apples. She's getting there. Her meds have kicked in, and her mum and dad have stepped up and promised to take Petal every Friday so she and Theo can have a date night—or sleep. Which is exactly what they've done for the first two. She spent thirty quid on organic ingredients in Waitrose last Friday, printouts of Deliciously Ella recipes poking out of her handbag, but in the end they were asleep by eight, with bellies full of Nutella on toast. The next morning, she'd sent me a photo of Petal, all gummy and wide-eyed. I cried when the text that followed said **My girl. Missed her.**

Today I'm back at Frank's, and when I go to let myself in, the door swoops open before my spare key even hits the lock.

"*You* have worked wonders," says Sam, standing

in the doorway of Frank's flat. He's sun-kissed and smiley, and when he holds my shoulders with large, warm hands, I feel like my heart is going to shoot out of my body and explode, like a dirty great firework above us both. I wasn't expecting to see him. I don't feel prepared, although I'm not even sure what I mean by that. He's a person, after all, not a bloody science exam. "You're a genius," he says.

"Well hello to you too." I laugh, and heat creeps up my spine. "You really think so?"

"For sure," says Sam, and he steps aside to let me in. "And it smells different in here—like, I dunno—is it . . . lavender?"

"Lavender disinfectant. Only the most *luxurious* of scents for Have a Go Frank."

Sam groans, pulls his mouth into a grimace. "Is he still being an ass?" he asks out of the side of his mouth.

"Oh, one hundred percent," I whisper, as I follow him inside, the heat of the flat hitting me the way it does when you step off a plane into a hot country. "Hates me. *Despises me.* And perhaps also the world, so I try not to take it too personally."

"If it helps, I think he secretly likes you."

"Sure he does."

"Trust me, Gallagher." Sam shoots a look over his shoulder at me—his dark eyes dancing with the secret inside joke of my now evolved

225

nickname, and I feel like my kneecaps might disintegrate. "But hey, come through to the kitchen. I have something for you."

"For me?"

We walk through the flat together. Sam looks good. *Again.* And I wish I had worn something different than the baggy oversized T-shirt and leggings I slung on in a rush this morning while Mum called for me from the bedroom, unable to reach her left slipper. He's wearing a white T-shirt, his arms muscular at the seams, and he smells of—ugh, I don't know, but that gorgeous Sam smell. Showers and fresh laundry and sun on skin. "I wish you'd just snog Sam," Charlie had said after I told her about Ed and me kissing. "And you keep saying you don't like him like that, but I have to say, dude, I don't believe you." And as I look at him now, golden and handsome and tall, I sort of wish I could too. *No, no, no.* Must keep remembering Jenna. Must keep remembering Jenna and Ed and screwed-up, bloody phone numbers left on smelly hospital benches.

"Hi, Frank," I call as we pass the living room.

"Hello," he answers, and although he says it as if he has a revolver at his temple, I feel a sense of victory.

"Well, would you look at that," I whisper. "One nil to Noelle Butterby."

Sam gives a deep chuckle and steps into

the kitchen. "Told you." Then he bends, rifles through a large hessian shopping bag on the floor, and when he stands, he's holding a huge bunch of freesias wrapped in peanut-brown paper. They are *beautiful*. Gorgeous and coral-reef pink, petals open as if ready to sing. "For you," he says.

"For *me?* Why—what for?"

"The old man's a jackass," he says dryly, "and you've done an incredible job, and so quickly. I was thinking about what you were saying about gut feelings and trusting your instincts, and then I passed these, and—I don't know. Gut instinct said I should take them—"

I open my mouth to speak, but it stretches into a wide, spontaneous smile. "Do you know—they actually do symbolize trust?" I say, and as I hear myself say it, goose bumps pepper my arms.

"Seriously?"

"Yup. And they're my favorites. First flowers I managed to grow from bulbs." I don't need a mirror to know that my face is totally ablaze with heat. Less Crayfish Face, more Lobstered to Fuck. "Thank you. Seriously, Sam, you didn't need to do this—"

"No, I know I didn't, but—well, I figured you're always the one that gives the flowers, so . . ." He trails off, reaches up to push his hand through his hair, his hand resting at the back of his neck.

"Thank you," I say again, and he smiles softly. "Will you keep them in water for me?"

"Sure," he says, and as he starts to fill the empty sink, water splashing onto the ridges of the draining board, my heart opens in my chest, like a box burst wide, sending sunbeams up and around my body.

Charlie says she doesn't believe me when I say I don't like Sam. And I don't think I believe me either. That question mark fades like smoke, to nothing.

Two hours later, Sam gets back from popping into town and we take a break on the balcony of Frank's flat. It's a warm, late August day, and the sky is the color of the ocean, and the clouds above are like swirls of cream in coffee. There's nothing up here, besides the sound of Frank's television and the distant chinking and mumbling of other people's homes through open windows.

"How're you doing over there?" asks Sam.

"Ish," I say, gripping the back of a garden chair and sitting down. "Can I say ish?"

"You can say ish." Sam laughs. He leans against the railing and the concrete of the adjoining wall in the corner, a tanned forearm resting on the metal rail. Then he produces two paper bags from behind his back. "Left or right hand?"

"What?"

"This is pasty roulette."

"You got *pasties?*"

"I got pasties," he says.

I can't stop the grin from spreading across my face. I lean forward, try and grab at a bag, see what's in what, but he retracts the bags closer to him. "Come on," he teases. "Play ball."

"Fine. Left."

He hands it to me, a square, white paper bag, and I open it up. "Still none the wiser," I say. "So, do I have to bite it to find out?"

"Yup."

And so I do, conscious of not spilling it all down my chin and looking up at him like he's caught me in the middle of a country fair eating competition. "Oh my God. A classic. I got the classic pasty. Cornish. *Perfection.*"

"Ah shit," says Sam, opening the greasy white paper of his own bag. "That means I have the wild chicken curry option."

"So your first pasty experience is an outlandish curry one." I laugh as Sam examines the pasty in his large hand. "You really are an adrenaline junkie."

Sam sinks his teeth into it and nods at me. "OK. OK, this is—good."

"You're a fan?"

"I think I'm a fan."

"Oh, well that's a relief," I say. "I'd have had to completely stop seeing you if you'd hated it."

"Nah." He grins. "You'd have orchestrated another blizzard. Stolen another key ring—"

"So you do admit it, then," I swoop in, a finger shooting up to point at him. "That maybe my key ring was yours, that maybe we had the same *nurse*—"

"*No.* It was a joke."

"But don't you—think it's weird, at least," I say, "that we keep bumping into each other, that there are all these coincidences, like . . . you keep showing up in my life." Those last few words fall from my mouth and I'm grateful there's a pasty to hide behind, although I drop a confetti cannon's worth of crumbs down my top as I do.

"I guess," he says. "But then it's a small world—"

"Not that small," I jump in, and Sam looks at me, says nothing. "My friend Charlie wonders if you went to the Green Day concert in Milton Keynes, back in 2004, the same one we went to."

Sam smiles, three creases in his forehead appearing, as if he'll humor me, nothing more. "Um, nope, 'fraid not."

"What secondary school did you go to?"

"St. Agnes High School," chews Sam. "In Oregon." He raises a mocking eyebrow. "Did you go to school in Oregon too, Noelle Butterby?"

I roll my eyes. "Oh, just eat your pasty."

We sit on the balcony for a while, looking out

230

at the blue summer sky to the leafy horizon, Bath sitting proudly in the distance with its biscuit-colored buildings standing tall like sandcastles. And as always when Sam and I are together, we talk about everything, and nothing, and it's there, the whole time, that churn in my stomach, the tingling skin, the heart racing just that bit too fast. But at the same time, it's like I can say anything. No posturing, no selling myself, and— God, is that what I do? *Do* I sell myself when I'm with Ed? And if I do, why? What am I trying to prove?

"You OK?" Sam asks.

I nod my head as if shaking off the thoughts, and say, "So, guess what, Samuel Attwood?"

He looks up from his lunch, licks his lips. "What?"

"I have said yes to something and I am definitely panicking, as you would say. In real time. Before your eyes."

"Oh yeah?"

"Candice at Jetson's."

"Post-it Candice?"

"Of Candice and Steve fame, yes." I nod. "She's asked me to do the flowers at her wedding. And I've said *yes*. Shitting myself. Like—properly shitting myself. But I'm doing it."

Sam stares at me, a slow, easy smile spreading across his face. "Noelle, that's amazing."

"Well, not quite amazing yet because I might

fuck it all up and I haven't even done anything yet, and last night I actually thought, I have the power to fuck their entire day up and—"

"No, but you did it," says Sam, factually. "You said yes. That's—that's brave."

I drop my eyes to my lap, pick away stray pasty crumbs. I can't look at him. Sometimes, looking into Sam's eyes makes me feel like I'm naked. Like he can see too much of me. "Thank you," I say. "But I'm not sure I'd have actually said yes, really. It was you, you know, talking about saying yes and panicking later and looking death in the face, and, OK, weddings aren't death— although I'm sure they represent that for some people—"

Sam chuckles, a rumble in his throat, his hand at the dark stubble of his chin.

"But I just thought fuck it. I wanna do it. For me. Because sometimes it feels like I'm fading into the background or something, and—nobody can see me. You know? But I thought—well, *I* can see me. Right? And this is what I want to do."

Sam hesitates, his brow crinkling beneath the dark hair he then swoops a hand through. But then he just says, "Yeah. *Right*. Definitely."

"Ed said he's going to help me," I carry on. "It's in Scotland, so I need to sort trains and stuff, but he's going to follow me up. Help. Stay over with me."

Sam straightens at that—his dark brows rise, and he shoves his hands in his pockets, stands rigid, shoulders broad. "That's cool," he says. "Ed the Ped, showing up when he's needed, that's good."

"Yeah. Really good."

"Yeah. Totally."

Silence follows, thick and loaded, like static. Sam kicks the bottom of the balcony with the toe of his sneaker, and I fiddle with the paper bakery bag in my hand. I pretend to see something in the distance, but it's pointless, because Sam hasn't looked at me once.

"I sort of want to take the sleeper train there," I say, words breaking the silence. "It's something I've always wanted to do. Since I was a kid."

"Then you should do it," says Sam, looking up at me. "When is it? The wedding."

"September twenty-eighth."

"Ah. Same as that charity event I talked about—the charity climbing thing?"

"And you seem *riveted* by that," I joke, and he laughs.

"Yeah, it's—not my thing. It's all suits and dancing and—" He shudders, makes a face at me then smiles, teeth grazing his lip. "But there'll be booze. And food, and there's a charity auction where they sell us off as guides or whatever. Last year it was at a ballroom in Manchester. *Me.*

A guy who likes hanging off rocks in his spare time, in a *ballroom*."

I giggle, but think to myself that he'd look perfect in a ballroom, in a suit, in anything. "And where is it this year? Oh—*shit.* You said Scotland! Didn't you? When you mentioned it before?" My heart starts to whoosh in my ears.

"Yeah. Yeah, it's in—"

"Edinburgh," we say together. Sam's eyes widen and his hand drifts slowly to his chin, at the same time I spew out, "Oh my fucking God. *Where?*" My voice is so high-pitched, I'm giving myself tinnitus.

"Uh. Some huge famous nightclub, according to Clay, my buddy—what?"

"The wedding. Candice and Steve's. It's at a hotel. In *Edinburgh.* Oh my *God.*"

Sam laughs, but it's a nervous, strained laugh, and he looks at his feet. "Weird," he says.

"*Just* weird? We're both going to be in Edinburgh, Sam. We are both going to be in Edinburgh at the same time, on the same weekend—"

"It's a big place," says Sam, and I stare at him. "And a small world. What?" He laughs.

I shake my head, curls bouncing around my shoulders. "Nothing," I say, when really, all I want to do is squeal, spill it all out on the phone to Charlie and Theo, or sit, like I'm in some sort of crime drama, and try and work out why this keeps happening—spread it all out, all the evidence, across the floor. If we hadn't had this conversation, we might've just been wandering around Edinburgh and yet again, bumped into each other. It *is* weird. It's weird and wonderful and it's bubbling away, the wonder of it, under my skin, as if it's going to burst through the surface.

"Maybe I'll bump into you," is all I say, and he says, "if I manage to escape the hours of speeches," and a part of me wants to grab him by his collar, ask him what *he* thinks it means. Because he always seems so annoyingly relaxed—almost dismissive of it. As if I believe in fairy tales or something, and he's far too old for such shit.

"Speeches," I say instead. "Sounds a bit like a wedding."

Sam nods. "Probably why I've never had one."

"You mean, why you never got married?"

Sam nods. "Jenna always wanted to."

"And why didn't you?"

He shrugs and looks down at the floor, kicks the balcony gently again, the way people might gently and pointlessly kick a tire. "I guess I've always just associated marriage with, you know, settled life, pets and kids and two vacations a year and white picket fences—" He smiles over at me. "I dunno, that's never been me. And it wasn't Jenna either, for a while, but . . ."

"It is now?"

Sam nods.

"Do you think you ever will?"

Sam looks down at his coffee, then looks at me with a slight smile. "*Cars* are for confessionals, Gallagher," he says. "Balconies are for pasties."

CHAPTER TWENTY-FOUR

The new autumn sun is shining extra brightly today through the misty train window, as if it knows—today is like no other for me. Today is a special day—the start of something. Today is the day that I am going to *Edinburgh*. Away from home. And not only that, but when I get to the other end, I'll be working *as a wedding florist*. Yep. Me. Noelle Butterby, *florist for events and weddings*. And Ed—he'll be joining me later, helping me, staying over with me, and in a five-star hotel no less. He just needs to finish his shift at the hospital. *Life*. I feel like I am living life, in this moment, with everyone else.

A woman scoots onto the train, pushing down the handle of a little ruby-red suitcase at her side and placing it onto the luggage platform. She smiles and finds her seat in front of me, leaving behind a lingering gust of sweet, orchidy perfume, and plugs in her earphones, sips from a coffee, the steam wisping from the little spout. I walk past these trains most days, hear them tear by in the distance as I wash up, or take out the rubbish in our tiny little cul-de-sac. And now here I am on one, and it's taking me miles away from my little safe world and into—well, the big wide world. A life that I want. A life I'd always hoped I could have one day.

The train driver speaks, muffled and deep, through the tinny speaker. He talks about the route, about the refreshments carriage and about the weather, as houses speed by in a watercolor blur, and I feel like I'm being carried away. Everything in this moment is perfect.

At half past ten, I listen to a podcast and break open the ham sandwiches I made last night as Mum shouted from the other room things she wanted to be sure I'd packed—"Deodorant? Paracetamol? Oh, and how many pairs of knickers have you packed? I don't think four is enough, Noelle. Think about what Dilly says. Always account for two accidents. An extra pair for a bug, and a pair for a hangover." And at quarter past eleven, three hours into the journey, a phone call cuts through my music, smack bang in the middle of listing down everything I need to do when I get to Edinburgh in my notebook with one of twelve spare pens I panic-packed.

"Noelle, it's me," Dilly's voice speaks through the phone when I answer. "I'm having a fucking 'mare."

My heart stops. "What? What's happened?"

"Van's conked out."

"What?"

"Conked out on the motorway. We're waiting for the AA. We didn't have any breakdown cover so we had to call them and sign up first—and then they said—"

"Dilly, I can't hear you."

"Well, I'm on the hard shoulder!" he shouts.

"But—but when do you think you'll be able to get home?"

Dilly sighs noisily as a lorry swoops past him, its horn blaring. "I'm sorry, Elle, but we're still in Newcastle."

At that, I stand up, as if to attention. A woman feeding a baby on the seats opposite looks up at me, her baby nothing but two tiny little kicking legs beneath a white cloth. I sit back down.

"W-What time did you set off?" I take a deep breath, but my heart is beating like it's running a minimarathon, like it's going to attempt it from here, if you don't mind, to sprint to Scotland on its own. "How can you *still* be in Newcastle?"

"Set off about half an hour ago, I reckon. Maybe forty minutes?"

"Dilly, it's *gone eleven*." I'm hysterical. And I know this because I *sound* hysterical.

I can't believe this. I cannot believe he would leave it this late. Mum's on her own and she isn't expecting to be on her own for long. Something bubbles up inside me, like hot, acidic waves. Anger. Sadness. Panic. This is what I mean. This is what I mean when I say that I feel like people don't see me.

"Dilly, you are supposed to be with Mum—"

"I know, I know, but what can I do, Elle? I'm not the driver, it isn't my van—Elle? Elle, are you there?"

I hang up, stare down at my phone as if for an answer to this total mess. Instead, I call Ian. It goes straight to voice mail. I stare down at the screen as a **sorry** comes through at the top of my screen, from Dilly—a pathetic little window that is absolutely no help or consolation. A fart in a hurricane, as they say, a drop in the ocean.

Mum is alone. Dilly is stuck. And I can't do anything about it because I'm on a fast train to fucking Edinburgh. In Scotland. Hundreds and hundreds of miles away.

Ed.

Ed finishes soon.

I quickly type out a text for him to call me as soon as possible, then another to Ian, and another text to Dilly to tell him to call Mum and tell her not to worry, because *Noelle'll sort it. She always sorts it.* And I'm ashamed when ten minutes later, Mum calls, and then she calls again and I watch the call taper off, because I know she'll be worried—and I don't yet have the solution, like I always do. I stand, pace the carriage as it rockets through the countryside. I want to get off. I want to stop the train. I feel sick. *I feel sick.* Like I might actually need those extra sodding standby knickers.

I go into the train bathroom, yanking open the

door and slamming it. I pull down the window and suck in gusts of cool, clean air. It'll work out. Something will work out. It always does. I look out at the passing greenery, the mossy blur of bushes, the endless blue skies. I think of Sam. I always think of Sam lately, when I don't know what to do. When I *do* know what to do. All the time, really. He's always there in my head. And like the universe takes pity on me, it throws me a bone. My phone vibrates.

"Ed."

"Hey, Nell," says Ed breezily, "I'm just heading to the station now. Showered at work. Got off a bit earlier—"

"Dilly's broken down."

"What?"

"Dilly. Did you get my text? He's in Newcastle still. Stuck on the hard shoulder."

"But—he said he'd be with your mum at midday—"

"I know, but his van, with his bandmates—it's broken down."

"Ah, shit," he exhales noisily. "Bummer. Look, do you need me to pick up anything?"

"No. No, actually, I was thinking maybe you could—" I swallow. Why does this feel so hard? *Why am I nervous?* It's Ed. The love of my life. Why does it feel like this, when all I'm doing is asking him for help? "Would you go and sit with Mum?"

Ed pauses, a painful, loaded silence. "What?" I can picture his face. Stone. A face that says, "I see not a single ounce of logic."

"I know, Ed, I *know* it's a lot to ask, but if you head there right now then she's got someone there from twelve, and then I can try and get hold of Ian or perhaps even Gary at number twenty-one just to—"

"Nell, no," says Ed. "No, I'm not doing that. I'm getting on a train and I'm coming to Edinburgh with you—"

"But I can't keep going to Edinburgh when—"

"This can't go on—"

"But right *now* I need to sort something and I can't stop this *fucking train,* Ed—"

I'm shouting now, and I know people must be able to hear me from the other side of the door. This mad woman who had it all together mere minutes ago, losing it slowly in a clinical train toilet that smells like pine and cheap body spray.

"Nell, this is a massive opportunity for you," says Ed. "You are not turning back and letting it be ruined."

"Please go back. Just go and sit with her." I'm crying now, my words shaking and pathetic.

"No, Nell. I'm sorry. I don't agree. And if I go, nothing ever changes, and I'll miss my train."

I close my eyes, lean my head against the wall behind me. A tear falls down my cheek. A montage of memories like this echoes through my mind. Ed irritated, Ed despairing of my ridiculous life. Mum and everything she did for me when I lost my way. Her gentle hands sponging my back in the bath, trays and trays of food brought lovingly to my bedside. She put me back together. And where was Ed? Ed was at uni, ticking his stupid, empty, bloody McDonnell boxes.

"Noelle, I care about being there for *you*. This is long overdue; this is—"

My phone bleeps in my ear. Ian is calling. "I'll call you back."

I hang up before Ed can say anything else. Within five minutes, Ian is getting into his car and heading for Mum. Dropping everything, just for her.

CHAPTER TWENTY-FIVE

S teve, *this* is the genius I was telling you about. Meet Noelle Butterby. You know Noelle, don't you? From work? Come on, you must recognize her now."

Big Steve in Sales bear-hugs me and pulls back, looking down at me with a wide, beardy, bristly smile. "Yes!" he bellows. "Of course I do. Ah, thank God for you, Noelle, that's all I can say. You've saved our bacon here."

"Oh, well, it's a pleasure. I'm honestly super excited." And it's the truth. I really am. I'd cried a bit on the train here, after Ian had shot round to Mum's. Ed had called a few times and I watched the calls ring through as the countryside blurred past my window. Confusion twisted in my gut, and I was teetering on the edge—I almost tipped over into it, into worry, into all-consuming despair of "I can't do this. Look. This is proof that I can't do this, that I can't actually have this, I'm not allowed this." But then I got a text from Candice, and a **You've got this Gallagher** text from Sam which warmed me through, like sunlight, and I felt like I could. I washed my face, ordered too much from the refreshment carriage, and answered a call from Ed (who explained calmly, black-and-whitely, why he said what he did, and we agreed to forget it, not let it ruin the weekend). By the time the train got in, I was fizzing with excitement again.

Candice pulls a barstool out and gestures to me with newly tanned arms and square, shiny manicured fingernails to sit down. "We're spoiled with you. Truly. Honestly, Steve and I were on your Instagram last night and I could barely contain myself. Your work is *lush,* Noelle."

"And you are way too kind," I say, and she wrinkles her nose at me and says, "Sit! Have some champers with us. Just a tiny bit, we won't keep you."

We sit at Bar Prince inside the grand and glittering Balmoral Hotel, and I can hardly believe I am here. It's bustlingly busy, full of guests and diners and drinkers, chatter and laughter and the thick smell of sweet cocktails and charred meat. The Balmoral is as full and as alive as the grand, noisy city outside, and I feel I could stand with my arms out and my eyes closed. This is where we used to dream of being, Daisy and I—a part of the world, lost in its busyness and noise and all the delicious *nowness.* I'm here. *I am here.*

Steve and Candice hold hands opposite me, their fingers intertwined, and a barman slides a shining glass of bubbles across the bar to me.

"So Martina, my wedding planner, has set

you up in a little room just off the banquet hall in which we'll get married and it's fully air-conditioned, meaning it's cold enough to keep the flowers nice and cool. Is that right?"

"*Perfect*. And did they say they had buckets?"

"A few, but not many."

"OK, good, well I've ordered more from the suppliers anyway. I'll go there just after I finish this. I parked in the car park just up the road from here. But if there's anything else you want, now is the time to say. I'll just add it to my list."

Candice grins at me, her diamond studs glistening in the buttery light of the bar. "Nope. I trust you. And your boyfriend is following you up, is he? Her boyfriend, Steve," she rubs his shirted forearm, squeezes it, "he's coming up to help, after his shift has finished. He's a *doctor*. Pediatrician."

"Oh, wow. Straight after a night shift," says Steve, champagne flute a ridiculous sight in his gigantic shovel hand. "That's love, that is."

"Oh, well, he's not really my—"

"I always think that's what true love really is," says Candice, dreamily. "If they make time for what's important to you, regardless of whatever they'd prefer to be doing."

"Aww," says Steve. "What about falling asleep with you on the bathroom floor when you're too hungover to move because *Steve, don't worry, it's only two piña coladas and I know my own limit thank you?* Does that count as *making time for what's important to you?*"

Candice laughs and slaps him gently on the arm. "Yep. Piña coladas *are* important to me."

I laugh, clink my glass to theirs, and say, "So come on, tell me how nervous you really are on a scale of one to ten!"

When Ed arrives, it's seven p.m. and I'm sitting cross-legged on the cool stockroom floor listening to music and making up a table arrangement. Blue hydrangeas. Gypsophila. Cream roses. I bound out to him, like an excited Labrador, desperately wanting to drag him into the Holyrood room, where Steve and Candice will be having their reception tomorrow. It's enormous and grandiose, with ten round banquet tables, plus a top table, all of which are waiting for their decorations—their flowers from—*me.* *Look at it!* I want to say. *Look at what I've made happen! We're here! We're in Edinburgh! We are somewhere in the world because of me. Not you this time, but me!*

Ed looks pale and disheveled, his hair damp with rain, but nevertheless flashes that wicked grin at me across the pearly floors of the lobby.

"Hey, Nell," he says, wrapping his arms around me. "I'm fucked."

"Nice to meet you, Fucked," I say, pulling back.

"Is everything OK?" he asks. "Dilly sorted?"

And although there's a part of me that wishes he would, I know he won't apologize for refusing to go and be with Mum, and really, should he? He wanted to be here to help me, he said it himself. Of course that is more important to him than Mum. I just wish sometimes that there was more warmth with Ed. Less "this is A, this is B, and you should do C, the end" and more "I understand. It's not perfect and always logical, but it's you, and I'm here."

"Fine," I say. "Dilly's almost home. Ian's with Mum."

"Good," he says simply, then he snakes his arms around me. "Come on, then, let's go see this room of ours. *I need bed.* And room service. Like, the biggest steak they've got. Dessert. Cheese. *Everything.*"

"I can't," I say. "I'm midway through the table arrangements."

"Oh, no, no, come on, take a break with me, Nell—"

"I can't. If I come with you now, it means I'll be working late tonight, and I want to make sure I get it all done, get it all perfect—"

Ed kisses me then, stops the words in their tracks with his soft lips, and it's a proper kiss this time. Slow, purposeful, his teeth grazing my bottom lip ever so slightly as he pulls away. "God, you look good," he rumbles against my mouth. "Seriously, you—"

"Look, why don't you go upstairs to the room," I swoop in, "have a sleep and then maybe in a few hours you can—Ed, for God's sake, we're in a *public place*." He nuzzles into my neck, lips against the skin sending an involuntary shiver down my spine. "I need to work."

"Fine," he groans. "Work me to the *bone* why don't you? At least let me get a coffee first."

Forty-five minutes later, Ed is splayed out on the floor of the stockroom holding ribbon between his teeth. "Are we done yet?"

"No."

"Let's just go upstairs. Look. I helped."

"For about half an hour!"

He groans again, pokes the arrow on my Spotify list. "I don't know why you still listen to bloody *Keane*."

"I love Keane."

Ed takes the hessian ribbon from his teeth and holds it in his hand. "It's mental all this stuff, though, isn't it?" he says.

"What, the flowers?"

"Just—well, they better be paying you loads for this. For sitting on a floor in a *cold, dark room*."

"Well, it needs to be a cold, dark room, to keep them fresh," I say shortly. "But it looks good, doesn't it, so far?"

"If you like flowers."

I look over at him, something sinking inside of me, like a rock, and he grins as if rescuing himself last minute. "They look amazing, you know they do." He sits up and brushes hair out of my face, fingertips grazing my cheek. "Like you."

I tut. "Smooth."

"I mean it." He leans, kisses me deeply, perfectly, *well-rehearsed,* and works his hand under my top, warm fingers skimming the wire of my bra. "Can we go upstairs now," he says into my mouth.

"Let me finish this," I say. "But then we're coming back down tonight."

"Of course."

"It's why you're here, remember."

"Mhmm." Ed's mouth smiles, his lips on mine. "It's why I'm here."

CHAPTER TWENTY-SIX

I knew it would happen. We were kissing. Kissing a *lot* when we got back to the hotel room. Then Ed had showered and tried to coax me in there with him, but I'd said no, and I'd sat looking out at the busy rainy city streets below as the water showered onto the stone tiles next door and Ed sang to himself. "You wanted this more than anything," said that voice in my head. "And now here you are. In a beautiful place with Ed. So why aren't you happy?" Ed had then appeared, a towel knotted at his waist, drops of water peppered across his toned stomach, and he tried it on again as we waited for the soft knock at the door from room service, kissing me at first, then moving his hand to my thigh, moving up, up, up, until I moved away, sliding across the duvet.

"No," I said.

"Why?"

"Because I'm here for work."

"But Nell, look at this place," he'd said, as if a beautiful hotel room and king-size bed were wasted if it wasn't shagged in at least once.

"I know, but—that's not why I'm here." Then we'd eaten cross-legged on the bed watching some boring quiz show, my eyes constantly on the clock, and when he'd kissed my neck I told him to stop and stood up.

"I thought we were away together," he said, shaking his head, and I had absolutely no idea what to say, so I went into the bathroom, locked the door, and showered. I let the water hammer my face, as if to somehow shake the thoughts in my head loose, arrange them into some sort of comprehensive order. But it didn't work. I suddenly felt panicked, like I needed to shove the door of the glass shower cubicle open and escape. I put on a face of makeup, took my time with the eyeliner flicks, with the smoky eye, and pinned my hair back, into some sort of messy updo, thinking the entire time, as I looked into my own eyes in the large hotel bathroom mirror, about what the fuck was going on—about what I was doing. Here, with him. He was all I'd ever wanted. I'd dreamed of this—of him coming back, of him realizing we'd made a mistake, and going back out together, into the world. So why didn't I want to be close to him, to have sex with him? Why doesn't it feel like I thought it would—*should.* It feels different. It feels wrong.

When I finally left the bathroom, Ed was passed out on the bed, and I'd felt relief that I didn't have to look him or my feelings in the eye anymore. I grabbed the key card and slipped out.

The Balmoral's lobby is jam-packed full of

black tie when I step out of the elevator, and I feel better now, lost in the noise and the din of a Friday night in the city. Tens of people in sharp, pressed suits and expensive dresses, shrouding the place in aftershave and perfume and raucous laughter, file slowly into the banquet hall opposite where Candice and Steve will get married tomorrow. They are meeting some of their guests tonight and having drinks in the bar, and they invited Ed and me to join them if I'm finished with the flowers early enough, so I wanted to be prepared—nice dress, nice makeup. Plus, I don't really want to be walking through somewhere as beautiful as this in my cruddy tracksuit bottoms. The Balmoral is too grand, and I am far enough from home to feel like it's a special occasion. I never get to dress up, but tonight is different. I blend right in, like I could easily slip into one of these little circles, titter a little laugh, and blend effortlessly into the conversation.

Outside in the car park, the drizzle has stopped and the autumnal sky is an amalgamation of pastel colors—as if the sky gods were inspired by fruit salad sweets—and I stand for a while, against the little hire van, looking up at it. Daisy. I always think of Daisy when I see a pretty sky, when I'm doing something new. She loved taking photos of the sky. She loved talking about all the people who are under it right now, and "isn't it weird, Elle, to think the people we'll fall in love with are under this sky right now," she'd say. What would she think now, if she could see me? Would she be proud? What would she think about me being here with Ed? Everything feels so confused and like a hundred loose ends, untied. I wish she was still here. I wish things were simple. I wish I wasn't me. I wish I wasn't so confused, and I wish I didn't feel so scared. To live. Because I am I think. I'm afraid to live too loudly. And I wasn't always like this, but I don't know how to get back there. I was definitely *there* the night we buried the time capsule, the moment Daisy took that photo of Ed and me. And I'd felt it so surely in my heart that my forever was in that photo. Not just Ed and me, but that photo was proof that I *had* forever, or what felt like it, ahead of me. My future was so bright. It was mine for the taking. The stars in the sky behind us just goading us to go ahead, take what we wanted, with both hands.

Two women walk by me holding hands. One of them says something to the other, and they tip their heads back, laugh, fingers spread at their chests, and I feel that pull. Sam. Sam always laughs at me. Nothing I've ever said has shocked him, embarrassed him, prompted him to try and fix it or change it. *Sam.* Ugh. All my thoughts end up back at bloody Sam Attwood. And to think—he's somewhere nearby. OK, he's right, it's a big place, but I like knowing that we're in the same city, that the same tufty, fire-tinged clouds above my head are floating over his too.

I open up the van and pull out the buckets I picked up from the supplier. I bet Candice feels like the world is hers right now. Everyone racing around for her, the brand-new chapter of her life just waiting for her when the sun rises tomorrow. And I think that's why I wish I had the camera, more than anything. So I could see photos of myself again, of who I used to be. That Noelle who dared to hope for bigger things. Before I almost died and accepted that I should be grateful for anything I was handed. Even if I didn't want it, it was better than not living at all, right? Daisy would give anything to still be here, like me. "Daisy doesn't know she isn't here," Ed would say to me, and it helped and hurt all at once. Daisy believed in the afterlife. Daisy believed you were bigger than just bones and a beating heart. I close my eyes. *Are you there? Send me a sign that you're there. I miss you. I'm sorry I don't do this enough. I'm sorry I don't talk about you, but I miss you every day, and I don't know what to do. I feel lost. I feel alone.*

I open my eyes, lock the van, sniff back the hot tears that are desperate to fall. I make my way back to the hotel. A group of women piles out of a taxi at the entrance, screeching with laughter. I think of Candice, of those beautiful flowers waiting for me inside, to be made into

255

something to be admired, to be photographed and remembered. I have dreamed of this for so many, many years, and I'm here. *I'm actually here.* I stop on the pavement. I can't sabotage this, ruin it for myself. This wedding. These flowers. This opportunity. Now. Now, not then. That's what matters.

I stand tall, look up at the gorgeous autumnal sky one last time, then carry the buckets up through the hotel doors, aware of how weird I must look in a tea dress and full makeup, carrying metal buckets like some sort of dusty laborer, but not giving a single shit. Yup. This is me. Noelle Butterby. Wedding florist. *Flower designer, don't you know.*

The lobby is jam-packed, like the bar before a concert, with people standing around chatting. Through the double doors of the banquet hall, I see others seated, wine buckets in the center of their tables, the room bathed in indigo disco lights.

A group stands before the doors chatting, all black tuxes and deep voices, and low music floats out from the inside. There's a stand beside the entrance, a crisp white page slotted inside the frame. "Climbing for Causes," it says. I stop, my feet on the shiny floor, a bucket at each side.

Climbing for Causes.

Climbing for Causes.

Oh my God.

And—

There he is. *Sam.* Of course he is. In the group of tall, black tuxes, Sam looks up, and before I can even register that he's there, our eyes meet, locking into place like two magnets. I feel like I want to cry at the sight of him. *You're here, you're here, you're here* beats my relieved, racing little heart. His face freezes, perfect pink lips parted mid-conversation as if straight from a photograph, and as if perfectly synchronized, we both break out into smiles. *What the fuck?* he mouths eventually. *I know!* I mouth back.

Of course. *Of course* Sam is here. And as much as it is completely ridiculous that he is actually here, in this same hotel, it also feels unsurprising. Here we are, yet again in each other's paths, and for what reason, I really don't know, other than— this is meant to be. Isn't it?

Sam breaks away from the group, all back slaps and hard nods, and approaches me, his dark eyebrows knitting together, but a stunned, lopsided smile on his handsome face. My heart bangs. My whole body feels as if it's just been slowly dunked in cold water. A mist of tingles and prickles across my skin. He looks gorgeous. He looks *so* gorgeous.

"The wedding," he says, gesturing to us both, and I stand, buckets at my side and look up at him.

"The charity event," I say. "Y-you said it was a—club?"

"It moved. Venue flooded, so we moved here—it was minibus mayhem, let me tell you, and—you—you have buckets," he says.

"I have buckets."

He flashes a playful smile. "Noelle, you look—" His dark eyes drift to my dress, then back to my face. I see his Adam's apple bob in his throat. "You look beautiful."

I swallow too, because I feel like something is swelling, blocking my airway, because I can hardly bear to look at him. He's the sun. He's the fucking sun. "And you . . . you really do suit a—well, *suit*."

He grins at me, and seeing him like this, somewhere new, miles away from everything, from Farthing Heights and stuffy launderettes, and in this glittering hotel beneath antique chandeliers, surrounded by noise and life and glamour, him in that suit . . . it feels too much. As if it's a glimpse, somehow, of what could be, in another life, in another world. Me in my dress, him in his suit, here together. And I think he feels it too, because we both just stare at each other for a moment, speechless. Then he steps forward and slowly, purposely, puts his arms around me, and it's the *first time*. It's the first time I've been this close to him, properly, slowly, feeling his warm, strong body against mine, his hands against my cold bare back. He holds me. He really *holds me,* not just like he did when he was consoling me in my mad Moomin pajamas. *Properly.* Like a perfect slotting together. And I don't even know if I'm breathing, or if I'm even *here,* but I never want to let him go.

"Hey, hey, hey, Attwood, what's going on here?"

We pull away as a large hand lands on Sam's shoulder, slapping him twice. Sam's face breaks into a smile. "Clay, this is Noelle."

Clay stands next to Sam, the total surfer dream boy, with floppy blond hair and tanned skin. Daisy would've fancied him. Charlie *definitely* pre-Theo would've ridden him into the sunset and back again (then totally broken his poor little wave-chasing heart). "Holy shit," says Clay, "Noelle from the traffic jam?"

Sam's cheeks color for the first time *ever* and he gives a deep nod. "Yup. That's right. Noelle, this is my buddy Clay—"

And before he can finish his sentence, Clay has closed his eyes, widened his long, shirted arms, and is saying, "Bring it in, Noelle from the traffic jam, bring it the *eff* in. You're a living legend. Do you know that?"

And when I laugh and hug him, my arms around his taut middle, he says out the side of his mouth into my ear, "If I'm honest with you, Noelle, I thought you might be a mirage he dreamed up.

259

You know, how people do, to get through a rough time. Make shit up."

"What did you just say?" asks Sam.

"Nothing, bro," says Clay with a wink. "Nothing."

CHAPTER TWENTY-SEVEN

Deep, bassy music from Sam's charity event emanates through the walls here, in my little stockroom, and I think of him. It's all I can do. It's a wonder I haven't subconsciously spelled his bloody name out in flowers. I wonder what he's doing over there, in that sparkling banquet hall. Laughing, drinking . . . *flirting.* He looked so handsome, I'd be surprised if he wasn't completely snowed under by a pile of beautiful philanthropists and climbers with strong bendy legs and insatiable libidos. But Clay. Oh my gosh, *Clay.* He talks about me to Clay. So much so that it didn't even take a second for it to register in his brain who I was. He knew instantly. Said he thought I was a mirage. A *mirage to help him through a rough time.* And of course, I keep wondering what that hard time is. Jenna, perhaps. His grumpy dad and the move. But whatever it is—Sam talks about me. He talks about me, like I talk about him.

We'd chatted in the lobby some more, and Sam had invited me inside to the event with him, and I so badly wanted to say yes, but I told him I couldn't, that I had to carry on with the flowers. Then he'd gotten lost in a flurry of conversation, so I'd ducked away with a meek wave. But when I looked over my shoulder, he'd done the slightest, quickest wink across the room at me, and I'd felt sick. *I literally felt sick.* Like I would never be able to eat again—not even the cheesy vegan pasta bake Theo makes that turns my veins to lard. *Can't-eat, make-you-puke love.* Is this what Daisy meant? Love. God, I can't even believe I'm considering those four letters. *Ed* is upstairs. He came to help me. But then—where is he? I'm alone in the dimly lit stockroom now, flowers everywhere, music playing softly, my back aching. It's just me.

A Joni Mitchell song begins playing on my phone, as something in the distance at the charity event strikes up with a hard, fast beat. I wonder if he's standing on the sidelines awkwardly, or if he's dancing now, laughing, Clay and him, pissing about. I turn up Joni on my phone. I wonder what it would be like to slow dance with him. To put my arms around his neck, sway close to him, to a song like "A Case of You," his strong arms solid and strong around me. *Argh.* Come on, Noelle Butterby, *come on.* You're tired. You have two table decorations left to do, and then you can go to bed. Sleep this off. You've had a long day, you're emotional, you're confused, and who wouldn't be? You're trying to jump-start your bloody career, chase your dreams, and all while Ed's asleep in your bed upstairs and Sam is next door being gyrated against by some opportunist *vixen,* when really you wish it was *you* he was pressed up against and—

"Shut up," I say out loud, groaning behind my hands. "Shut up, shut up, shut up, brain, I cannot deal with this now, I have so much to do—" *Knock, knock, knock.*

Shit. I freeze.

"Hello? E-Ed?"

The door is pushed open, flooding my little dimly lit stockroom with warm, yellow light. Sam's handsome face peers around the door. "Hey," he says. "Need any help?"

"God *yes,*" I say casually, but I feel as though I'm melting into the floor, like lava. "Yes, definitely. But I couldn't possibly take up your time, you must be so busy next door—"

"No, no, the auction's done," he says. He moves, filling the frame, then comes into the room and closes the door behind him. The light dims again—just us, Joni, the flowers, and the little chrome desk lamp in the corner. "Now it's just dancing and drunk people and Clay trying to talk random people into sleeping with him."

I laugh as Sam slips off his suit jacket and folds it over his arm.

"Is it working?"

"Oh, it always does." Sam lowers himself to sit next to me on the floor, his long legs out in front of him. "Eventually. When he finds a willing participant."

"Ew."

"Right?" Sam laughs, that delicious crescent dimple a prod in his cheek. "So, come on, what am I doing?"

I smile at him and pass him three roses the color of vanilla ice cream. "Hold these."

"Yes, ma'am."

I start to slide flowers into a sponge of oasis foam for the table arrangements—classic really, like Candice wanted. Pale blue hydrangeas, cream roses, white daisies, and sprigs of gypsophila. Sam holds the flowers and watches me work. I can feel his eyes on me in the dim quiet, nothing but soft music playing, and find I have to concentrate on breathing. In and out. *In and out.*

"So, where's Ed the Ped?" he asks.

I don't look at him and carry on with the flowers.

"Upstairs, asleep."

"Oh."

"And where's Jenna?" I shoot back before I even know what I'm asking.

"Um." He clears his throat. "Jenna is in America."

"She never comes over," I say, and I'd blame the one glass of champagne I had at the bar with Candice and Steve, but that was hours ago, and I don't think Dr Pepper and a cheeseburger makes someone feel brave. But maybe it's being here. Maybe it's tonight.

"Yeah, I know." Sam loosens his crisp, white collar, leans back on his hands. "So—Jenna slept with someone else," he says directly. "Last year."

I feel a hot slice through my chest. "What?"

"It went on for six months. Or so she says. But, you know, I'm never home and I can't exactly say I was a *great* boyfriend in the last, I dunno, God knows how many years—"

"But—still that's—"

"Yeah. I know." Sam nods, presses his lips together, and I realize I've done nothing but try to slot in one single daisy for the last two minutes. The way you do when you're distracted, or read the same line over and over in a novel. "And so, we decided we'd try," says Sam. "Make time for each other. Daily scheduled calls, weekly video calls, me going back as much as possible, Jenna looking into visas, because we both wanted this new start, new place, and—I thought it was what I wanted."

"And it isn't?"

I'm frozen now, and it feels like time has too, the flowers a heap in my lap.

"No," he says quietly. "I don't know. We're Skyping, we're calling, we're even *writing* to each other, and I go back and we have date nights and we do *all* the right things, but . . . I don't know."

I nod. I can say nothing else. Because I feel like those hands, always hiding things so close to his chest, have fallen a little. And I understand. It's me and Ed. That's how I feel about me and Ed.

"I'm starting to realize that sometimes something that worked for so long just doesn't anymore," I say and I feel sad as I hear myself say the words. "No explanation. It just—stops."

Sam smiles at me ruefully, bows his head once, in a nod. "We're meeting on our anniversary," he says. "In three weeks. To talk about where we go from here. With a counselor." He winces when he says that, as if he just witnessed a near-miss. "October twentieth. Stick or twist."

"Like Steve and Miranda," I say. "In *Sex and the City*. If they want to be together, they have to meet on the Brooklyn Bridge."

Sam chuckles softly, but I have no idea if he gets the reference.

"What does Jenna think about all this?" I ask, although I feel like I'm in purgatory. Am I being his friend? Do I even *want* to be his friend when actually, all I think I want is to kiss him, to wrap my arms around his neck?

Sam blows a long breath out of puffed cheeks. "She just says I run," he says. "That I'm never there and all I do is run—and you know, she's used to me being away. For work. It's always been that way. But now she suddenly wants to slow down, change things, and—I don't think I want that."

There's silence, and I teeter on the line, between friend and something so much more. "And do you think you run?" I ask.

"Maybe," he says guiltily. "Not knowing what's going to happen, when it's all going to be over—I find it comforting to just keep going. Standing still—ah, I dunno, Gallagher. Maybe I'm scared. To stop."

"Why?"

Sam looks at me. You could hear a pin drop. "When my cousin took his life—it changed everything. I was eighteen when it happened, just like him, and he was—God, he was wild and funny, but so deep and clever and autonomous, you know? And one minute he was there, and then not, all in a fraction of a second. Our lives changed—instantly. In the time it took Bradley to—" He stops talking, as if it's too painful to continue, and swallows. "And that could've been me. It's hard to describe what it does to you."

I nod slowly, tears budding in my eyes. "I lost a friend. I was a similar age and she was," I take a deep, deep breath, "killed, and I felt like it should've been—" Me, my brain whispers, but I trail off, fiddle with the flowers in my lap.

"The friend with the balcony?" asks Sam, and I nod, smile, heartened and warmed because he remembers—he always remembers the little things, as well as the big.

I think he's going to carry on, but he doesn't, he just nods. And as if synchronized, as if Sam's words have prompted the fog to clear, I know we're the same. Because I've spent my life being too scared to start living. I've been too afraid to live too noisily. I should settle for what I've got, even if it isn't what I want, because I'm not meant to be here. And Sam. Sam is too afraid to *stop* living, because he believes it's only a matter of time before it's taken away. Both of us scared, for seemingly opposite reasons that are at their heart, the same.

I swallow down the lump in my throat. "You said you're never there," I say into the darkness. "But you're there for your dad. And you're here now. Aren't you?"

"Yeah," he says thoughtfully. "And I always seem to be. When it comes to you."

And suddenly it all feels too much. That Ed isn't here. That Sam is. That he is again and again, and this feeling. This bloody feeling in my gut—that something that has sat between us both, fizzing like electricity since that night on the motorway. I look at him, my shoulders sag—I give up, universe. I give up.

"Where did you go to school?" I ask.

Sam laughs a low rumbly chuckle and shakes his head. Our faces are so close, I can barely breathe. "You know where I went to school."

"But don't you want to know?" My words are so quiet, they're barely there. "Don't you want to know why this keeps happening?"

Sam stares at me. He's so close, I can feel his breath on my face. "Why do we need to know?" He picks up a white daisy from the floor, slowly brings his hand to my face and pushes it into my hair. He runs a finger down my cheek and says, "I'm just glad that it does."

Move closer. I want him to *move even closer.* "You can't still think that this is random."

"I don't know," whispers Sam as Joni plays softly on. His breath tickles my lips.

"You were my pen pal."

Sam's face breaks into a smile inches from mine and he retracts a little, and *God,* were we going to kiss? If I hadn't said anything, would he have actually kissed me?

"What?" He chuckles.

"I was meant to have a pen pal in November 1996, and you said you broke your leg in 1996 and—my pen pal had to be reallocated. Remember? My pen pal from Portland."

He laughs deeply. "Holy shit," says Sam. "Maybe I was. I mean, I don't remember anything about a pen pal but—"

"You were," I say. "I know you were."

Sam leans and gently adjusts the daisy in my hair.

"I want you to know something," he whispers, words barely there, his nose inches from mine. "You said nobody does but—I see you, Noelle. I do."

And I close my eyes, and safe behind the lids, they fill to warm pools, and I don't know why. Because he said he sees me, I suppose. Because I've known all along, somehow, that he does.

"I like how it sounds," I whisper. "When you call me Noelle."

Sam smiles in the darkness. *"Noelle,"* he breathes against my lips.

Flutters prickle their way down my body, turning it to jelly—my spine, my stomach, my groin, my knees, my toes. "Again."

"Noelle," he says again, then Sam inches closer and I close my eyes, but I can feel him, warm, strong, secure against me. He presses his lips to mine—warm, soft lips that taste like whiskey and chewing gum, and as he moves, deepens the kiss, and warm stubble prickles against my face, I swear my whole body feels like it's alive, and I'm nothing now but stars.

CHAPTER TWENTY-EIGHT

T he woman needs a hobby, Nell. She's driving me mad with all of it. Do you know she called me seven times in two hours about canapés? She's ordered from some deli near us and I feel like saying, just invite some of Dad's mates over, stick them in the lounge with the piano, and let them get drunk, you know? Nell? *Nell?*"

I blink, look beside me at Ed who looks bright and pink-cheeked and rested. As if he actually spent the night in a five-star hotel with a king-sized bed—the exact polar opposite of how I feel this morning.

"Sorry. I was miles away."

"Stop worrying. They're flowers, remember. Just flowers." Ed smiles gently. "You nailed it, Nell. Even better without my help." He yawns, ruffling his wild brown hair, a slice of toned stomach appearing beneath his navy-blue T-shirt. "Jesus, man, how long're they going to take seating everyone? I need breakfast. I'm fuckin' starved."

The breakfast queue is long today at the Balmoral—there's a sort of chaotic chatter in the dining room as people are squashed onto tables, and more of us wait here at the grand, bright entrance in a big, straggled crowd more than a queue. And I'm relieved as Ed takes out his phone and scrolls, because I can barely string a sentence together. Because I can't stop thinking about last night. About Sam and that gorgeous kiss and how it had gone on for what felt like forever but was probably more like ten seconds before Sam's phone had buzzed and it was Clay, who couldn't find his hotel room. We said goodbye then, in the hazy dim light, and Sam had asked if I needed his help in the morning because he'd booked a stupidly early breakfast and wanted to head out early. *Yes,* I wanted to say. *Yes, and never leave.* I wanted him to kiss me again, wanted to squeeze every moment of time out of the world to spend with only him. But I said no. Because of Ed. Because of Jenna. Because he runs. Because frankly: I am fucking terrified of everything that I feel. It feels like there's a tornado inside me, gathering speed, gathering more and more information and confusion and emotion, until it's just going to take flight, and take me with it.

The people in front of us are seated, and the waitress smiles at us but doesn't speak, and taps away on the iPad on the podium in front of her. The restaurant is crammed with people, and the din of griddle pans and cutlery on plates, and the smell of toast makes my stomach rumble. I haven't eaten. I haven't slept. Even my hands are shaking. Nerves, I told Ed, for the wedding and the flowers later. But it isn't just that. It's Sam. It's the kiss. It's Ed and it's the flowers and this hotel and the confusion and the speed everything seems to be going, and it's all swelling until it's a saturated sponge in my skull. I press a hand to my forehead. Ed eyes me and says nothing.

"Good morning," the waitress says with a smile. "Your room number, please?"

"Morning," I say. "It's 231. Under Butterby. Noelle Butterby?"

The waitress runs a slim finger down the bright screen of her iPad. "Ah yes." She looks over her shoulder and studies the brimming restaurant. "We've had a few double bookings," she says as if to herself, and Ed sighs.

"How do you have *a few* double bookings?" he asks me, but loud enough for the woman to hear.

She looks at him and gives a stiff smile. "We took in a last-minute booking of twenty guests and a charity event of ninety-six yesterday when the other venue flooded. It's been a stretch. Don't worry, we will get you seated, but we may have to wait for—"

Oh my God.

Oh. My. God. Waves rush into my brain, drowning out the waitress, drowning out Ed and the restaurant chatter, and I know they're all still talking because their lips are still moving, but all that's in my head is *static*. Like someone just pulled the plug.

Sam. He's at the table, just over the way, with Clay. The both of them sitting at a table for four, coffees and plates and newspapers spread over its wooden top. There are two spare chairs on either side of them. Sam looks up from his cup and—he's seen me. Fuck, he's seen me. My belly flips over like a fish. I'm going to vomit. And before either of us can react, Clay sees me too.

"Hey!" he shouts across the restaurant. "Hey, it's the mirage! Join us!"

Ed looks at me with half-confusion, half-amusement. "You—you know this bloke?"

"It's—no—the other one—it's Sam. The American. Well. That's his friend. You know. Sam. Who I clean for. The, uh—his dad. F-Frank. C-cleaner?" Oh my God. I can't speak. It's like my tongue is an overgrown fucking clam in my mouth and my brain is no longer a brain, but a joint of roast beef instead.

The waitress looks at me hopefully. "Are you happy to join?"

"Uh, I don't think—"

"Well if it's our only chance of getting some scran." Ed looks at me and gives a big shrug. "I'd sit anywhere if I'm honest."

The waitress looks at me expectantly. I look at Sam, who gives a small, comforting smile. A smile that says, "It's cool. It'll be fine."

"OK," I say, standing tall like someone who

is absolutely cool with this. "OK, sure. Makes sense."

Clay and Sam stand up as we approach the table and God, why does Sam have to be so tall, and why does his tired, didn't-get-much-sleep-last-night face and disheveled bed-hair make me want to bury my face into his neck? And yup, just like that, my hunger pains have disappeared completely. *Can't-eat, make-you-puke love* . . . No, no, shut up, not now.

"Eh, see, this is nice and cozy," says Clay, his lips pale, his eyes bruise-like with the rings of someone hungover and still drunk. "How's it going, Noelle? And is this your—" He eyes Sam for a moment, then me. "Your—"

"This is Ed," I jump in.

"Her date. Her helper. Her *slave*." Ed grins and holds his hand out.

"Ah, I should've known a queen like this would have a slave. Have many." Clay winks at me, a teasing blue eye, and they shake hands roughly. I can feel Sam's eyes burning into me, but I don't dare look at him, into his eyes, at his lips, the ones I was kissing last night . . .

"Morning," says Sam, and Ed holds out his hand, ever cool, ever confident. "I'm Sam."

Ed shakes his hand, but his brow creases. "Sam," he says. "Oh—you're . . . shit, you're— *no way*—I know you."

Sam doesn't react, he just looks at him, and

I don't think I have ever seen Sam stone-faced before, but he is. Right this moment, he is. His jaw is set, his shoulders are back. What is Ed talking about? He knows him? "You do?"

Ed laughs, but his cheeks pinken. "Yeah, I— your dad. You brought your dad into rheumatology. Few weeks ago. We—we had a chat."

Sam nods, but he's still standing tall and rigid. Sam's tall, yes, but standing like this, he looks *enormous*. "That's right. I remember."

"You're Frank's *doctor?*" I ask.

"No," cuts in Sam before Ed can reply, then Ed clears his throat, a balled fist at his mouth.

"No, no that's Pragya, isn't it—Doctor Laghari, I mean?" he says.

Sam nods once.

"I filled in on her surgery," says Ed to me, then he turns back to Sam. "And how is he, your dad?"

"Frank? Yeah, he's good." Sam smiles a tiny smile as Clay laughs, and says, "Holy shit, so you're a doctor? Oh—" Clay downs a shot of espresso. "Let me scoot round there and we can all sit."

"Actually," says Sam, "we're kind of done anyway, right, dude?"

Clay pauses, fixes his eyes on Sam. "Um." He looks down at the empty espresso cup in his hand. "Yeah? Yeah, I guess if you want to—"

"You don't have to go—" I start, although I really don't mean it, because I'm relieved

276

I haven't gotten to sit at the table with both of them. My head feels fit to burst, to explode all over the restaurant like a detonated pumpkin. Ed and Sam have *met*. They've *had a chat*. Sam thinks Ed is a twat. I'm not exactly a body language expert, but that much is clear.

"No, no," says Sam, "we've taken up enough space for long enough and they're super packed, so . . ."

Ed nods and holds out his hand again. "Well, it was good to see you again," he says, laughingly. "The world's never been so small, eh?"

Sam gives a nod, then looks at me. "Good luck today, Noelle," he says, and before I can even register what just happened, before I can take in the icy, icy stare from Sam to Ed, they're gone.

I tried. I tried really hard to sit with Ed, in the loud, overbearing dining room of the Balmoral, but in the end, I couldn't. I stood up—frankly, in the manner of someone having an adverse reaction to a drug—and my chair squeaked suddenly on the hard, shiny floor. "Sorry," I said, as Ed looked up from his newspaper. "I need to check something. With Martina. Can't sit still." And thankfully, he seemed to buy it. He didn't seem to notice my fluster or the fact I was the color of the white marble floors or that I pushed a slice of toast around my plate like it was a bathroom tile and not food. He just said he'd go up to the room and pack, ready for our train. And I'd torn outside, as if the hotel were filled with twenty-foot-deep water, and the outside was air.

I stand now, against the cold, ornate walls of the hotel. I need to think, but I can't seem to grasp a thought long enough to understand it, and I can feel my heart rate quicken—a freight train, going so fast, it's just a blur on the horizon. I fix my eyes on the huge window of a shop opposite and *inhale, hold, exhale, inhale, hold, exhale.* Why does this keep happening? The gasping for breath, the racing heart. It's as if I am still and stationary and the whole world around me is on fast forward. Panic. Panic like I used to, when I lost my way. Last time, a kind mental health nurse had suggested I wasn't listening to myself—I wasn't digesting something I was feeling, not looking it in the eye. What is it? What is it I'm feeling?

Confusion. Overwhelmed. Like I want to withdraw from Ed because something niggles at me when we're together and I don't know what it is. And Sam. I want to run toward him and away all at once. And questions. So many questions flood my brain, squash into every crack. If I'd gone to Oregon with Ed, would I have met Sam? If I'd never gone to the time capsule event, would I have taken the job at Frank's? Would I have met Sam for the first time then? Or would we have chatted in the hospital waiting room? Would we have even talked at all? Magnets. The same planes. Meant to be? *"I'd mention your soul mate,"* Daisy's voice drifts through my mind, *"but I don't want to make your eyes roll so much they get stuck in the back of your head, because you want to be able to look at him. Because he'll be totally hot. Charming too. And so tall, he'll give you a neck ache."*

My phone buzzes in my pocket, my shallow breath deepening again, slowly but surely. It's a reminder. It's ten to ten. I need to go back and put the final touches to the flowers and put them on the tables, at the ends of the pews, deliver the bouquets. That is what I'm here for. Candice and Steve. Everything else will have to wait until that long train ride home. I can't have a mini emotional meltdown now. Not here. Not today.

I wander back through the doors of the hotel, my feet squeaking on the polished floor. And then I stop. Because Ed and Sam are by the elevators. They're talking—well, Ed is, and seriously and quickly, and Sam's jaw is set again, and he nods, once. Ed is bent close to him, like he's explaining something complicated, all hand gestures and serious eyes, and I know all his faces—well, most of them. I know when he's sad, or he's angry, and he looks—stressed. *Irked.* Are they arguing? *Why* would they be arguing? Did Sam tell him that we kissed? No. No, surely not, why would he do that? Life is not a Nicholas Sparks novel.

"Um—hello?" I call, and although it's loud and bustling in the lobby, with voices and music and telephones ringing, they both look up. Ed's face breaks into a huge, too-big-to-believe grin. Sam gives a tiny, barely-there shadow of a smile.

"Hey you," says Ed. "Just catching up. Talking about climbing. Mount Hood."

I look at Sam, who dips his head. "Yeah," is all he says.

"So, I'll go and get the bags together," says Ed with another big smile and that weird look again in the eyes—what would I have said that was, when we were together, that look? A secret, maybe. Something he's not telling me. "Meet you over in the stockroom?" Ed looks at us, to and fro, then disappears into the lift, leaving Sam and me alone in the lobby, a stretch of shiny floor between us.

"What were you two talking about?" I ask. Neither of us moves.

Sam puts his hands into his pockets, his shoulders stiff, but that stone-faced jaw relaxing. "Just climbing. Dad. Stuff."

"Stuff?"

Sam nods, then his face softens. "Are you OK?"

I shrug, feel emotion bubble up inside me. "Yes," I say. "No. No. I don't know. Can I say ish?"

"You can say ish," repeats Sam sadly, but he doesn't smile this time or say anything else.

"So you two met already," I say.

"Well, I wouldn't say we *met,* we just—"

"Do you think I was meant to meet you, Sam?" I say, words rushing from my mouth. "The more I keep thinking of everything, the more I'm here, the more I'm with you—"

"Noelle . . ."

"Don't say that it's random. You *know* it isn't. I think we were—" I realize my voice is too loud, and I step closer to him, lower it, shrink the words small, so they're just ours. "I think we were meant to meet. If Ed and I hadn't broken up, if I had moved to Portland—"

"If." Sam takes a breath. "Noelle, I drove myself crazy with *if*s for such a long time, and I *can't* believe in ifs and signs and—"

"But why? Why can't you just say it is?" He says nothing, but my mouth keeps moving because of course it does. "Why can't you just see that this *is* fate and or at least might be—"

"Because I can't."

"But *why?* I feel—*something*—"

"Noelle!" A shrill, excitable puppy dog voice cuts right through our words.

Candice calls across the lobby from the open double doors behind me, a golden croissant balancing on a small white plate, her hair in rollers, a dressing gown tied at the waist. "Mum. Mum!" she says, turning. "This is Noelle. This is my florist!"

281

Sam smiles at me, softly. "Go be with your people," he says. Then he leans and presses his warm lips to my forehead. "I'll see you soon."

And I know now that I will. Regardless of everything, of every *if* in the world, I know that I will.

When I let myself into the hotel room, Ed is on the phone. He quickly hangs up.

"It was, uh—Mum," he says, rolling his round eyes. "Droning on again about Dad's seventieth. Did I tell you I'm not allowed a plus-one—"

"Ed, Candice has asked me to stay," I say into the quiet room. The TV on the wall is just an inch away from mute, a football commentator barely audible, a footballer rolling around clutching at his leg. "For the ceremony and the reception."

Ed's brow creases, his lips turn down at the corners, as if trying to work out an impossible sum. "But our train is in two hours."

"I'm going to get the sleeper train home tonight."

Ed scrunches up his face as if he's just stepped in something disgusting. "Nell, sleeper trains are grim—"

"I want to take the sleeper train," I tell him. "I'm being paid and I can afford it, and I want to stay."

Ed turns his phone in his lap, breathes a noisy inhale through his nose. "OK," he says.

" 'Course, Nell. You should stay," and the look he gives me makes me want to cry. I see Ed. I see the boy I fell in love with, the man I flat-hunted with, the man I loved with every piece of me for so long. "Are we OK, Nell?" he asks feebly.

"I don't know." The words catch in my throat. "Maybe—maybe you coming here with me was too soon."

He looks down at his lap, rubs a rough hand over his face. "Right," he says. "OK. So, I'll go, then. Get the train?"

I nod stiffly.

"All right, then," he says defeatedly. "OK."

I feel numb as I walk back down the corridor away from Ed, as I take the elevator down, as I cross the lobby and walk down the aisle between lines of white, uniform chairs—everything prepared and lined up, ready for guests and moments to be made, my flowers, the backdrop of so many memories forever.

I push open the stockroom door, switch on the lights, and I'm almost winded myself at the sight of everything I've done. The floor is brimming with color, a sea of pearly cream petals and powder blues, like blueberry swirled yogurt. The flowers—*my* flowers, all neat and waiting patiently in their big silver buckets. They look exactly how they did in my head, in every daydream I ever had about doing this. I've done it. I have actually done it.

I jam open the door of the stockroom, and quickly but meticulously, I pin flowers to every aisle seat's edge. I carry table arrangements to the Holyrood room, I buzz and fizz as I place them down, as Martina, the wedding planner, gawps at them, takes photos. This is what I want, I think, as I deliver the bouquets to Candice and the bridesmaids, watch their eyes light up, watch them hold these beautiful puffs of hydrangeas to their stomachs. I want this. A life of color. Sam's right. It could all be over in a heartbeat. And I don't want to wait anymore.

Later, I head back into the dark, empty stockroom. On the back of the door, there's a Post-it Note stuck on it: "Proud of you," it says. "Love, Sam x."

CHAPTER TWENTY-NINE

O"f course you were meant to meet him in fucking *America*." Charlie looks to the ceiling. "Jesus guide me, we've been saying this for*ever*. The traffic jam, the hospital waiting room—none of it is a coincidence, my friend."

"But what does any of it even mean?" I ask. "Theo? Honestly, it's a mess. *I'm* a mess."

"This means you've always been linked to him," says Theo as if he's just told me something as simple as he needs to purchase a loaf of bread. "From birth, most likely. And there are probably moments you were meant to meet before. It's more than just the hospital and his dad's flat. More than just the traffic jam."

"Totes," says Charlie, bouncing a gummy, dribbling Petal on her hip. "Isn't that right, my girl? Is Auntie Noelle meant to be with tall, dark, and rippling wet at the top of a mountaintop Uncle *Sam?*"

I groan. "I don't know."

"Yes you do."

"You're meant to be together," says Theo, a miniature cucumber in his hand, which he crunches into a second later. I remember Charlie for a moment, back when she first met Theo, saying, "He eats these little cucumbers the way normal people eat like, a Twirl or an Alpen bar. It's so Greek and exotic."

I groan again, bury my face in my hands, rest my forehead on the countertop. "Then what's the point of Jenna? What's the point of Ed?"

"You weren't ready?" offers Theo, the way someone offers an answer during a quiz.

I shake my head. "I don't believe that. Me and Ed—we had so much and . . . well, Sam's been with Jenna forever and she helped him through everything, and that's where he is now—well, will be, two weeks on Monday."

"Where's he going two weeks on Monday?"

"Twentieth of October," I say. "Their anniversary. They're having a meeting with their bloody couples counselor. Like Steve and Miranda in *Sex and the City*. On the bridge. Make or break. To decide."

I haven't heard from Sam since the hotel. I punched out numerous text messages to him on the way home, watching the dark night rush by from my tiny little box on the sleeper train. But I didn't send one of them. And neither did he. I don't know when he goes back to Oregon, to Jenna. I don't know if he's working, or how long he was in Edinburgh after the event. I didn't see him, nor Clay, although I looked for him, every single time I ducked out of Candice and Steve's beautiful wedding. I kept imagining what it might be like, to see him standing across the lobby again, in that suit. To cross the floor, take his hand . . .

"She cheated on him and he loves you," says Charlie factually, reaching over and taking the rest of Theo's cucumber. "Don't forget those minor details."

"He doesn't love me, Charlie," I say. "OK, can we talk about something else?"

Theo nods gently, a soft, therapist's smile on his face. "Let's talk about Charlie's birthday."

"Oh yes," says Charlie clapping. "*How* do you fancy going glamping? Oh, come on, Nell, don't give me that face."

"The bugs—" I start.

"There are no bugs in January."

I laugh. "True. But nobody camps in January—"

"But they do *glamp*." She reaches over and squeezes my arm. "Come on, the little huts are even heated. And that's plenty of time to sort stuff for your mum. And we might have to share a bog, but there is *heating and a bed*."

I fold my arms. "And this is what you want to do for your birthday?"

Charlie nods. "I made a list," she says sheepishly. "Of all the things that are authentically me. Alan, my therapist, asked me to. And being outside, camping, adventures, *hikes* . . . that was on there. Oh. We could do a hike soon too."

"Then it's a deal," I say. "Glamping, hikes . . . sign me up."

"Don't you remember we were meant to go camping," says Charlie. "You, me, Ed, and Daisy. After you guys finished college. I was going to bring that bass player. The one with the arms. Remember? Soz, Theo."

Theo laughs, rubs at his thick black beard.

I nod. "I do remember."

"Maybe you can bring someone," says Charlie. *"Sleep under the stars."*

I groan again. "Oh yeah, like who? Who would I bring? The Storm? Gary at number twenty-one? I mean, I could bring Ed, but you might drown him in a nearby stream."

"Oh, *you know who* I want you to bring." Charlie giggles, thumbing the charm hanging from a choker at her neck—a plastic cocktail glass today, complete with umbrella.

"Oh sure, 'Hi, Sam, I know you're about five thousand miles away doing a Steve and Miranda with your long-term cheat of a girlfriend, but fancy coming to shit in a local port-o-loo in the woods with me?' "

Charlie throws her head back, laughs throatily at that, as the bell above Buff's shop door jingles.

Theo looks up, straightens, and gives his best proprietor's smile.

"Good morning, Mrs. McDonnell," he says obliviously, and Charlie and I turn in what feels like slow motion to see Ed's mum standing in the doorway of Buff in a puff of perfume, a handbag over her shoulder, her short hair blond and bouncy on her head.

"Hi," she says. "I've just come to pay up in full. For the canapés."

She eyes Charlie first, smiles tightly. Then her eyes settle on me. They widen in unison with her mouth.

"Oh my goodness—*Noelle!*"

"Hi, Helen."

"My God, it's been such a long time!" The green kite-shaped earrings in her ears swing. "Do you—do you work here?"

"No," I say. "I just popped in to see Charlie. Theo's Charlie's husband."

She looks at Charlie again, who nods at her and raises a little feeble hand.

"Oh," says Helen. "Of course. Small world." She turns back to me, crosses her slim arms across her chest. "And how are you, Noelle? You look—" Her eyes linger over me for a moment and I curse myself for wearing the shitty tracksuit bottoms with the bleach stain on the knee shaped like Pac-Man. "Ed's back. Did you know?"

In the corner of my eye, I see Charlie turn to look at me.

"Um—yeah. We bumped into each other, actually."

"Really?"

My heart sags then. Ed and I haven't spoken much since Edinburgh. He's called a few times and we've chatted, caught up, and of course, it's been easy. But it always is with Ed and me. We just pick up where we left off, fill the silences with waffle and small talk. But I feel wounded that he hasn't told his mum. But then he's always said she butts into his life—maybe he concealed it because he doesn't want her to know his business. She was always like that. She liked to know the ins and outs, the plans we all had, to get those McDonnell boxes ticked.

"Did he tell you about Alistair? His birthday?" I open my mouth to reply, to say of course, he said you're boring him shitless, but she swoops in. "No, I don't suppose he did. He isn't going to stand in a street harping on about a birthday, is he, after bumping into you by chance." Helen laughs and reaches into her bag for her purse, all the while waffling about everything Ed has already told me. About how Alistair has never let her organize a birthday party, has always had golfing weekends, and how she's trying to prove she is capable and also that he'll enjoy it more, and I stare at her as she speaks, and think, *Your son was with me all last weekend. He was in Edinburgh with me.*

I nod along, I smile, I say, "Oh wow." I even

compliment her manicure. I know how to play Helen, I did it for long enough.

"I've been so selective," she says, "and do you know, I think that's the key. A select amount of people. My boys and their partners make six. Plus, Alistair's brothers and their wives, makes ten, some old colleagues. We're at thirty-two. Quality over quantity, I say. Couples, no children, you know."

Helen pays for the canapés and praises Theo over and over, as if I have no idea who he is or what he's capable of, despite standing right *here,* as his friend. Helen always did this. Made me feel like a hollow person with no idea how to operate in real life. I once introduced her to a photographer I used to clean for, to take photos at Ed's brother James's wedding, and she would talk about him as if it wasn't me who introduced them. As if she understood him much more than I ever would, and it took her half the time to do so.

She hovers in the doorway, still droning on about the party, about James, about Borneo, as she picks and weighs up shiny red apples in her hands from the outside fruit and veg boxes. I follow her out into the gray October chill, the dutiful listener as I always was, and she starts telling me about Ed.

"The hospital wanted him to stay over in Oregon," she says.

"I know."

"And I think he was tempted, you know, because the way of living over there is so fantastic. Their flat over there—*half* the price of rent here, and right round the corner from work, so they could get there and back within minutes."

"Right," I say, but *they.* Who's they?

"—well—he recommended him for it, for the job here, and I said to Alistair, I said I know he's happy out there but—"

"I know," I cut in. "I know, and he missed home. So he took it."

Her hackles are up now, invisible porcupine needles—I've interrupted her, Helen's worst nightmare, and she tilts her head to one side, a predator sizing me up.

"We've seen a lot of each other," I say, hating that I'm flustered. "In fact we went to Edinburgh together this past weekend. I had a wedding up there—I designed the flowers. As their florist. And Ed came with me. To help."

Helen says nothing, but her nostrils flare.

"Is that why he said he came back?" she asks, almost musically. "To England?"

"Sorry?"

"That he missed it? Is that what he told you?"

I nod, reluctantly, pull my cardigan around myself as a breeze picks up. "Yes. He told me everything."

"Right." She shakes her head, looks vindicated all of a sudden. "No, I'm just surprised. I actually didn't think he was too pleased to be back at all. Planning to leave again, last time I checked, meet up with her in Virginia, as planned."

"Virginia? Meet—" I start. But I stop myself. It's what she wants. I can tell, the way she's looking at me. Tossing scraps, hoping I'll go for one. "Yes. I know. He said," I lie instead, and she gives a titter of a laugh. A laugh she'd always give after delivering an insult disguised as banter.

"Oh, well, who knows?" she says with a theatrical sigh. "I'm only his mother and we know boys give nothing away. I'm sure your mum would say the same. Anyway, must dash. Nice to see you, Noelle. Always such a novelty bumping into someone from your past, I find."

And yet you asked me nothing about myself, I want to say, so I don't see what the novelty would be exactly, Helen and your horrible, puke-colored earrings.

"Enjoy the party, Helen," I say. "Best of luck for it."

"Oh, it'll be a dream," she says, and she clops off across the damp cobbles, as rain starts once again to spit from heavy, charcoal clouds.

Theo appears behind me. "I wish people wouldn't handle my apples," he says. "They never do it with care."

And then something opens up in my chest, something that feels like a chasm. I think of what Helen said. *My boys and their partners make six.*

I think of that photo. Ed and the woman on his Twitter profile with the auburn curls. The way Helen said *they*. Twice, was it? Three times? And Virginia. Isn't that what that guy in the hospital said, the night of Mum's accident—"Didn't fancy Virginia, then?" and what had Ed said? *"Fuck knows."*

"I'm coming with you," I say to Theo.

"What? Where?"

"To deliver the canapés for Ed's mum's party tomorrow. Can I come?"

CHAPTER THIRTY

"Hi, this is a message for Noelle Butterby. This is Ruth at Jerome's College. We're calling everyone who left their details on Facebook and otherwise to let them know the rescheduled time capsule event will go ahead as planned on the eleventh, to coincide with our open evening. The event starts at seven p.m. We hope to see you there."

Theo stands in his dark, closed shop dressed in a checked shirt and bow tie and his jet-black hair is combed over to one side in a quiff. He looks like part Teddy boy and part barista.

"Theo, I've never seen you in your canapé delivery getup. I love it."

"And I love yours." He grins at me. "Noelle, you look perfect."

"Do you think?" Nerves dance in my belly. I'm wearing a red midi wrap dress with a pleated skirt that I saw on an Instagram influencer I follow. She's tall like me, has big hips like me, and I'd never bought anything via Instagram before, but I knew I had to buy this. I used the money I earned from Steve and Candice's wedding, and the second I put it on, I felt like I could stand a little taller. This dress is the sort of thing I'd dreamed of wearing, in the future. The dress of my daydreams—something the future Noelle Butterby would buy when her life had begun. But what's the use of anything if it's always so far in the distance you can never quite put your hands on it?

Charlie appears behind the counter, Petal in her arms.

"Fuck me." She whistles. "You look out of this world. Like—why do I feel like I'm going to cry? God, I actually am. Elle, you look way too good to be delivering posh twats their bloody olives and fat lumps of cheese." She grimaces in Theo's direction. "No offense, baby." Then she looks at me. "Elle, do you really think you should go? I love that you're going for this, but—I don't really understand what *this* is."

I'd felt the same after I'd said it, and on the walk home, I went over and over in my mind the conversation with Helen, and the fact I've known this whole time there was something that didn't feel right about Ed and me. The way I'd sit in that little flat with him and feel like I was in someone else's world—intruding or something. But now I don't think it was the flat. I don't think it was bad decor like that bloody splodged glass bowl he kept his peanuts in, either. I knew something wasn't sitting right. *I knew.* My heart did, before

296

my head caught up. I think Ed did meet some-one in America. I think she's waiting for him, in Virginia. And us—well, maybe that's why I want to go to the party. So I know what it was. So I can look at him, standing in that house without me, and know that there is no Ed and Noelle. There hasn't been for a long time.

When I got home, I was relieved to find Ian sitting on the sofa with Mum. He's been around a lot lately, and both of them, both Mum and Ian have seemed happier. Mum even talked yesterday of going to lunch at a new café in town that Ian keeps raving about. "Perhaps we could get a takeaway first," she said, and Ian beamed and said, "What a good idea," and I had to stop myself grabbing her by the shoulders proudly, and dancing with her around the living room.

I'd sat opposite them, on the armchair, and as new, fresh anger bubbled beneath my skin, I'd told them everything about Ed, and it felt so good to open up—to lean on my mum, to not have to be the pillar for once. I cried, which I did and didn't expect all at once. I didn't want Ed anymore. But that didn't stop me feeling used, or something. Something to be picked up, tried on like an old coat.

"And you think she'll be there?" asked Ian. "This woman."

I nodded. "Yeah—and I think I need to see it with my own eyes. For closure."

That's the thing—my world's been stuck for a while, and I think Ed knew it. He thought he could come home and "turn back the clock," as if I'd been waiting for him all along. And I guess in a weird way, it worked for me too, stepping back in time, to safety, old routines.

"I think I want closure," I say to Charlie now, as she pats circles onto Petal's chubby little back.

"But if Ed has a girlfriend—"

"He won't tell me, Charlie. I've asked him. And—it just seems obvious to me now."

"But why do you need to *go* there?"

"I want to see it, Charlie. I know it sounds mad or unhinged, but I feel like I need to go there, to that house, to the McDonnells', and see him there without me. To feel it; to say goodbye. I want to let go. And I don't think I ever have let go. Of much at all, actually."

Charlie looks at me sadly, the corners of her eyes crinkling. "I get it," she says. "My therapist, Alan, he always says if you can physically do something to move on—write a letter and burn it or something, or actually *have* the person or thing in front of you—then there's more chance of *really* dealing with something. Releasing it."

We pack up Theo's little van with the canapés, and Theo checks and double-checks the amounts before he closes the doors. Charlie follows us out and kisses Theo goodbye, and he gives Petal and Charlie matching forehead kisses.

"That *dress*." Charlie grins at me, then gives a wink. "Go show those old stuck-up crones what Noelle Butterby is made of. And whatever you do, have a drink ready to throw over him. Posh people love a drink-throw. Invented it." And I see a glimmer of Charlie Wilde, then. That girl who would meet Daisy and me from college, her hair the color of Easter egg foil, slinging her arms over our shoulders and whispering, "The guys in this place look dull as *fuck*."

We drive away, Charlie waving, making Petal's chubby little woolly cardiganed arm do the same. A parent. A mother. And I realize I do want that. A little unit of my own, yes. But I want to make things happen. And not just someday. I'm ready for someday to be now.

Pulling up to Ed's parents' house is the most surreal experience. Everything looks exactly the same. The purple wisteria covering the biscuit-colored brick, dangling above the front door in beautiful, heavy cones; the old wooden Georgian windows and their pristine shutters. I remember the first time I came here. *Ed's rich,* I'd thought. And then I felt myself shrink to a speck. I'm not sure I ever fully puffed up to full size again around them after that.

The gravel driveway is full of cars and one huge black and bright purple Harley Davidson that screams "midlife crisis," but Theo parks up on the road outside. He loads canapés into a trolley, as I watch from a distance people standing and talking in the amber glow of Ed's parents' high-ceilinged living room. I can't see Ed yet, but I know he's inside. Nerves churn in my gut as Theo locks the trunk. *No.* No, I need this. I need to walk into that house, standing tall, completely myself, and I need to stare everyone in the eye. If someday is going to be now, then I have to stop being afraid. We are supposed to let go of things. We are supposed to make room for new. Things are meant to change. *Say yes, panic later.*

Theo and I follow Helen's emailed instructions to go around the back of the house. She always did this when they had barbecues. Guests at the front, family and any sort of "help" as she put it, around the back, like ugly cattle, hidden out of sight. In the vast back garden, there's a wet sheen on the neat, trimmed grass, and I almost slip and lose the tray of food in my hand. And of course, Helen is *right there,* looking at me like I'm a cat who's just puked on the kitchen counter.

"Oh," she says. Her eyes are wide, a hand at her chest, holding a champagne in the other. "Noelle."

"Mrs. McDonnell," says Theo with a smile. "I have for you the best canapés and the best extra pair of hands."

I look down at the single tray of slightly squashed miniature quiches in my hands and at the huge case of food Theo is holding and see Helen's eyes do the same. "Yes," I say. "I'm the help. Where would you like us to put them?"

"If you both just come through and arrange them on the platters on the counter. Then you can leave." When she says that part, she's looking at me with eyes that I'm sure are part laser beams.

We follow her inside, into the huge farmhouse-style kitchen. It smells the same—vanilla bean and lavender reed diffusers that sit in every alcove, potpourri, last night's garlic. And there isn't a thing out of place. Absolutely nothing has changed. And yet: everything has.

Helen stands guard at the kitchen door as a woman in chef whites checks and checks again something in the oven that smells like baked chicken and red wine, and I can hear the din of voices and laughter and Rat Pack songs playing on a stereo. The same music. The same thin, white crockery, the same golden chandeliers, the same *everything*. And yet as I stand here, in the kitchen, arranging canapés on a huge white ceramic platter, I don't feel it, like I used to. The speck. They are just people, like me. I might not have money or doctorates or trips to bloody Borneo planned, but they are just people. I never had to fit in. I'm not a puzzle piece trying to find its place and I never have been. These are just people, and these are just bloody platters purchased from John Lewis, and Helen is just a bored old professor with grown-up sons who have flown the nest.

"Nellie."

Ed stands in the kitchen doorway, in smart trousers and a sky-blue shirt, the top button open. He looks pale and surprised.

"Hiya." Helen eyes us both nervously as if we're a horror show that's about to start.

"Hi, Theo."

Theo nods at Ed. "You all right, mate? Hope you don't mind that I brought some help."

Ed laughs nervously, then glances at his mother, eyes wide like a small boy in the teacher's office. "N-no, no, not at all."

There is deathly silence for a moment—well, nothing but the sound of Theo peeling back the cling film, and the woman in chef whites opening and closing the oven as if she's doing it only to give her hands something to do because even *she* feels this is awkward.

Something wordless passes between Ed and Helen, and then she disappears, the kitchen door closing softly behind her.

"Nell, can we—" Ed gestures with a tilt of his head to the outside, to the McDonnells' huge back garden, black through the huge patio doors.

"Yep, all good," Theo says looking up from the platter. "I'll take it from here."

The grass crunches under my heels, and we walk until we're several meters from the house. I can hear the trickling of the fountain behind me, of Ed's parents' pond. Helen used to call it the lake, and they'd all laugh, Ed and his brothers, and make fun of her. "I know pond doesn't sound as good, Mum," Tom would laughingly say, "but I'm sorry, that's what it is. A bloody big pond with a fountain stuck in the middle."

"What are you doing here?" Ed asks, a chuckle in his voice, but it's one of disbelief, of "what're you bloody playing at, Nell?"

"Is your girlfriend in there?" I blurt.

"What?"

"Your girlfriend," I say. "The one waiting for you, in Virginia."

"I—" He reaches a hand behind his neck then, and scratches. He gives me that sideways wince, and I think he's going to pull some smooth line out of his arse, but then his eyes close as if surrendering. "So, Sam told you."

"*Sam?* No," I say. "No, he didn't. What does Sam know?"

Ed sighs, drags a hand through his hair. "We talked at the hospital. Just—bedside stuff, you know. His dad talked about his first wife and marriage and girlfriends and—"

"You told him you had one."

Ed nods slowly. "And I thought he might tell you—obviously, I didn't know who he was." And now it makes sense. Sam's iciness, his set jaw, their serious-looking words in the hotel lobby.

303

"And if you had known who he was, what, you would've just pretended?"

"Nell, I'm sorry—"

"I asked you." My words cut through the silence of the garden, and the fountain in the blackness trickles on.

"I didn't know what to say," Ed says woundedly. "It's complicated, Nell."

I laugh—it's a titter, just like Helen's. "Ed, even for you that is—"

"We were engaged."

The words land, as if right there, on the grass between us. Three little grenades.

"We're not at the moment. And she isn't here. Claudia—" Claudia. She looks like a Claudia. A Claudia, I think, as I look in through the Georgian double doors into the warm, high-ceilinged living room, would fit right in, in there. "And I don't want to lie. I never did. But it isn't over, Nell. We're taking some time. She was offered a job at the same time as me, but in another state, in Virginia, and—"

"She's a doctor?"

He nods, almost embarrassed. As if he expects me to make fun, to call him predictable. A cliché. "Oncologist," he says. "And I know I should've told you. But it all sort of went wrong, you know?"

I shrug, say nothing.

"Things happened all at once," Ed carries

on. "We had an engagement party, she started booking stuff, then her dad, he gave me his mum and dad's wedding bands, and it all suddenly felt really *real* and—then Tom called me about the job. About coming home. And she didn't want me to go, but I didn't want to go to Virginia, and so we sort of broke it off. A break, I guess. Then I came home, and I saw you, and everything was—"

"The same," I add.

"*Yeah.* And it was easy, in every way. To pretend that I never left. That things never got complicated, that things were how they'd always been. For a moment, I even thought maybe we could—I don't know. Pick up where we left off."

Raucous laughter bursts from the house and we both look over at it, looming and grand, behind us, watching us how it has so many times over the years, in this garden.

"I don't think we could ever do that," I say to Ed sadly. "Not really."

"No," says Ed. "No, I know."

Because you don't love who I am, I want to say. You love who I could be. The Noelle who leaves her mum behind, who doesn't care deeply, who wants to study business, make loads of money, who wants to move away from this little town and buy big homes and work through that checklist. And I want to see the world, yes of course I do, and I want adventures, and I want

305

my hobby to be my job. But I don't want to leave my family behind. I don't want to leave this town completely.

"Is that why you never accepted me on Instagram?"

Ed looks at his feet, then at me, his face tipped to one side. His eyes close again, and he nods. "There's a lot of photos on there. Of us."

And it hurts. I'd be lying if I said it didn't. And I don't want to be with Ed. But regardless of how "done" a relationship is, there'll always be a small part of you—a small, whimsical part— that wonders what would've happened if things had been different. Would his Instagram be full of me if I'd gone with him? Or would we have ended up here anyway, regardless, in this cold, dark back garden.

"I'm so sorry, Nell," says Ed. "I should've been honest when you asked me. But I saw your face in that moment and—"

"I know you well enough to know that there was something." The fountain sloshes in the darkness, and the distant sound of cutlery chinks from the kitchen. "I just didn't know what. And I don't think I wanted to believe it. I'd missed you too much. And then there you were."

"I know."

"It was almost too easy."

Neither of us speaks for a while, and we both stand silently, our breath making clouds in the dark night. Then Ed gently takes my hands in his. "For what it's worth," he says, "I loved you, Noelle. I was a goner when I met you. I loved you instantly. That smile. That mad curly hair . . ."

Warm tears bud in my eyes as he twirls the end of a curl in his fingers and drops it. "And I loved you too."

"God, I know, Nell," he says softly. "I know you did. And we were good. For such a long time, we were so good."

"Were," I repeat, and Ed nods, and brings my hands to his mouth. He kisses them, one each. "Were," he says.

Music grows louder inside the house and laughter floats out from the open kitchen door. I see Theo's silhouette, waiting in the kitchen, zipping up his coat.

I lean and kiss Ed's cheek. "You better go in."

Ed swallows and doesn't say another word. I wipe my tears quickly on the back of my hand. I don't tell him I'll text him this time. I don't tell him I'll meet him, maybe, for coffee by the station, after he finishes work. I don't even ask him if he'll be at the rescheduled reunion next week. Instead, I release his hands.

"Bye, Ed," I say, and I walk away. I leave him there on the grass—my past, and my comfort blanket—the dark, starry sky above our heads, our only witness.

CHAPTER THIRTY-ONE

When I arrive at Frank's with a bag of food and hot drinks from Starbucks, he's sitting on his armchair among boxes, like a fort. He smiles at me. The man fucking well *smiles*.

"Morning, Frank," I say. "I bought you a tea. Just in case the kettle was packed."

"It wasn't," he says. "But George over there packed the mugs."

George, Ian's squash partner, appears in the doorway from the kitchen, a barrel of a man. "Sorry," he says, a vape cigarette in his sausagey hand. "My fault." He grins at me. "It's lovely to meet you at last. What a job you've done here. Ian said you'd be a dream, and he wasn't wrong."

"Ah. Thank you."

Frank says nothing, but he nods, and I like to think he agrees. George ducks back out into the kitchen. "I'll get back to disconnecting the washing machine," he says. "Bloody thing won't budge."

Frank's moving day has come around quickly, and you'd hardly know that the flat I found when I knocked on 178A that day at the start of summer, the one Sam showed me around, *awks as fuck,* is the same one we sit in now. I feel proud of myself, really, for the job that I've done. But mostly I feel proud to be part of this. This is a new start for Frank—the moment he walks away from something he's frightened to let go of. And I hope, in some way, I've helped him feel able to do that.

"Sam's going to be back late," he says gruffly. "Can't make today. Said he'll get in on Saturday instead, which is no bloody help to me, but George is here. And his daughter said she'd help. So."

My heart stops. "So he *is* coming back?"

It was over a week ago that Sam and Jenna were to meet. On their anniversary. I keep imagining it, taunting myself with it, a big stick over the head. Sam, windblown and handsome, some beautiful, grinning, long-haired beauty running up to him, throwing her arms around him; Sam spinning her around, the cameras panning out, sodding Bon Jovi ballads playing—

"He'll be back as far as I know, love," he says, and we both sip at our teas slowly, a mirror image. "And I should thank you," says Frank easily, as if the kind words have been there, waiting, all along. "For all your hard work."

I soften, like ice cream in the sun. "Are you sure you mean that?" I tease. "And you're welcome."

"Sam said you were a blessing, but—well, I thought you were a bloody nuisance, to be honest. All that chatting."

"To *myself* thanks to you." I laugh. "Nuisance. That's mild though. I was sure you wanted me dead at one point."

Frank laughs huskily, then sits back in his chair and looks at me, knobbly hands wrapping around his takeaway cup. "He likes you, my Sam. I mean, Christ, I don't know much. But I know that."

My heart thrums in my ears. "Well I like him too—"

"No, I mean he *really* does. He changes when you're here. Sort of . . ." Frank opens a hand on his lap. "Opens up." He looks up at me. "Sticks around. Makes plans. He sort of just wanders about, otherwise, you know. Lost."

"Really? Sam doesn't really seem lost to me."

"Mm," considers Frank, swallowing a mouthful of tea. "He never quite got over it. Losing Bradley. His cousin. You know?"

I nod.

"He was only a kid but . . . things that happen when you're young—I think it does something to you. Mucks with your blueprint. Keeps you stuck." He takes another long, shaky sip. "But then again, none of us have been the same since. I don't even see my brother anymore, Bradley's dad. Did he tell you that?"

"No." I shake my head. "No, he didn't." There's an ache in my chest as Frank speaks. I was stuck. I have been stuck. And it sounds like Frank has been too. He's lonely. Without his nephew, his brother, and a lot of the time, Sam too. All of them separated by this one awful event. And when you're lonely, I suppose it's easy to be sad and jaded with the world.

"What actually happened?" I ask, pressing a stray piece of brown parcel tape down on a box beside me labeled "DVDs."

"He hasn't told you," says Frank, but it isn't a question. He seems unsurprised. "No, he doesn't talk about it."

I think of Daisy, and how I rarely say it all out loud either. For so many years, I worried that if I said it out loud, people would be judging me—thinking that I might've been able to stop it, that it could've been me, that they'd want the details—the gossip. People do love a tragedy. I'd also worry, too, that somehow, if I said it aloud, that something out there would get wind that I was still here, still alive, come back and fix it.

Frank looks down at his tea, then at me. "I always sort of blame myself. He was wild, and my Sam was so sensible, so strong and kind. Still is. And—well, his cousin, he looked up to him. And when Sam'd come over, we'd get him to chaperone, keep an eye on him, and looking back that was such bloody pressure to put on him. He was a kid. Wise before his years but a teenager. And that's when it happened. Sam left him alone—split second, really—"

"God, that's awful."

"Happened on his watch, I suppose you'd say. He'd just gotten out of the hospital. We thought he'd be fine, once he got home, settled."

I think back to the day I got home from hospital after I lost my way, and Mum, I think, had been shocked at how far from "normal" and better I was. I felt unsafe at home, wobbly, too free. I think she expected me to get home, sleep in my own bed, and wake up, fighting fit, just like you do after the flu or a stomach bug. Poor Sam. Poor Bradley. He went home way too soon.

"That's so terrible. Sam must've—"

"Yes," says Frank. "He had a terrible time, did Sam, for a while. Blamed himself."

My heart aches in my chest. Sam must've carried such a heavy load around. And I know it so well. Because I slip so easily into blame. For Daisy. Because of the times I went over and over in my head what I could've done to save her. And because of Mum. Did I cause the stroke, that time I lost myself? All that pressure I put on her, all that worry. I wish he were here. I wish I could tell him I understand. That he doesn't need to run, just as much as I don't need to hide.

"Anyway." Frank breathes in deeply, puffing a breath out of his veiny cheeks. "I think he comes back. For you."

"For me?"

"Yes. For you."

Frank chuckles, a deep, throaty smoker's chuckle. "It ain't for me, darlin'." He laughs. "I don't suppose we'll ever be poster boys for father and son. I've made my mistakes. I know I have. But Sam—he comes back for you. I know that much."

I look around Frank's empty flat, the TV mumbling, the soulless woodchip, the lack of photos, of ornaments and collectibles. I can almost feel the ghost of teenage Sam loping about this flat, never feeling like he quite fit in. And now it's an almost clean slate for someone else.

"What about Jenna?" I ask.

"Oh." Frank rubs a hand over his thin mouth. "Well, Jenna's . . . Jenna's a good girl. Nice. Sensible. She sort of scooped him up and nursed him back to life. But they shouldn't be together, though. No, not now. But that's the thing. I think they feel they're tied—that they owe something to each other."

I nod. "I know what that's like," I say to Frank.

"You and me both, darlin'."

Frank and I drink in silence for a while, no sound except for the television and George on the balcony, chatting on the phone.

"If you want my opinion," he says, "I think he's scared."

"But Sam doesn't strike me as someone who

gets scared. He climbs mountains. *Icy* mountains. With lions."

Frank shrugs. "Safer to climb a mountain than to risk getting your heart broken."

CHAPTER THIRTY-TWO

As I descend the stairs, the house is deathly silent. It's been almost two weeks since I saw Ed at his parents' house, and tonight is the rescheduled time capsule event. There is no silk dress tonight. Just jeans and a sweater and as many layers as I can pile onto my body. My phone is fully charged, my car is stocked with snacks, and is it bad—and I asked Charlie this, this morning—if I'm hoping it snows more than it ever has tonight, and Sam, who flies in today, gets stuck next to me again? Weirder things have happened, especially where we're concerned. Because I *miss him*. God, I really miss him, and every day since Edinburgh, I've missed him and thought about him, over and over, like a tape stuck on a loop, until my head and my heart ache all at once.

I reach the bottom of the stairs and turn, and stop dead. Mum, Dilly, and Ian are all sitting at the kitchen table. Mum's eyes are rimmed red, Dilly's too, and Ian looks up at me and smiles sadly.

"Oh my God." I pause. "Oh my God, what's happened?"

"Nothing to be concerned about," says Ian gently.

"Come and sit down, darling," says Mum, her words thick. She pats the flat of the table with her dainty hand. "Come on. Next to Dilly."

I don't even remember or register the steps to the table. One minute I'm at the bottom of the stairs, the next minute I'm at the table. *Shit.* Someone is ill. Someone has something to tell me and it's going to be—

"Ian took me to the doctor today."

Bile sloshes in my stomach. "Oh my God. Mum—"

"No, no, I'm fine," she says. "I'm fine, I'm not ill. I'm OK." Mum reaches over the table and squeezes my fingers with cold, clammy hands. "But—well, I'm not, am I, Noelle? Not really. Living like I do. It's not OK, how things are."

Tears spring to my eyes. I don't think it'd take a lot to tip me into floods of tears tonight. I'm already a big ball of fit-to-burst emotion, thinking about going back to the college tonight for the last time, to pick up Daisy's camera, to take a final walk around the grounds where I feel like I left a part of myself, all those years ago. But hearing these words come from Mum's mouth— the tears fall easily. Melted waxwork face, all over again.

"So, Ian and I. We went today to see the doctor.

And I've been given these—" She pushes a white box across the table. "And . . . I've signed up to this thing. A group therapy? Local, it is. There's a long waiting list, but in the meantime, Ian knows someone at the squash club. A counselor. And we saw her today, too, didn't we, Ian? And he says he'll help with the cost. If we need it." Mum beams at him, tearfully, and Ian gives a stiff, proud nod.

"She says we start small," he says. "Not to think of a return to normal life, to life before the stroke, even. But a new normal. To move forward and find what that new normal is for her. And for all of you."

Dilly puts his bandy arm around me and squeezes me into him. I cry into his shoulder, turning the fabric of his thin, pink T-shirt shoulder damp. "Oh, snot. Great. Cheers for that."

"You smell weird. Like jam." I cry into his shoulder. "Like, really strongly."

"Get fucked, Elle." He laughs, but when I pull back to look up at him, his eyes are watery, too, and it makes me want to cry even more.

"I saw the wedding," he says. "On your Instagram. Elle. And you *have* to go for it. You fucking killed it. It looked *amazing*."

"I want to, Dill," I say. "I do want to."

Ian clears his throat behind a tight fist. "And that's why I'm moving back next door."

"What?"

Ian's pale face glows pink now and he entwines his fingers together. "The rental agreement is almost up and they don't want to stay. And frankly, I missed all of you. I missed Belinda—your mother—more. More than I could ever say, in fact." Mum smiles at him, tears glittering at the edges of her eyes. "And I know I'm not in any way family. I know I'm just your neighbor and what I think really is irrelevant, I suppose. But—" He looks down at the tablecloth, presses a finger onto one of the polka dots. "I would very much like to see you happy, Noelle."

Rain thrums against the window and the fridge whirs, and tears fall, one after the other onto the table like little puddles.

"And you—" Mum says, squeezing my hand again. "You have been my shining light. But it's not fair, Noelle. It's not fair that I'm holding you back. There have been times in the last few months that I've really seen it. You . . . *so* happy, so different. And I worry you're letting your life pass you by, for someone else, and . . . at the cost of *you*."

"Mum, I—"

My phone buzzes. A reminder of the reunion, as if I was ever going to miss it or forget it.

"I—I'm so sorry, I have to go. I've got the bloody college reunion and—I don't even have to go, really, I can just stay here with you—"

"*No.* You go." Mum smiles a watery smile. "We'll talk more tomorrow. That's if I haven't grown two heads on these new meds." She looks at me, pulls a face and laughs. "I'm joking."

Ian reaches behind him on the kitchen counter and puts an envelope on the table.

"Oh, and I meant to give you this. Your final week's wages. From Frank. George passed it on." He slides it across the table. "Frank was ever so pleased, apparently. Loves the new ground-floor maisonette. He said you made it feel like home."

"I'm glad," I say, a pang of something in my heart at the sight of the envelope, my name written in Frank's spidery scrawl. "And Ian?"

Ian looks up at me.

"You are family, by the way. You're as much a part of this family as I am. We wouldn't be without you."

Ian's eyes shine. "Well," he says, swallowing. "Yes. OK. Thank you, Noelle. That is very kind."

iMessage to Charlie: Hi love. So I've been wondering—is Theo's parents' coffee stand still available?

iMessage to Noelle: WHAAAAAAT

iMessage to Noelle: FOR YOU? Please say yes, please say yes!

iMessage to Charlie: Yes! Just making inquiries, that's all. It might be totally not doable. But YES! YES! FOR ME!

iMessage to Noelle: Oh my God. I am DEAD. D E A D. And crying. Bloody hormones. Pathetic. They're turning me into a right sap.

CHAPTER THIRTY-THREE

The reunion looks exactly how I imagined it would. The grounds are lit up with floodlights, like they were almost sixteen years ago. There's music playing—the tinny, bassy notes of a distant live band—and barbecue smoke billows in the distance. It looks *alive*. With people and cars and noise, the very same stars splattered across the sky.

At the entrance, a young woman beside a table of labels smiles. She wears huge feathery eyelashes and her eyelids are powdered in hot pink, fading to canary yellow.

"Take a tag and write your name on it," she grins excitedly. "And then you can go on in. The college is open, too, if you'd like a look around."

Something fizzes inside me as I move inside the building with a little crowd, through the reception area, and outside to where the whole courtyard is lit with fairy lights. Excitement, I suppose. *Hope.* Because this is where I left it, all the hope I had once. And I can have it again.

A band plays loudly, the barbecue sizzles and smokes, and people stand around in little groups, like a mini music festival. I stand still, my feet on the concrete, and look up at the window of the

English classroom Daisy would wave to me from. Her beautiful face. Her beautiful, happy face full of life. One minute she was there, and the next, gone, destined to be written about once or twice in a local newspaper, and slowly forgotten by most.

I close my eyes. "I miss you," I say to her in my mind. "I don't know what's going to happen," I say to her, "but when I close my eyes, I know you're watching me and you're there, saying, *Go on, Elle. Go out there and have adventures. It's all waiting.* And I believe you. This time, I believe you."

I open my eyes then, and for a moment—I freeze. Because I think I see Sam. *Sam.* Of course I think I do, I see him bloody everywhere. It's like I'm hallucinating lately—had too much Calpol or something. The back of someone tall, jogging through town. The sound of anyone with the slightest American twang to their accent. Dilly and Mum were watching a film the other night and butterflies fluttered in my gut as I heard someone say the word "dollars." I miss Sam. I miss his voice and his lips and the way he makes me feel alive and seen and perfect, just as I am. Not for who I could turn out to be. It's true what I wanted to say to Ed—that he loved me for who I could be. Not who I am. *Love.* It is love with Sam. At least what I feel for him. *Shit.* Well, there it is. Noelle Butterby is in love. It should scare me, but it doesn't, and I can't help the grin that seems to take over my face—so large, it'd crack plaster. A passing stranger side-eyes me and looks slightly haunted, so I hide it behind my hand.

I take a tour of the college, and drift aimlessly through the college grounds, the air thick with woodsmoke, the occasional bang of faraway fireworks. Things I'd forgotten reveal themselves as I wander, like the pages of a pop-up book, and with them, rushes of memories. Ed's arm slung over my shoulder; Daisy, the way she'd gaze over at Lee, smoking in the distance. How happy we all were.

I buy a hot dog, like Daisy and I did fifteen years ago. I watch the band, like we did, and then I buy a nonalcoholic cocktail from the beer tent and make my way inside. I want the camera. I do. But if it's lost—I've made my peace with that, I think. I have Daisy in my mind. I have the Ed and Noelle of back then in my mind too. No camera will bring her back—bring anything back for that matter. She was a kid. I'm an adult. And I don't have a corner sofa or a sweater-wearing husband. But I am here. The Noelle of right now, is right here.

In the large reception area, people are crowded around walls of old photos, and I slip into an open space by one of them that's drawn quite a crowd. And I'm not prepared for it. But there

323

she is. Daisy's face beneath a laminated sign that says Gone Too Soon. Daisy Cheng. Age 17. Beside her is another student I don't recognize. Robert "Duff" Duffield. Age 16. There are more than anyone would expect. Smiling, frozen-in-time faces. And then—it's him. It's Lee, and my heart aches at the sight of him. He's laughing in the photo, blue eyes and floppy hair, and I realize I never really knew what he looked like. Not properly. I never got close enough. He was just that smoking kid Daisy would shyly wave at. And I feel shame, then, prickle my body. I was so consumed with the grief of losing Daisy that I hardly thought about him. He was alive for a whole two weeks after she was. Mum had read the small, heartbreakingly almost offensively small article in the local paper aloud.

"He's in hospital," she'd said to me. "You just concentrate on yourself, love. Daisy would want that."

And then I'd heard, weeks later, that he'd died too. I hardly remember how I knew, just that I did. Whenever I think of that time, it feels like every memory is underwater. Slow and blurry and muddy. I don't remember entire weeks, entire months, but I remember some moments with crystal-clear clarity, and I remember feeling relieved. There'd be no trial, no analyzing of what happened, no anger and blame pinned on an eighteen-year-old boy that never ever wanted it to happen.

Bradley "Lee" Goody. Age 18.

I never realized his surname was Goody. I never realized he was a Bradley, either. He was just Lee to us—the person who crashed the car that killed Daisy, and nothing more. Sometimes I'd feel shame. Our grief felt so enormous and important that I would forget there was another family feeling the same, somewhere close by.

I move away and toward the reception desk, which is crowded with people queuing for their items and envelopes. I'm ready to go now—say goodbye. I'll ask for the camera and then I'll go, whether it's there or not.

But I feel sick. I feel swirly-headed, and my feet won't move. I feel like everything is too loud. Something is bubbling inside of me, opening a black, deep hole.

Bradley.

Bradley "Lee" Goody.

No.

No, no, no.

Then I see him.

Across the crowded room, at the front of the queue. And it's him this time, undoubtedly. It's not someone who looks or sounds like him. It's Sam, and although relief floods through me, because I've missed him, every single day, I can't unfreeze my feet from the spot. I'm in quicksand, stuck and sinking. And now he's seen me. And in his hand is an envelope. And I feel like I'm going to faint, that the ground is going to fall away beneath me.

He raises his other hand in a wave, as if I've just bumped into him in the street or the supermarket, but his brow crumples, confused. I must look as mad as I feel. My mouth is hanging open, my eyes are squinting—the face of someone trying desperately to join the dots in a room that's too crowded, too noisy, a room that feels as though it's swaying from side to side now.

He moves through the crowd. My head spins, but I know.

I know, I know, I know.

"Noelle," he says. "Hey, what are you doing here—"

"That's Lee's," I say, looking down at the envelope in his hand. Sam's eyes shoot down to his hand, as if he'd forgotten he was even holding it. And I see it. A camera through the clear plastic. "Lee," I say, my heart racing, my head rushing. "Lee was your cousin."

Sam nods, then he freezes. "Yeah. Yeah, he was."

"Daisy," I say. "Daisy was my best friend."

CHAPTER THIRTY-FOUR

Daisy seemed to be secretly relieved when I told her I wouldn't join her in Lee's car. I beat myself up about it for such a long time, making up versions in my head that had Daisy looking sad or disappointed when Ed came along and said, "Come with me, Nell. Don't let me go on the train on my own. *Pleaaaase?*" In so many versions my brain dreamed up to torture me, in so many bad dreams, Daisy begged me to stay with her. She cried, she got really angry at me—snarlingly angry. "Why the *fuck* would you leave me?" she'd spit. "So, what, you're just blowing me off for your boyfriend? Is that what you're doing? You could've stopped him. You could've changed things."

But the reality was so different. She gigglingly stumbled over the grass with me, then stopped and pointed out his car. A white Golf in the distance, low to the ground. "There he is," she'd said. "Next to that really tall one with the dark hair. That's his cousin. But look. Look at him. Look at that super sexy surfer hair."

"Fit," I'd said.

"Both super fit. Well. Even you can see that from the back, and you can a tell a hottie from the back, you know," said Daisy. "It is scientifically proven. But they are. Trust me."

Then Daisy had put her arms around me and cuddled me tightly. Her hugs were always tight, as if she was squeezing something out of me. "I hate weak hugs," she used to say. "I'd rather they didn't bother, if they don't mean it. What's the point? Hug me or don't at all.

"Do you know he told me I had the sexiest mouth he'd ever seen?" she'd squeaked and I laughed into her ear. She always smelled of vanilla, a perfume she used religiously, from a baby blue bottle.

"You do have a sexy mouth."

"You wait till you hear his voice," she said, jiggling about on the spot the way people do when they're bursting for a wee. "It's slightly like . . . I dunno . . . Canadian or something. Or maybe he's just weird, like one of those blokes out of Busted. You know, they sort of talk American when they're from, like, Taplow or something. I like weird."

"*Is* he Canadian?"

She linked my arm. "Oh no, he's from Bristol, I think. You'll know what I mean when you hear his voice. But his cousin is full-blown American, so I think he gets it from him. You know, it rubs off." And we'd laughed giddily then, like we might never stop.

We walked together across the soft grass, green

and lush and cushiony, and the floodlights lit us up as if the sun were shining. I think that's why my last memories of Daisy are as if the sun were shining on her like a spotlight, turning her brown eyes copper, twinkling as if excited by the world and all that was waiting for her.

"His cousin is proper tall, isn't he?" Daisy said. "And you know, I love our Ed, but it's sort of a shame you're not single, Elle, because I can really see you with a tall man."

I laughed, and she squeezed my arm.

"*I'm serious!* I can see it if I close my eyes. You and this super tall guy with like . . . I dunno . . . a little twinkle in his eye and strong arms and . . ." She put a hand forward, to Lee's cousin who was now walking off, his hands patting his pockets. "I mean, look at those shoulders . . ."

She stopped, conscious of Ed being behind us now. " 'Cause you know, Ed might have that smile and those bloody Colgate teeth, and all that boring knowledge all the girls in biology *love*." She looked at me and smirked. "But Ed's a proper fucking short arse. Like he could probably fit into my size threes."

"I'm a size nine, actually, thanks very much."

I felt Ed's arm around my waist, warm and tight.

"A very generous nine," I said, and Ed kissed the side of my face.

"Size nine is quite pathetic, Edward," said

Daisy. "Lee is an eleven. His cousin probably struggles to find shoes. The sign of a real man."

I stopped on the grass. I remember how smoky my hair smelled from the barbecue, the way I lifted a bunch of curls to my nose. "How can you know what size Lee's feet are," I'd giggled, "but have no idea what his proper name is. Or where he lives. Or if he's seventeen or eighteen or even *nineteen*."

"Because I find out the important stuff up front. Shoe size. Ability to write a poem . . ."

"His real name?" asked Ed, laughingly.

"Yeah it's like, Stanley or Bradley or something. Anyway, Edward, you've got to go."

"Have I?"

"Elle, come in Lee's car with me on the way home. *Please*. Then you can meet him."

"Bloke on the plumbing course? The one with the hair?"

"Yup."

"Well, you're not stealing my girl," said Ed, nuzzling his nose into my neck. "I'm coming too."

"No way. He's not got the room. You are *not* getting in."

"What? So I have to go home on my own?"

Ed groaned and pulled me toward him as we stumbled along. "Get the train with me, Nell. You'll be third wheel. Nobody likes a third wheel, nobody *wants* to bc a third wheel—"

"She won't be. Nell can scope him out, approve of him, and then we'll drop her off. *Then* it's to the twenty-four-hour Maccy D's and a snog in the car park."

"And when is it you're going to check out his feet?" Ed asked. "Is that after a Big Mac or before?"

And we'd all burst out laughing, there under the stars, under the bright floodlights, our breath making fog in the air.

"Seriously, come with me, Nell. She's got a *date*."

I really did weigh it up. I didn't want to be third wheel. I wanted to be with Ed. But then I wanted to be with Daisy, meet this boy she never stopped talking about. But I could meet him another time, right? A time I wouldn't be a third wheel, awkwardly squirming in the back seat with his cousin or whoever it was, as they made out in the front. There was no rush—we had plenty of time. "I should *really* leave you to it," I said. "If you're gonna be snogging and stuff. Unless you want me to come, and then of course I will—"

At that moment, Lee called over. "Daisy!" he shouted. I can still hear that part swirl through my brain, if I think hard enough. It was so loud, it echoed.

"I don't see a car full," I whispered.

"See," said Ed. "His tall mate with the special shoes is even walking off."

"God." She looked over her shoulder where Lee was still looking, smiling, a cool, lazy hand in a wave. She waved back and turned back to us, her eyes bright, two little lime-green studs glittering in her ears. "Maybe it is just us two."

And then Lee had called again, and then Daisy had sort of started walking backward, her mouth in a rigid, tight, excited grin, all teeth and sparkling eyes.

Love you, she'd mouthed to me. "I'll text you, Elle."

"You better."

And she had. It was her last ever text. **He seriously just reached over and squeezed my hand. My heart is dancing! WHO KNEW THE HEART COULD DANCE!**

And I waited for Daisy's "I'm home" text, but nothing came. I was asleep until Ed shook me awake at our train stop and we walked home together, tired and lazy, blue lights streaking through the town. I'd tutted at the shrillness of the sudden sirens. Sirens I later found out were for Daisy and Lee. And would've been for me, too, if I'd just gotten in the car.

CHAPTER THIRTY-FIVE

In the distance, the band plays loudly, and the smoke from the barbecue billows like a smoke signal. I stand on the wet grass, hugging my body, relieved that I wrapped up in layers before I left tonight. But still, I shake. From head to toe, my teeth chattering.

"Are you OK?" asks Sam.

I nod, look up at him, the wind turning the lines of tears on my cheeks ice-cold. "I think so. Are you?"

"I think so," he says, and he brings one of his gorgeous hands to his chest and pats it once. "Heart's still going."

"Mine too," I say.

Neither of us says anything else, and I watch as our breath clouds in the cold air of the field we both stood in all those years ago.

Sam was meant to get in the car that night. Drive, chaperone, keep Lee from speeding. I was meant to get in the car too. And if I had—

"I would've met you," I say shakily, an icy breeze whipping through my hair. "If I'd gone with Daisy, to Lee's car. If you hadn't walked away—"

"But if we'd got in—" Sam stops, and he

333

doesn't finish his sentence. We would've died, I think, and something weighs down on my shoulders, unbearable. We were meant to meet in the car, that night. But if we had, Sam and I would've died.

"He was lucky to get out alive," he carries on sadly. "We knew that, he knew that. The car was—" He winces, his eyes closing momentarily, and I nod, because I know. Mangled, they said. Nothing but bent, crushed metal and smashed glass left. "He was in the hospital for two, three weeks. For a while, my uncle didn't tell him what had happened to the girl. To Daisy. And I think he knew what would happen when he did—"

I open my mouth to speak, but I can't—tears fall. Freely, one by one. A tragedy, for everyone. It really was. The guilt Lee would have let weigh him down, and the way Daisy, I *know* would've pleaded with him not to carry it.

"He'd been out of the hospital for two days," says Sam. "Then he did it. We'd been—" He looks up at the sky, smiles so sadly to himself, I feel my heart break right there, behind my ribs. "Playing video games. Mario Kart. And he convinced me to go out, grab some food and— of course I did. I was pleased that he was eating. And then—that was it."

I wipe away tears with the back of my hand, the wind chilling them on my skin. "I'm so sorry, Sam."

"Me too," he says.

Distant music floats over from the reunion, guitars and a too-loud bass, and the silhouette of two people in the distance drunkenly stumble over the wet field. "I wonder if—all this time, they've been trying again," I say, tearfully. "To make us meet."

"Who's they?" Sam asks, but he smiles at me, softly, blue moonlight reflected in his eyes.

"I don't know."

"Fate?" he offers, but this time, there's no teasing, piss-taking smile.

"Yes," I say. "I like to think so. I mean, I don't even know what I believe, but I believed for a long time that it was fate that I met Ed, that it was fate that he stopped me getting in the car and then . . ." I blow out a long breath into the air, the vapor from my lips like blue smoke. "When Ed and I broke up, I thought, well, what was it all for, then? Maybe it isn't fate, maybe it's choice. Maybe it's always been a choice. And then I met you."

Sam looks up from his feet, at me, his gorgeous eyes lingering on mine. "And then I met you," he repeats.

The band in the distance strikes up with a new song and there are some cheers—wine and beer firmly in systems now, inhibitions thrown asunder, inaudible singing, shouty and out of tune.

"Do you remember why you walked away? The reason you didn't get in?"

Sam nods, drops his gaze to his feet again. "The keychain." He looks up at me, from under his dark hair. "The keychain. I noticed it wasn't on my keys and I turned, for—a minute really, that's all, to look for it on the ground."

"The heather? The one on my keys?"

He nods. "I thought that's where I dropped it. I mean—maybe I did, but I think—"

"My key ring is yours."

Sam's face breaks out in a shy, reluctant smile. "I mean—it feels stupid to argue with that at this point."

"It is," I say. "I know it is. And—the heather. It *did* protect you."

He laughs, drags a hand through his hair and gives a boyish shrug. "That's my mom's take too."

Someone is saying something into a microphone now in the distance, and something spits from the sky in the dark. Rain. Sleet.

"Did you—were you really on your way to the airport?"

Sam gives a deep nod, his teeth grazing his lip. Sleet flurries down, the drops turning from falling to drifting the longer we stand here. "I was. But I was going to swing by the college, pick up Bradley's stuff, and then—I don't know, Noelle, I couldn't face it, so I didn't. I've never been able to face it, to say it out loud—"

336

"And the camera. You were the one that called up asking for the camera."

Sam nods again. "There's a photo of us on there. Bradley and me. I don't have any pictures of us together, and Daisy gave it to him."

"The camera?"

"Yep." He smiles, his eyes drifting as if watching the projection of a memory play out that I can't see. "She'd already handed her envelope in, completely forgot she still had the camera in her hand. So she gave it to him to put in his. He didn't want to put anything in his. Wasn't his scene, really. The party part was, though." Sam laughs to himself at those final words.

"So you met her," I say, the realization a warm hug. "You met Daisy."

"Yeah," says Sam with a smile, as if he worked this out long before I did. "She was— a firecracker, right? This ball of energy, shouting at me to smile, to cheer up, look at the camera, look *hot*."

I laugh—warm belly laughter. Daisy met Sam. She died knowing who he was—the man I'm in love with. She met him before I did.

And I am as sure as I have ever been of any-thing, as I look at him now, across this frosty, dark field, the college lit up behind us like a stage. I love him. I love Sam Attwood. I do.

"I knew there was a reason I kept bumping into you," I say, tears sliding down my cheeks. "I know you didn't. But I did. I think I knew deep down, all along."

Sam looks at me sadly. "I tried," he utters. "I mean, I kidded myself, I think. But I liked you from the second you got into my car. And then everywhere I turned, there you were, and when you *weren't,* I couldn't stop thinking about you and I—I tried. You were like this—I dunno, you lived in my head." Sam laughs, a hand at his straight jaw. "I couldn't explain it. I can't . . . how I feel when I'm with you, Noelle."

My heart feels like it's ten times too big for my body, that it's full of helium, full of air, and I'm going to float up into the sky like a balloon. And I think of Jenna. I think of their anniversary and Steve and bloody Miranda—and the tears fall faster.

"I love you," I say croakily, letting my arms fall to my side. "I really do, Sam. And I know that it's too late, and it's inappropriate probably, and I talk too much, but I don't talk about what I feel and what I want because I feel like it doesn't matter, but—it does. And I don't expect you to say anything back. But I do. I love you, Sam. And you can know that and walk off with it, and know it and—take it up bloody mountains with you."

Sam's eyes shine under the moonlight, and he laughs, a flash of white teeth. He strides over, closing the gap between us on the dark, grassy field, and ducks his head. "Why would it be too late?" he whispers.

"Your—anniversary—" I start to cry. "Steve and Miranda. The bridge. The—"

Sam brings a hand to my cheek. "Noelle, I never went to the bridge. Well, the bridge that's a therapist's office, actually." He laughs again. "Well, I mean I went. But to say it was over."

"Really? But you didn't text or call or—"

"But I wanted to give you and Ed space."

"Me and *Ed?* But you knew that was doomed, that he was engaged and—"

"Noelle." Sam takes both of my hands in his, strong and warm. "At the hotel, we talked, and he asked me to not tell you what he told Dad and me. And I said I wouldn't, on one condition— if he was serious about you. But if he had no intention of being with you properly, then he should walk away. Because you deserve to be happy, Noelle. And God, of course I did *not* want you to be happy with him, like a selfish asshole. I wanted it to be me. But I knew how much he meant to you—I didn't want to be that guy that stood in the way."

"He doesn't," I say, shaking my head. "You mean everything to me. *You* do."

I hold his warm, handsome face in my cold hands, prickly, rough stubble beneath my fingertips. I have waited and waited for this.

"Ditto, Gallagher." He smiles down at me, then

his warm lips are on mine, his hand cradling my face, fingertips in my hair, and our kiss is soft but urgent, as if it's everything we've been waiting for. It's a promise, to the world, to the universe, to fate, that we are here. Finally.

Sam draws back, looks deeply into my eyes.

"I've gone my whole life without feeling the way I do when I'm with you," he says. "I don't want to go another day."

"Then let's not," I say.

"Let's not," says Sam, as familiar snowflakes start to drift from the sky.

CHAPTER THIRTY-SIX

"This is *some* bullshit," puffs Charlie. "I'm fucking freezing."

"It's not freezing, Char, it's invigorating," I say. "Can't you feel it? Smell it? Adventure. I thought adventure was on your *authentic you* list."

"Yes, adventure *was* on my authentic me list, Noelle—*shit!*" Charlie slides on the leafy verge, grabs hold of Theo's arm, "But dying on a hike with Captain America was *not*. I booked glamping pods for my birthday. With heating. With a *toilet*."

"Ah, come on, Charlie," says Sam. "It'll be worth it when we get to the other end."

"It will be once I get there and unleash the massive bottle of prosecco in my rucksack. Mum has the baby until the morning and I would very much like to be drunk by noon."

Sam smirks over at me, the winter sun on his skin, and my belly flips over. My boyfriend Sam. Sam, my actual *boyfriend*.

"I've packed some lovely cordial," says Theo, sniffing deeply and looking out across the woods as if he is enjoying every tiny moment—taking it all in. "Elderflower. Homemade."

"Which will taste lovely added to my prosecco," says Charlie again.

We all laugh, and I hold on to Sam's hand as we tread uphill, wet leaves sliding under our feet. I bought walking boots and *over trousers* for this. And for the climb Sam is insisting we go on, in the spring, in Wales, not far from his work. "It'll be a baby climb, I promise," he said, sitting on the edge of my bed on Christmas Eve, his eyes closed, and when I'd walked out in my plastic trousers and walking boots, I told him to open his eyes, threw a leg up on the bed and slapped my knee. "These shoes don't do baby climbs," I'd said with a laugh, and his eyes had widened.

"Holy shit." He laughed, pulling me onto his lap.

"Merry Christmas."

"It's the sexiest thing I've ever fucking seen," he'd said against my mouth. *"My baby climbs."*

It's been six weeks since the time capsule event, and they've passed in a total beautiful whirlwind blur. Sam went back to Snowdon for work, and I met up with Theo's parents to talk to them about renting the coffee kiosk. And eventually, after one sleepless night; multiple chats with Mum and Ian; and a mad evening scrawling in my notebook, working out every eventuality, good and bad—I struck a pencil through it all, took a deep breath, and said yes. I have a lot to set up—a ridiculous amount that feels like my very own icy baby mountain—but in eight weeks, I will be opening my own little florist kiosk. *Me!* Noelle Butterby. Age thirty-two, almost three. I've said yes, and if I need to, I'll panic (a lot) later.

Charlie's designing the sign and the logo. Theo said he'll supply some truffles for the opening, and Dilly is compiling a list of flower-related songs he wants to perform on his acoustic guitar on the day (which I haven't totally agreed to yet, but he's promised me The Storm won't turn up with any sort of drum, and he'll keep the set short). But today, we're having a picnic, Sam and I—me and my *boyfriend Sam, thanks very much*—and Theo and Charlie. Charlie had put "be in nature more" on her therapy list, and when I'd told Sam, his eyes had glinted and he'd said, "Let's go on a hike. Call them, set up a date. I know this cool place nearby," and I felt like I was going to burst as I dialed Charlie. "Tell them it's punishment for booking us a goddamn *glamping pod*," he'd called out, and after, we'd sat talking. About camping again, just us two (no tents). About climbs, and holidays, and endless nights together. About long-haul flights. About hot-air balloons.

"Look," says Sam now, his strong hand gripping mine. "We're almost there."

"You want us to climb up there?" asks Charlie, as if he's just shown us the erupting volcano we have to scale.

"It's just a verge, but wait until you see the view."

"Prosecco," chants Charlie. "Think of the sodding prosecco."

It feels dangerous to be this happy, and I'm sure it will for a while. When you're scared of something for so long, it has a way, as Frank said, of becoming part of your blueprint. You tell yourself it's just not for you—that you don't make the rules, and all those things everyone else seems to get, just aren't open to you, aren't available. But they are. Anything is, as Sam has made me see, as *I* have made me see. And who says you can't draw another blueprint? Rub parts out over time, replace the lines and paths the more you tread them.

Sam pulls me up and I pull Charlie to the top of the verge, and the view in front of us knocks the breath from my lungs.

"Fucking hell," breathes Charlie. "Are we in Mordor or what?"

"Close." Sam laughs. "We're about fifteen minutes from your house. Look—" Sam points, one hand protectively on my back. "Just over there is the church."

"Oh my God. Look at it. It looks like—I dunno, a Christmas village or something. Like something out of Postman sodding Pat."

"Beautiful," says Theo, and I look at Sam, who's already looking at me.

"Well. You *definitely* took us on a hike," says

Charlie, and she puts her fist out to him. Sam bumps it with his with a smirk, and Charlie leans and kisses his cheek. "Thank you. I needed this, Cap." She looks out across the town. "I feel *alive!*" she shouts. "I'm ALIVE!"

"Our little town," says Theo, visibly moved, his proud little face sandwiched between a thick woolly hat and hand-knitted scarf Jet apparently made. Jet and his torso.

"So, Sam," asks Charlie breathlessly. "Do you think it could become your little town, too? What's the plan?"

"Charlie," I say, but I can't help but melt into laughter into Sam's shoulder. Charlie Wilde. Charlie fearless bloody Wilde. Sam and I haven't talked about that yet. About what will happen—with his job in Wales, with me down here. We're just dating, at the moment, I suppose, but it all feels so hopeful, so exciting, that I don't care. I know we're right where we need to be. I know we will always find a way. Those fifteen years apart showed me that.

"Hey, Char," says Theo. "Help me set up this picnic, eh?"

"Totes," she says, then she holds her arm out, like a Shakespearean actor. "Fill me to the tip with those tomatoes of yours, my love." She laughs. "Open my eager third eye."

"And this is before prosecco," I say to Sam, and he laughs.

Charlie and Theo wander off together, Charlie giggling at his side, to a flat piece of the grassy verge we stand on top of, and we watch as they fan out a purple picnic blanket on the cold, hard ground.

"I've never had a winter picnic before," I say. "Outside. In a wood. On a hill."

"There's never a bad day or a bad place to eat, if you ask me." Sam smiles, and I lean and kiss his gorgeous, soft lips.

"Motorways," I say. "Balconies."

"Rental cars," adds Sam, and I lean my head on his shoulder, gaze out to the tiny model village— it looks like something you'd buy from a garden center for Christmas, to put in the window, to play cheesy Christmas carols. "Can you see out there—the little church?" Sam asks.

I nod against his shoulder.

"And then just over there—see, that's Dad's old apartment block."

"Uh-huh."

"And there's the park. And somewhere over there, a tiny microscopic speck, is his community garden."

I nod again.

"That he gave to me," says Sam, turning, his mouth to my hair. "And I'd like to give it to you. If you want it. No pressure, no *nothing,* but you said you want somewhere to grow stuff, and your garden at home with your mom is—"

I lift my head up, meet his gaze. "Are you serious?"

Sam smiles. "*Yeah.* It's all yours. If you want it. From me to you. Well. From Frank to you, really. I'm just the middleman."

I laugh, hold his face in my hands. Sometimes I hold his face and I want to squish it, kiss every inch of it, "eat it, sink my teeth into it," as Charlie says about Theo's. I never really got it. Thought it was yet another one of their "things," like reiki, like Theo's little cucumbers, like Charlie's third eye opening post–fruit consumption. But I do now. I get it totally.

"*Thank you,*" I say to Sam. "Oh my God. Seriously, thank you."

"I'll give you the keys," he says. "Before I go back. Then you can go and explore your little patch of *dirt*."

"I love it already," I say. "My very own little patch of mud."

CHAPTER THIRTY-SEVEN

'Ere, check the fitty out," says Dilly, tuning his guitar.

"What?"

"Over there. Getting off the train. Fucking arse on it."

"Dilly."

"What?" he gawps, twisting a knob on his guitar. "Look at him, the man's made of marble or something."

"Will you just get on with tuning the bloody guitar and start—I don't know, strumming away or something, sing, make yourself useful. God, where's bloody Theo?"

Dilly sighs, rakes a hand through his butter-cream swirl of hair. "Stop being so nervous, Elle. The stall looks great. The flowers look great. And you—well, you're dressed like curtains to be fair, but you look great too. So, chill, yeah? Seriously."

Today is the day. The opening of Noelle's, my own little florist shop in the train station. Mine. *My own little shop.* I can hardly believe I am saying those words. And Dilly's right, it really does look great—just how I imagined it would. When opened wide, the wooden shutters have shelves on, full of beautiful in-bloom flowers, some made up into bouquets, some bunched loose, in sections, for bespoke requests. Charlie's sign sits above my head, beautifully painted on driftwood, my name in tattoo-like calligraphy across it in white and orange, and entwined around the letters, the green stalk and the plump petals of a daisy. It's tiny. It's beautiful. It's *mine*. A place to do what I love, in a place where people come and go and explore and have adventures out in the world and come home again. Or don't.

"What's the time?" I ask nervously.

"Eight thirty. Oh, look. Charlie and Theo." Dilly holds a hand in the air, does a big swoop of a wave, like someone trying to find their friend in a nightclub.

Charlie trots down the platform, a huge flower-shaped helium balloon in her hand, her mouth wide, her hand in the air as if she's at a concert. "My girl!" she shouts. Morning commuters look up stiffly from their coffees. "My girl has *done it*. Fuck me, I'm going to cry. It looks amazing. Doesn't it, Theo? *A-mazing*."

Charlie speeds toward me, throws her arms around me, and then wraps the balloon's ribbon around my fingertips.

"For you." She beams, tucking my hair behind my ears. "I'm so proud of you."

Theo glances up at the shop's sign, then down at me. He lets go of the stroller where Petal is sitting, a huge croissant in her chubby hands, and presses the brake on. "Congratulations, Elle," he says, circling it, to hug me. "This is just how I saw it. I always knew."

"Visualized it," says Charlie with a wink. "In the sweat lodge."

"With Jet, no doubt," I say.

" 'Course," she giggles. "Post–cunnilingus class."

Charlie and I laugh loudly, our happiness echoing around the station, bouncing off the walls, and Theo takes our photo. I hold Petal and pose, and Charlie presses her face against my cheek, and Dilly shoves his head in the frame and makes a stupid face, and I feel full of it—to the brim. With happiness. With love.

Then I hear her familiar voice.

Mum. It's *Mum.* She's here, and she looks beautiful, the sunshine on her face, her lips in her favorite ruby-red lipstick, wearing knee-high boots and the fur coat she'd swish out in after performing in clubs. Mum. My amazing Mum. And when she sees me, she bursts into tears. I had hoped so much that she would come. She's starting small, and coming here with her walking stick—a stick Dilly had painted hot pink and stuck diamantés on—is a big step for her. Huge.

"Oh, Elle. Oh, Elle, this is just beautiful. *Beautiful.*" Then she opens the lapels of Ian's beige Mack and cries into his chest.

"Well done, Noelle," he says sensibly and measuredly, a hand patting Mum's back. "A very well done. I've already left a Google review. Did I tell you? I'm a local guide."

Everyone stays for Theo's cacao rosewater truffles, Candice and Steve turn up, having snuck out of the office on an unofficial smoking break, and Dilly sings two songs, while Mum watches and claps and sings along, and my heart feels like it's going to propel out of my body at the sight of her bobbing from side to side, watching him live, like she used to. She's here. I'm here. And we're scared, *definitely*—I for one am shitting myself—but we're doing it anyway. We're living now. Because now is all there is.

I look behind me at my little flower shop, and at everyone—well, almost everyone—I love in the world. And I think of something Daisy once said, something she'd written for her English paper— that the only way to live forever is to leave parts of yourself behind. And that's what this is. A part of me.

I turn on the platform, a cold breeze whipping through my hair, the smell of greasy sugared doughnuts floating from a bakery two doors down. And there he is. The final piece. Sam. Making his way down the platform. Tall, handsome, strong, *can't-eat, make-you-puke* levels of gorgeousness. He carries a huge bouquet of flowers in his hand, the color of sunrise.

I walk a few paces forward to meet him on the platform. Dilly plays and sings behind me; Mum, Theo, and Ian watch him; Petal sleeps on; and Charlie chats to a passing commuter, a tray of truffles in her hand, arranged on a foil platter.

"You're here." I beam at him, and Sam grins down at me.

"What's up, Gallagher." He leans down, kisses my lips softly, a slow hello. "Sorry. Ran a bit late with Dad. But I'm here."

"You're here."

"Live and in color," his voice rumbles in my ear, then he straightens, looks past me at the stall. "Jeez, look at this. This—Noelle. It looks incredible."

"It really does, doesn't it? And *these*—" I gesture at the flowers in his hand, jiggle about on the spot excitedly.

"Oh, they're not for you," Sam says sternly, shaking his head, then his face breaks into a wicked smile. "OK, fine. Take 'em. They're yours." He laughs. "We can't have you giving this little town flowers and nobody giving them to you, right?"

"Oh my God, I love them. They're *asters*," I say.

"Yep. I know. I actually did my research," he says, passing them to me, the paper crinkling in our hands.

"Did you?"

He nods, brings a hand to my face, holds my chin softly between his thumb and finger. "They mean patience."

My heart dances. "That's right," I say. "They do."

Patience. Patience is what got us here. It could've happened fifteen years ago; it could've happened so many times since. Who knows how many times we passed each other, just missed one another, like two ships passing in the night. But it wouldn't have been the right time. But I feel sure that now is. The invisible red thread. It may have tangled, but it never, ever broke.

"Oh, and I also got you this." He pulls a rectangle from inside his jacket. It's wrapped in thick, red paper, lined with silver stripes. "Something for when you're ready."

I hold the thick rectangle in my hand. Daisy's photos. It must be.

"Thank you. And now of course, I feel like *you* should have something."

Sam bends and kisses my forehead. "Nah," he says. "Already got everything I need." He smiles down at me, as his hand slides down my arm and grips my hand. "Come on. Let's go see the fam."

Behind me, Dilly finishes a song and I hear Charlie shout, "Well, if it isn't Captain America!"

Sam laughs, raises a hand in a wave, and together, we walk toward my little shop, my family, my friends, my future. My forever.

EPILOGUE

The sun is beginning to go down, painting the train station in a marmalade glow. Rush hour over, and one single bouquet of flowers sits beside me in a bucket. Mine. My asters, from the man I love. I sit on the tiny little round stool in my kiosk. I closed half an hour ago, but I just want to sit here. Take it in, my first day as a business owner; take in my *life,* as the sun goes down, marking the end of another day.

I take out the gift from Sam and unwrap the paper, and of course it's what I expected it to be. But it's not a photo album. It's a photo book, bound like a paperback novel. I take a deep breath, listen to the rumble of a train approaching, the tweeting of birds bedding down, the chugging of a shop's shutter going down. I turn the page.

The first photo is Daisy's feet in pink tatty Converse on green frosty grass. The next is a deep blue sky, a blurred mass. The next, the college, all sandy brick and railings. And then: *there we are.* Daisy and me. Smiling, tight arms enveloped around each other, a tangle, cheek to cheek. Love. Friendship. The world at our feet. And it isn't hard to look at it, as I thought it would be. It doesn't crumple me into tears like I thought it would. It only makes me smile, makes my heart swell with love for her. With hers, for me. That I know how it feels to love someone, like I loved her.

Another photo of the sky—the moon this time, pearlescent and glowing. Daisy always loved the moon. Said it made her feel small and insignificant when the world was on her shoulders. Then Lee. *Bradley Goody. Age 18.* Blond, blinking, his eyes closed, but face pink with life, cheeks bitten by the cold. And beside him, young, tall, and skinny Sam, his large arm wrapped around Lee's shoulder. I stroke a thumb over it. Who'd have known we'd end up like this—that we'd end up here. Me and the boy in the photograph.

I flick through the pages. I'd forgotten the awful quality of some of these old photos—wrong sort of light, a flash on when it should be off, the blur, the orbs of light. Daisy would *love* the new cameras we have on our iPhones. She'd document her whole life. She'd be an influencer, I bet, because you couldn't help but watch her. I'd give anything to watch her do an Instagram story, or a post, all poetic in the caption, and all style in black Dr. Martens and long, flashy skirts and sunglasses against a graffitied wall in the photo.

And then there it is. The picture I was so sure was a snapshot into my future. My forever.

Ed and me. Our faces pressed together, young and happy, our fingers entwined, and in the background, the white glowing plate of a full moon and crowds of kids, young and happy too, like us. But my eyes find something, at the same time my heart locks into place. Just on the left, distant and blurred, standing on the outskirts of a crowd, but unmistakably 100 percent him—Sam. Sam Attwood. In the background, small, in the distance, but inches away from the image of me.

Sam and me. Me and Sam, in a photograph. The photograph of my forever.

"Hey you," he says now, popping his head around the door, a delicious smile on his face. "You ready?"

"Yes," I say. "I'm ready."

ACKNOWLEDGMENTS

This part—as much as it is my favorite—always feels so daunting to write. Because while writing might be a solitary profession—just me, my laptop, and many, *many* cups of coffee, most of the time—it takes a village to bring a book into the world, and without each and every one of them, I probably wouldn't even have an acknowledgments page to write. (And of course, I'm always so worried I'm going to forget someone!)

Firstly, I owe so much to my incredible agent, Juliet Mushens, at Mushens Entertainment. Juliet, thank you so much for your advice, your guidance, kindness, and friendship (and for calmly listening to my insane "I'm going to delete my book and move to the woods to live off-grid, sorry, bye" voice notes). Without you and your fire-extinguishing, I'd be a little lost koala.

A massive thank-you also to the whole Mushens Entertainment dream team and co-agents, and to the simply brilliant Jenny Bent at the Bent Agency, New York.

To my brilliant editor, Charlotte Mursell, thank you so much for your hard work, passion, and excitement, and for completely "getting" me and the stories I want to tell (even when those stories are a mere wobbly skeleton of what they'll end up becoming!) Thank you to Alex Layt and Lucy Cameron, and the entire lovely, hardworking team at Orion.

To my US editors, the amazing Emily Bestler and Lara Jones—thank you for your vision, your encouragement, and your cheerleading. It is an absolute *dream come true* to work with you both, as well, of course, as the whole incredible team at Atria/Simon & Schuster.

To the many talented writer-friends I am fortunate enough to have: you are the best faraway work colleagues I could ever ask for. Thank you to my bestie Gillian McAllister, to L. D. Lapinski, Lynsey James, Lindsey Kelk, Hayley Webster, Laura Pearson, Stephie Chapman, Rebecca Williams, Lia Middleton, Nikki Smith, Holly Seddon, Hina Malik, and so, so many more of you who make my tiny, little world feel big and wide and warm. You are at the proverbial water cooler in my phone, rain or shine. Your beautiful words make the world a better place.

To my beautiful friends who accept and love me for the old-before-my-time, Friday-nights-in-my-pajamas hermit that I am. You know who you are. Thank you.

Mum and Steve, Dad and Sue, Bubs, Vicky, Alex, little Lottie and Max, Nan, Grandad,

Alan, and Libby. You are the warmest, proudest, funniest family of all. I'd be lost without you, and your love.

To my three beautiful babies, and to my Ben: thank you for loving me. Thank you for being my safety and my home. Thank you for accepting me for all I am (and blowing smoke up my arse and telling me I'd win MasterChef every time I nail the Sunday Yorkshire puddings).

And to you, the readers. To everyone who has read my books, reviewed, reached out, spread the word, made beautiful posts. Thank you. Without you, I wouldn't be able to do this.

Center Point Large Print
600 Brooks Road / PO Box 1
Thorndike, ME 04986-0001 USA

(207) 568-3717

US & Canada:
1 800 929-9108
www.centerpointlargeprint.com